G000140541

The last thing Rowan had wanted was to leave London and go to live in the Lake District – but by the terms of her father's will she and her stepmother Antonia were stuck with each other. What was far worse though, was that Rowan was also stuck with Carne Maitland, Antonia's cousin – who was the one man in the world Rowan wanted, and who was totally out of reach.

SUMMER OF
THE RAVEN

by

SARA CRAVEN

MILLS & BOON LIMITED

15–16 BROOK'S MEWS
LONDON W1A 1DR

First published 1981
Australian copyright 1981
Philippine copyright 1981
This edition 1981

© Sara Craven 1981

ISBN 0 263 73590 7

Set in Monophoto Baskerville 10 pt solid

Made and printed in Great Britain by
Richard Clay (The Chaucer Press), Ltd.,
Bungay, Suffolk

CHAPTER ONE

Rowan transferred the weight of the shopping bag wearily to her other hand, and paused to catch her breath before mounting the remaining stairs to the flat. Just for a moment, she thought nostalgically of the lift which had operated so smoothly between floors in the previous luxury block they had lived in, but it was the only thing she did regret. She had never liked that flat, and never regarded it as home. Now, as she looked around her at the chipped paint and peeling wallpaper, then down at the worn lino covering the stairs, her lips twitched in spite of herself.

'So this is home?' she asked herself with a kind of desperate gaiety.

And the answer to that was – yes. It was the only home she had now. The cottage in Surrey which contained all her happiest memories had been sold to buy the Knightsbridge flat, and now that had gone too.

She sighed and hoped very much that Antonia would have a cup of coffee at least waiting for her, but it was doubtful in the extreme. Antonia had spent most of her life in an environment where cups of coffee and meals appeared as long as there was a service bell within convenient reach. Antonia had been born to be a rich man's wife, and Rowan's father, Victor Winslow, had filled the bill admirably as a doting and indulgent husband.

Rowan had always taken the background of money very much for granted too, until two years ago when the plane that was carrying her father to New York had crashed without survivors, and a series of long and ultimately embarrassing interviews with solicitors and accountants had revealed how very little money there was after all.

There was some money left in trust for Rowan when she was twenty-one from her late mother's estate, and there was a small income for Antonia and herself, dependent on certain conditions. And the main one was that she and

5

Antonia should live under the same roof until she, Rowan, was twenty-one or until she married, or Antonia married again, whichever came first.

It wasn't a condition which had held much appeal for either of them and Rowan had been quite willing to renounce her allowance and seek her independence, but when she had suggested this, Antonia had become almost hysterical.

Before she had married Victor Winslow, Antonia had enjoyed a marginally successful career as an actress. She'd done some television work and a few minor stage roles – it was at an after-the-show party that she had met Rowan's father – and Rowan had assumed that Antonia would resume her career. But this, she soon discovered, was the last thing her stepmother had in mind. At thirty-seven, Antonia Winslow was an outstandingly beautiful woman with auburn hair and enormous violet eyes. She could have knocked half a dozen years or more off her age without causing anyone to raise a sceptical eyebrow. But the life of a pampered wife of a tycoon suited her far better than the rat-race of acting. Antonia had no wish to have to sell herself in the market place all over again. She was quite content to accept the allowance, and Rowan was made to see that any attempt to carve out a life for herself and thus deprive both of them of this income would be arrant selfishness.

'Your father obviously wanted you to stay in my care,' she had declared tearfully. 'They were his last wishes, Rowan, and you can't ignore them. Even you wouldn't be so heartless.'

Rowan accepted the implication that she was a cold fish without comment. There was, she supposed, a certain amount of truth in what Antonia had said, but what she could not understand was why her father had imposed such a condition, knowing as he must have done that all too often a state of armed neutrality existed between his second wife and his daughter.

When he had married Antonia, Rowan had been twelve, a slender gawky girl with her light brown hair, pale skin and wide hazel eyes. She had a brace on her front teeth and she bit her nails, and no one could have described her as a pretty child.

Antonia could possibly have enjoyed a pretty child, someone to dress up and take around with her, and reflect her own charms, although there would probably have been friction of a different kind in the years ahead. There was no friction with Rowan of this nature. If Antonia had ever asked 'Mirror, mirror on the wall, who is the fairest of them all?' the mirror would have given her the answer she wanted.

But from the first, she simply hadn't been interested in Rowan, and had made it perfectly plain, and Rowan had looked back at her with clear scornful eyes that seemed to see that beneath the expensive clothes and flawless complexion there was a mean, rather spoiled little mind.

Now, at nineteen, Rowan was a little more tolerant. She had few illusions about her stepmother. She recognised that Antonia was lazy and selfish, and lived consistently beyond both their means, but at the same time there could be a curiously helpless and childlike quality about her.

Antonia, Rowan thought cynically, always has to have someone to look after her. First it was Daddy, and now it's me, and I have to do it for Daddy's sake. It wasn't, she realised, that Victor Winslow wanted her to remain in Antonia's care for a few more years. It was the other way round, and it came to her rather sadly, that in his own way Victor Winslow had also been rather selfish.

She had managed a little independence for herself. She had been forced to abandon her 'A' level course at boarding school, because the money that was available wouldn't cover the remaining fees, but she had enrolled at a local college of further education and was in the throes of a two-year course there. If she was successful, it had occurred to her that she might try for a degree on the Social Sciences side at one of the Polytechnics.

Life was by no means perfect, but there seemed to be a certain order and pattern emerging from the frank chaos that her father's sudden death had left. Money was always in short supply, largely thanks to Antonia's ideas of budgeting. This was why Rowan did the shopping herself now, on the way home from her classes. She did a lot of the cleaning too, and most of the cooking, and tried to fit her studies in as best she could.

Every so often, Antonia would bestir herself and announce that she was going to get a job. She had done a little demonstrating at various exhibitions, and some clothes modelling in the restaurant of a West End department store, relying heavily for these breaks on contacts she had known in her acting days, but she was not reliable and the offers of work were rarely repeated.

She had even managed at one stage to become a partner in a boutique which was about to open. Rowan had been frankly appalled. Where, she had wanted to know heatedly, had Antonia got the money to invest in this chancy venture? Boutiques came and went like April showers, and often their erstwhile owners found themselves facing the Official Receiver.

But Antonia had waved her objections irritably aside. They had backers, she said, people who were not afraid to risk their money on possible success. She was so evasive on the subject that Rowan guessed this unknown backer had to be a man, but she was neither shocked nor disturbed by the knowledge. Her father had been dead for two years now, and Antonia was a man's woman in every sense of the word.

Rowan herself was still thin rather than fashionably slender, and her brown hair remained as straight as rainwater, and about as interesting, she thought detachedly. Her teeth were straight now, but she still bit her nails on occasion. The chances, she decided objectively, of her getting married before she was twenty-one were remote in the extreme. Her only hope was that Antonia would beat her to it, preferably with someone who could keep her in the style to which she had been accustomed.

This mysterious backer, whoever he was, seemed hopeful. And he must have money to burn if he was prepared to risk it on the prospect of Antonia undergoing some kind of sea-change into a successful businesswoman.

She had waited resignedly for the inevitable crash. Neither Antonia nor her partner, another ex-actress called Alix Clayton, had any real working knowledge of the exigencies of the rag trade. They assumed blandly that they would get by because of their eye for style and colour, and that their friends would flock to support them. As it was, they lasted a bare three months before the sad 'Closing Down Sale' notices went up in the window, alongside the announcement that the lease was available again.

Rowan had wondered uneasily how much liability Antonia would have to bear for the failure of the business, but nothing had ever been mentioned on this score. The boyfriend, she decided drily, must be besotted as well as rich if he was prepared to write off that kind of loss. Or maybe he was doing it for tax reasons.

Anyway, Rowan thought as she pushed her key into the door, she'd heard nothing more on the subject, and at least Antonia had been fairly subdued since, with no more wildcat schemes for making her fortune in the offing.

The air in the small living room was thick with cigarette smoke when she entered, and Antonia was lying on the sofa in the act of lighting another from the previous butt.

'Chain smoking, yet?' Rowan dumped the heavy shopping bag down on the table.

Antonia surveyed it sourly. 'What have you got there?'

'Nothing very exciting,' Rowan said lightly. She ticked the items off on her fingers. 'Mince, stewing steak, carrots, onions, potatoes, spring greens . . .'

'God!' Antonia shuddered. 'You should get a job catering for some kind of works canteen. Well, have fun with your nice mince, sweetie, because I shan't be here for dinner tonight, thank heaven. I'm going out.'

Rowan sighed. 'You could have told me,' she observed with resignation.

'I couldn't tell you because I didn't know myself until an hour ago,' Antonia returned. 'And I shall probably be late, so don't bother to wait up for me,' she added with evident satisfaction.

Rowan went into the tiny cramped kitchenette and began stowing the meat away in the ancient refrigerator, and piling the vegetables into the rack that stood beside the sink unit. She would make do with a poached egg later, she decided. She did the odd bits of washing up that had been left for her, then made herself a cup of instant coffee and carried it back into the living room. She set the cup down on the table and took her college file out of the bag, together with the reference books she had brought from the library that day.

'More work?' Antonia queried without interest. 'You know what they say – all work and no play . . .'

'Makes Jill a dull girl,' Rowan concluded for her rather bleakly. She'd heard it all before. And she also knew that if she never lifted another finger as long as she lived, it would make her no less dull to Antonia.

'You ought to get out more – enjoy yourself a little,' Antonia declared. 'You could look quite reasonable if you just took a little trouble with your appearance. As it is, no one would dream that you were nineteen.'

Rowan opened one of her books and studied the index with minute interest.

'I'm not really concerned about appearing in other people's dreams at any age,' she remarked rather shortly. She was used to Antonia's sniping by now, and didn't let it disturb her particularly. Besides, she knew quite well that Antonia was quite satisfied that she appeared to be much younger than she actually was. It wouldn't have suited her book at all to have a grown-up stepdaughter; she would have considered it ageing. When they had first moved to this particular flat, Rowan was quite aware that Antonia had informed some of the neighbours that she was her younger sister, and she had never bothered to correct this impression. If that was what Antonia wished people to think, then it was all right with her.

Antonia got up from the sofa and wandered across to look in the long mirror what was fixed to the wall.

'I'm putting on weight,' she complained, turning sideways to study herself. 'It's all this starchy food we eat. I shall have to go on a salad diet for a while.'

'Do you realise what salads cost at this time of year?' Rowan frowned as she tried to concentrate on her reading. It would be more sensible, she thought, to forget about trying to write an essay until Antonia had gone out, but on the other hand, Antonia was clearly in one of her difficult moods and Rowan wanted to avoid an overt row if possible. She shrank from scenes and raised voices, and always had done. Usually if she buried herself deeply enough in a book at times like this, Antonia contented herself with a few shrewish observations on her intellectual abilities and then relapsed into sulky silence.

'That's all you seem to think about – the cost of things!'

'Well, someone has to,' Rowan said temperately. 'If we're careful, we can manage, but . . .'

'I'm sick of being careful – sick of managing!' Antonia's face was flushed with temper and her eyes were stormy. 'Cooped up in this damned hole, day in, day out! At least you have that college of yours to go to.'

Rowan had to smile. 'Well, you could always enrol for a course yourself if you wanted. And you do get out. You go anywhere you want, and you know it. You play bridge each week with Celia Maxwell and that gang and . . .'

'I haven't played with them for weeks.' Antonia passed her hands over her hips, smoothing away the non-existent surplus.

'I didn't know that.' Rowan gave her a surprised look. Bridge had always been one of Antonia's passions.

Her stepmother's lips tightened sullenly. 'There's a lot you don't know. It's all very well for Celia. When she loses at bridge, all she has to do is stretch her hand out to good old Tom and he'll pay up without a murmur. She doesn't realise it isn't that simple for all of us.'

Rowan laid her pen down and regarded Antonia with startled eyes and parted lips.

'Toni, do you owe Celia Maxwell money?'

'Yes, I do as a matter of fact. Quite a hell of a lot, if you must know. I went on playing because I thought my luck was bound to change, only it didn't. It just got worse.' Antonia's tone was bitter. 'And if you don't pay your debts in that circle, you're soon *persona non grata*.' Her voice sharpened. 'And don't look like that, for heaven's sake. You must have known I played for money.'

'I suppose so.' Rowan pressed a hand to her head. 'It just never occurred to me before. What are you going to do – ask Mr Tomlinson to advance you some of next quarter's allowance?'

'I asked him already,' Antonia snapped, 'and the answer was no. Instead I got a sermon on extravagance. My God, he'd never have dared when your father was alive!'

'Maybe it would have been better for both of us if he had

done,' Rowan said soberly. 'Will – will Mrs Maxwell insist on your paying?'

'I don't know what she's planning. We're not exactly on close terms at the moment.' Antonia sounded petulant. 'But I'll find the money somehow. I'll have to. Celia could make things damned uncomfortable for me if she wanted to.'

'I wish you'd told me before,' Rowan said unhappily.

Antonia's brows rose. 'Why? What good would it have done? What good has it done now?' she asked. 'Now I have you looking down your nose at me as well as old Tomlinson. Well, just don't imagine I'll stand a lecture from you. I'll manage without any help from you.'

'Is it this man?' Rowan bit her lip as she met Antonia's inimical stare. 'The one you're going out with tonight, I mean. Is he the one who advanced the money for the boutique?'

'Yes, it is – if it's any affair of yours.' Antonia flounced back to the sofa and sat down, lighting another cigarette.

Rowan hesitated. 'Do you think it's wise – to put yourself so much in his power, I mean?'

'My God!' Antonia gave her a look full of derision. 'You sound like the heroine of some Victorian novelette! Miss Puritan herself. This is the 1980s, sweetie, and the permissive society has been here for quite some time, although I can see it may have escaped your notice,' she added with a curl of her lip. 'You should give up writing essays and start on moral tracts. Everything in this world has to be paid for, my dear, even marriage with your estimable father.'

'That's a vulgar, hateful thing to say!' Rowan said passionately.

Antonia was not offended, she appeared instead almost amused. 'But the truth, sweetie, often is vulgar and hateful, as you'll probably find out before you're much older. I was younger than you when I realised what life was all about.'

'I hope I never do, if that's the case.'

'That's rather a forlorn hope.' Antonia's voice was bored. 'You not only look like a child, Rowan, you are a child. But even you will have to grow up some time. And now I'd better do something about my nails. I wish to God

I could afford a decent manicure.' She got up, flicking ash casually on to the carpet, and wandered off towards her bedroom.

Rowan sat staring down at the table feeling utterly wretched. She supposed that ultimately it was none of her business what Antonia did. Her stepmother had her own life to lead, and her own values to lead it by, and she had not the least right to interfere. But at the same time, she felt that if she had kept silent she would in some strange way be letting her father down.

By the time she was ready to go out Antonia had recovered her good humour. She looked striking in swirling chiffon patterned in jade, peacock, lilac and gold, and she wore long gold ear-rings, and a collection of bracelets on one wrist.

'Goodbye, sweetie.' She tapped Rowan carelessly on the shoulder as she went towards the door. 'Don't read too much or you'll get wrinkles and damage your eyesight. See you later.'

Rowan watched her go, and then on an impulse got up and went over to the window. The April sky was fading into twilight, but she could see quite clearly that there was a car parked just outside the front door of the flats. It was long and low and sleek, in some dark colour, but she could not catch a glimpse of the driver. No doubt he would be dark and sleek too, she thought with a grimace of distaste. She moved back as Antonia came into sight, and returned to the table and her studies. Pride forbade that her stepmother should glance up at the window and catch her peering out at them like a gossipy neighbour. But at the same time her ears were pricked for the sound of the car drawing away, even though common sense told her that those kind of engines rarely made any sound.

She found herself wondering where they would go. Out to dinner, of course, as Antonia had said – to some restaurant where the lights were low and the prices correspondingly high. And where did people go after that? Perhaps to some fashionable night-spot like Annabel's, or even to one of the gaming clubs where Victor Winslow used to take his wife. Antonia had a passion for all games of chance.

Rowan stifled a sigh and pushed her books to one side. She could not concentrate tonight. She got up and walked across the room and stood studying herself in the mirror, much as Antonia had done, but without the same satisfaction. Antonia was right, she thought soberly; she did look like a child. In sudden dissatisfaction, she lifted the long straight fall of hair and piled it on top of her head experimentally. Other girls wore this style and managed to look graceful and careless; she looked merely untidy. She pulled a face at herself and let her hair fall back around her shoulders again.

She was too thin. Her top half was all collarbones and shoulder blades, and her breasts were too small. Her lower half looked good in the denim jeans she usually wore, because her hips were slim and she had long legs. Taken all in all, she thought, she looked totally colourless.

She remembered with painful vividness a remark she had overheard Antonia making to one of her cronies in the early days of her marriage. 'Oh, the child is no bother. Darling, she's so quiet, she's practically non-existent.'

That's me, Rowan told herself ironically, Miss Non-entity, and she made herself a small mocking bow.

She cooked herself the promised poached egg and ate it without appetite while she watched an old film on television. Then she switched off the single bar of the electric fire that she had been using, emptied the ashtrays, switched off the lights and went to bed with a glass of hot milk.

Their flat occupied the top floor of a large Edwardian house, and had been attics and servants' rooms. As well as the living room, and the kitchenette which had been divided off from it, there was a large bedroom, occupied by Antonia, and a smaller room which had been divided into a minute bathroom and a boxroom. It was this latter that Rowan slept in. She had barely room to move round, but at least she had privacy. She would have hated having to share a room with Antonia.

She undressed and got into bed, then felt under the pillow, extracting a notebook and a ballpoint pen. This was her own time, and Antonia was not the only one to have a secret. Rowan wrote short stories. She had begun at school, encouraged by her English teacher, and she tried to write a little bit each evening before she went to sleep. She had always kept it from Antonia because she knew she would laugh at her. Of course, she was used to Antonia laughing at her really, but she didn't think she could bear to have scorn poured on this. She had no idea whether what she wrote was any good. In fact, she rather doubted it. One day she would acquire a secondhand typewriter and send some of her work out to magazines, but not yet. If there was going to be a sad awakening for her, she did not want it to be quite so soon.

She was quite satisfied with her evening's endeavours when she closed the book and slipped it under her pillow again. She switched off her bedside lamp and was soon dreamlessly asleep.

She did not know what woke her. She only knew that she was sitting up in the darkness, her heart thumping, listening intently. Then she realised what she was hearing. Someone was moving round in the living room. She sighed and her whole tense body relaxed in relief. It was only Antonia.

Yet Antonia did not have so heavy a tread, she thought with sudden unease. Nor did she normally bump into the furniture. Then she heard an unmistakably masculine expletive, and without considering the wisdom of her action, she pushed back the covers and jumped out of bed.

She flung open her door and took a step forward into the living room. She saw him at once. He was tall and lean, with tawny hair springing back from his forehead and curling slightly on to his neck. As Rowan entered, he turned to look at her and she saw that he was very tanned, as if he spent a lot of time abroad, and that in contrast his grey eyes were almost silver. He wore a dark green velvet dinner jacket and a frilled and ruffled shirt with a casual elegance that was in no way effete.

She had the craziest feeling that she knew him, that she'd seen him somewhere – perhaps in a newspaper or a magazine, but his name eluded her and the reason he had been photographed.

Then she looked beyond him and with a little cry of alarm she saw Antonia lying on the sofa, very white. The man had been bending over her, and there was a glass in his hand.

Rowan started forward. 'What have you done to her?'

He stood very still and looked at her, a long hard stare encompassing her from the soles of her bare feet to the top of her head, and she blushed to the roots of her hair, realising what a spectacle she must make in her schoolgirlish gingham nightdress. It was a good job it was opaque, she thought, as she hadn't bothered to throw her dressing gown on over it.

'Who the devil are you?' His voice was low and resonant with the faintest drawl.

'I'm Rowan Winslow.' Her voice faltered as she stared anxiously at Antonia.

'Rowan?' He frowned. 'Oh, yes, the child. I'd forgotten . . .'

Antonia stirred slightly and muttered something and he turned back to her.

'What's happened to her?' Rowan took a further step into the room, her hands tightly clasped in front of her. 'Is she ill? Did she faint?'

His mouth twisted. For the first time she noticed a slight scar on his face near the corner of his mouth.

'That's a delicate way of describing her condition,' he said sardonically. ' "Passed out" is the more usual phrase.'

'What?' Rowan's eyes went disbelievingly from his face to Antonia's unconscious form. 'You can't mean that – you're saying that she's . . .'

He nodded. 'As a newt,' he said pleasantly. 'If you'll indicate which is her room, I'll put her to bed. And you'd better get back to your own before you catch your death of cold.'

Rowan was not listening. 'You took Antonia out and got her drunk,' she accused hotly. 'That's a swinish thing to do!'

He gave her another more searching look. 'I took her out, yes.' His voice was cool. 'But I can assure you that her over-indulgence in alcohol was all her own idea.'

He bent and lifted Antonia into his arms. She was no lightweight, but he held her as easily as if she were a doll. There was something vaguely obscene about her helplessly dangling legs and the way her head lolled back against his arm, and Rowan swallowed uncomfortably.

'Her room's through there.' She pointed. 'If – if you'll just put her down on the bed, I'll do what's necessary.'

His brows rose. 'Aren't you a little young to be coping with this sort of thing?' he demanded. 'Or is it quite a normal occurrence?'

She was just about to give an indignant negative to both his questions, when it occurred to her that perhaps it was no bad thing in the circumstances that he thought she was much younger than she actually was. If Antonia had been drinking to that extent, he could hardly be stone cold sober himself, and it was very late, and they were practically alone together.

'It isn't at all a normal occurrence,' she assured him rather bleakly. 'If you'll wait a moment, I'll fetch my dressing gown.'

It was a warm, unglamorous garment in royal blue wool which had seen service during her boarding school days, and she felt oddly secure once its voluminous folds had enwrapped her.

When she got to Antonia's room her stepmother was already lying on the bed. The man was standing beside the bed, looking down at her, his face sombre and rather brooding.

'Do you want me to help you with her dress?' he enquired as Rowan came in. 'Your wrists are like sparrows' legs and you might have difficulty turning her over.'

'I shall leave her as she is, thank you,' she replied with dignity, resisting an urge to tuck the offending wrists out of sight in the sleeves of her dressing gown.

'As you wish,' he sounded totally indifferent. 'But if she's – er – ill in the night and ruins an expensive model gown, she's unlikely to thank you.'

'It's really quite all right.' She sounded like a prim old maid, Rowan thought despairingly. 'You don't need to stay. I'm quite capable of looking after her.'

He smiled suddenly, and she felt her mind reel under the sudden, devastating impact of his charm. Suddenly he was no longer an intruder – the stranger who happened to have brought Antonia home. He was very much a man to be reckoned with in his own right. Absurdly she found herself wondering how old he was. Possibly Antonia's age, she thought, judging the hard, incisive lines of his face. Perhaps a year or so younger.

'Do you know,' he said slowly, 'I almost believe you are. The question is – who looks after you?'

She was blushing again, and the disturbing thing was she didn't really understand why.

She gave him a formal smile. 'We really can manage now.' She looked down rather uncertainly at Antonia. 'I – I'm very sorry about all this,' she ventured, then wondered vexedly why she should have said such a thing.

'I'll tell you one thing,' he said softly. 'Antonia will be a damned sight sorrier when she wakes up. She's going to have a head like a ruptured belfry when she eventually opens her eyes, so I'd keep out of her way if I were you.'

He nodded to her and walked out of the bedroom. Rowan padded after him to the living room door, where he turned and subjected her to another of those lingering head to toe appraisals.

Then, 'See you,' he said lightly, and went out.

'Not if I see you first,' she thought as she secured the latch and shot the bolt at the top of the door. And then she realised with frank dismay that she didn't actually mean that at all. In fact, she didn't know quite what she did mean, and her mind seemed to be whirling in total confusion, although that could be because she had been startled out of her sleep.

She leaned against the door for a moment and took a long, steadying breath. It was then she remembered that she had never found out who he was.

She went slowly back to Antonia's room and stood looking down at her. It was true, it was a lovely dress, and sleeping in it would do it no good at all. It was a struggle, but eventually she got Antonia out of the dress, and hung it up carefully in the wardrobe. Then she pulled the covers up over her stepmother's half-clothed body, flushing a little as she remembered the stranger's half-mocking offer of assistance. He was probably adept at getting women out of their dresses, whether they were conscious or unconscious, she told herself scornfully.

At least he'd had the decency to bring Antonia home, she argued with herself as she switched out the light. But then, returned a small cold voice inside her, what other course was open to him? Antonia's condition had ruined the natural conclusion of the evening for them both.

Usually Rowan slept like a baby, but when she got back into her chilly bed, sleep was oddly elusive and she lay tossing and turning. In the end, she sat up in bed and said fiercely, 'This is ridiculous!' and gave her pillow an almighty thump as she did so.

She had met an attractive man; that was all that had happened. She had met others in the past, she thought, her mouth trembling into a rueful smile, and they hadn't noticed her either. Nothing had changed, least of all herself. He was very adult, and very male with that tanned skin and those pale mocking eyes, and he had looked her over and seen what there was to see, and he had called her a child.

'Perhaps that's what I am.' She squinted sightlessly through the darkness towards the window where a paler light was beginning to be perceptible through the thin curtains. 'A case of arrested development, small breasts, chewed nails and all.' The thought made her smile, but it did not lift her heart, and when she fell asleep she dreamed the small unpleasant dreams that cannot be recalled to mind the next day, yet hang about like an incipient headache.

The next day was Saturday, so there were no lectures, but she had to go to the library to exchange an armful of books, and there was the weekend shopping to be done. She breakfasted quickly on toast and coffee and looked round Antonia's door to see if she wanted anything before she departed, but Antonia was still sleeping like the dead.

Rowen bought vegetables and fruit from a street stall at the corner on her way home from the library and agreed with the vendor that winter really did seem to be over at last, wriggling her shoulders in the pale warmth of the sunlight.

She felt almost cheerful as she walked in at the front door and came face to face with Fawcett, their landlord. He was making his weekly rent round, and she said smilingly, 'Good morning. Did Mrs Winslow hear you knock? If not, I can . . .'

'I have the rent,' he said rather dourly. 'I'm very sorry to hear that you're leaving us. You've been good quiet tenants. I could hardly have wished for better.'

Rowan stared at him. She said at last, 'I don't quite follow—are you giving us notice?'

He looked quite shocked. 'On the contrary, Miss Winslow. Your stepmother told me herself that you would be leaving at the end of the month.'

'Oh, no, there must be some mistake.' Rowan drew a long breath. She said urgently. 'Please, Mr Fawcett, don't advertise the flat yet. My—my stepmother hasn't been well lately and . . .'

'She certainly didn't look very well.' His lined face was suddenly austere with disapproval. 'But I hardly feel there's any mistake. Mrs Winslow handed me her notice in writing. Perhaps it's a matter you should discuss with her rather than myself.'

Rowan was breathless by the time she reached their front door. She pushed the key into the latch and twisted it, and the door gave instantly. Antonia was on her knees at the sideboard and she looked round as Rowan marched in.

'I'm looking for old Fawcett's inventory,' she said without preamble. 'It must be around somewhere, and I'm damned if I'm leaving anything of ours for the next tenants.'

'So it's true.' Rowan dropped limply into one of the chairs beside the dining table. 'What have you done? I know it's not Knightsbridge, but it's clean and quiet and cheap and he doesn't bother us.'

Antonia got up from her knees. 'You don't have to sing its praises to me,' she said shortly. 'I'm quite aware of all its dubious advantages, including the low rent. Unfortunately even that is more than we can afford just at present.'

'Since when?' Rowan began to feel as if the world was tottering in pieces all around her.

'Since last night.' Antonia came over and sat down on the opposite side of the table, facing her. She was very pale, and her eyes were narrowed as if the light was hurting them. She looked across at Rowan's suddenly bleak face and gave a small rather malicious smile. 'But don't worry, sweetie, we won't be sleeping on the Embankment just yet.

We do have another hole to go to.'

'One that we can afford?' Rowan moved her stiff lips.

'Rent-free, my dear, in return for services rendered. Only not, I fear, in London.'

'Not in London?' Rowan repeated helplessly. 'But Antonia, I can't leave London—you know I can't!'

'I had no idea you were so devoted to the place,' Antonia retorted. 'I always had the feeling you preferred that place in Surrey.'

'Well, so I did,' Rowan stared at her with sudden hope. 'Is that where we're going—Surrey? Oh, that won't be too bad. I can easily . . .'

Antonia shook her head. 'So sorry to disappoint you, but our destination is several hundred miles from Surrey,' she said rather harshly. 'We're going to the Lake District, to a place called Ravensmere. I don't suppose you've heard of it and I understand it's too small to have appeared on any but the most detailed of maps,' she added with a faint curl of her lips.

Rowan listened to her in stunned silence, then moistening her lips, she said, 'I—I don't believe it! You even hated the place in Surrey. You said it was too remote, and now you're actually considering going to the other end of England.'

'I'm not considering anything,' Antonia said flatly. 'I'm going, and you're going with me.'

Rowan shook her head. 'No way,' she said steadily. 'I have a course to finish and exams to take, in case you'd forgotten.'

'I've forgotten nothing.' Antonia drew her pack of cigarettes towards her and lit one irritably. 'Perhaps you've forgotten that all-important clause about our sharing the same roof until you're twenty-one.'

'Indeed I haven't. We'll just have to tell Daddy's solicitors that we found it—impossible to comply with.'

'We'll do no such thing,' Antonia returned inimically. 'That money is a lifeline as far as I'm concerned, and you won't find it so easy to make out as you seem to think once it's gone.'

'I'll manage.' Rowan lifted her chin stubbornly. 'And if it means that much to you, you could manage too. We can catch Mr Fawcett and tell him you've changed your mind about leaving and . . .'

Antonia's hand shot across the table and gripped Rowan's arm. She had been on the point of rising, but she hesitated now, almost pinned to her seat.

'Unfortunately, it's not as easy as that.' Antonia paused. 'You remember all the trouble that Alix and I had over the boutique's closure?'

'Not particularly,' Rowan said drily. 'It seemed to me at the time that the pair of you had emerged virtually unscathed.'

'But not quite,' said Antonia with a little snap. 'I'd arranged all the financing, as you know, and I believed that my—backer was prepared to write the whole thing off as a loss.' She paused again. 'But I was wrong. He's demanding payment in full.'

Rowan gasped. 'But when did you discover this?'

'Last night.' Antonia stubbed out her half-smoked cigarette in the saucer of a used coffee cup. 'By the way, just as a matter of interest, who put me to bed?'

'I did, of course.'

'There's no "of course" about it.' Antonia sounded almost amused. 'It wouldn't have been the first time Carne had seen me without my dress, you know. I presume he did bring me back, and didn't just abandon me to the mercies of some taxi driver?'

'There was a man here.' Rowan felt a betraying blush rise in her face and mentally kicked herself.

'Was there?' Antonia nodded gently, her eyes absorbing Rowan's overt embarrassment. 'I've known him for years, of course. His mother and mine were some sort of distant cousins—hundreds of times removed, of course, and too boringly complicated to explain or even remember. But Carne and I did see a lot of each other at one time. We even nearly got engaged. He was hopelessly in love with me,' she added.

In spite of herself, Rowan found she was visualising that dark, proud face with its cool, sensual mouth, and trying to imagine its owner in a state of hopeless love with anyone. It was not easy.

Without thinking what she was saying, she asked, 'How did he get that scar?'

'My word, we were observant,' Antonia mocked. 'I've no idea, actually. I expect one of his women bit him. But don't get any ideas, sweetie. He eats little girls like you for breakfast.'

'How desperately unconventional,' said Rowan, trying for lightness. 'Has he got something against cornflakes?'

Antonia was not amused. 'You know what I mean,' she said petulantly. 'He is out—but out of your league, ducky, and don't you forget it.

'I'm not likely to.' Rowan felt suddenly listless. 'Anyway, it's unlikely that we'll ever meet again, so let's drop the subject.'

Antonia sighed abruptly and her shoulders seemed to sag. 'Would that we could,' she said. 'But that's what I've been trying to tell you. It's dear Cousin Carne to whom I owe all this money, and as I can't repay him in cash he's insisting that it has to be in kind. He has this house at Ravensmere which an old aunt looks after for him. But she's got arthritis now, or some crippling thing, so the idea is that I go there for a while and act as his housekeeper in her place.'

There was a long silence as Rowan stared at her in utter disbelief. Then, 'Oh, God give me strength,' she said, half under her breath. 'Is he serious?'

'Of course he's serious. That's the deal. I go up to this mountain hellhole of his for as long as it takes while I— purge my contempt, I suppose.' Antonia's lips thinned. 'He's also offered to pay off any other debts I may have, including Celia's, so I can't accuse him of being ungenerous.'

'It's not a question of that.' Rowan shook her head. 'You don't even know how to keep house. Does he know that?'

Antonia shrugged. 'The subject wasn't raised. He knows I ran the Surrey house and the other flat without any problems. Naturally, he wasn't a frequent visitor because your father, to speak plainly, sweetie, was jealous of him.' She gave a little knowing smile that made Rowan feel sick. 'Not altogether without cause, I may say.'

Rowan pushed back her chair and got to her feet. 'That being the case,' she said quietly, 'the last thing you'll want is my presence in the house. I'm sorry you're in this mess,

Antonia, but it's of your own making, and there's nothing I can do about it. From now on we go our separate ways.'

'Oh, but we don't.' Antonia's eyes glittered as she stared up at her stepdaughter. 'I have no intention of serving my term and then finding myself without a penny. I do have— plans, naturally, but I also intend to keep all my other options open, and I'm not seeing your father's allowance just whistled down the wind. Besides, the deal includes you. I told Carne about Victor's will, and he was most understanding.'

'How good of him!' Rowan's eyes flashed. 'But I would prefer not to be carted round Britain like so much excess baggage. I can manage to support myself for the next two years. There are grants and . . .'

'And what about me?' To her horror, Rowan saw enormous tears welling up in Antonia's eyes. 'Your father wanted us to stay together, you know he did. You're all of his that I've got left. You can't leave me, Rowan!'

Rowan was aghast. 'That's cheap blackmail, and you know it,' she began roundly, but Antonia was crying now in real earnest.

'Rowan, you've got to come with me. It will only be for six months or so at the most. You can go on with your course afterwards—do what you like. If you don't come with me, then the whole arrangement is cancelled and Carne is going to make me bankrupt. He threatened to last night. Why do you think I drank so much?'

'But he hardly knows of my existence . . .'

'Of course he does. And there's another thing.' Antonia bent her head over her wedding ring, twisting it aimlessly on her finger. 'I—I let him think you were younger than you actually are. You don't look your age, Rowan, you know you don't. It wouldn't be any hardship to pretend— just for a little while.'

'How old?' Rowan said baldly.

Antonia concentrated on her wedding ring. 'Sixteen,' she returned after a pause.

'Sixteen?' Rowan sank back on to her chair, her legs threatening to give way beneath her. 'Antonia, you are unbelievable! You can't do this to me.'

'And you can't do it to me,' Antonia retorted sullenly. 'They take everything from you when you're bankrupt. There was talk of an investigation after your father died, but it was smoothed over. If Carne bankrupts me, the whole thing could start again. Do you want to see the Winslow name dragged through the financial mud?'

'No,' Rowan acknowledged. 'But I don't think it will come to that.'

'Oh, yes, it will,' Antonia said softly. 'For one thing, Carne has never forgiven me for marrying Victor. When he offered to back me in the boutique, I thought it was an olive branch, but I realise now that he just wanted to have a hold over me. It was as if he knew the boutique was going to fail.'

'Well, he wouldn't have needed much business acumen to tell him that,' Rowan said drily. 'What is he? Something in the City? I thought I knew his face from somewhere.'

Antonia grimaced. 'Well, it's more likely to have been the gossip columns than the financial pages. You've heard of him, of course—I'm surprised his name didn't ring a bell. He's Carne Maitland.'

'The painter?' Rowan could hardly believe her ears. The most surprising element in the story was that Antonia should be even distantly related to one of the most famous portrait paiters in Britain and have failed to mention it.

'The very same.' Antonia smiled lazily, her tears forgotten. 'Did you notice his tan? He's been out in one of the oil states, painting a sheik. They're about the only people in the world who can afford his prices these days. Of course, he doesn't need the money. His parents each left him a fortune, and he still has the controlling voice in the family business. Painting was always his hobby when he was a child, but everyone was amazed when he went to art college and began to work at it seriously. Who says you need to starve in a garret to be a success?'

Certainly, Rowan thought, not the critics, whose laudatory remarks had greeted every new canvas in recent years. He had had some dazzling commissions of late, including the obligatory Royal portrait, and had fulfilled them brilliantly. And he was Antonia's distant cousin, and a former lover, to judge by her words.

She got up and went over to the window, gazing down into the busy street outside with eyes that saw nothing.

'So I can tell him it's all right?' From behind her, Antonia's voice sounded anxious. 'I can tell him to expect us both?'

Rowan moved her shoulders in a slight shrug. 'Tell him what you like. That's what you've done up to now, isn't it? I'll come with you, but for Daddy's sake, Antonia, not yours.'

And not mine either, she thought, as she began the weary task of locating the missing inventory. Because the last thing she needed was to find herself in Carne Maitland's orbit again. She could still feel the lingering scrutiny of those silver eyes, and the memory disturbed her more than she cared to acknowledge, even to herself.

Not that she had anything to worry about, she told herself ruefully, as she caught a glimpse of her reflection in the long mirror. The beautiful, the rich and the elegant—those were the type of women with whom his name was most often linked, and she didn't qualify under any of those headings. Quite apart from the fact that he regarded her as a child, she had no doubt at all that he found her looks and personality about as fascinating as a—stewed prune.

And that was meant to be a joke, so why was she finding it so hard to smile? Rowan sighed, thankful that the tenor of her thoughts was known only to herself.

This could prove to be the most difficult summer of her life. And she thought, 'I'm going to have to be careful. Very careful.'

CHAPTER TWO

THE motorway was far behind them, and the towering fells had closed in as if they were entering some secret citadel. Antonia was driving and Rowan sat beside her, the map open on her knee, although they hadn't needed it so far as everything was so well signposted.

Rowan had never been to the Lake District before, and she supposed she could hardly be seeing it for the first time under better conditions. The soft blue April day was warm and the sun sparkled everywhere—on the grey-blue slate that faced the houses, on the rippling water, on the last traces of snow in the sheltered hollows of the fells, and on the masses of daffodils blooming wherever the eye could see.

She had read Wordsworth's poem, of course, but she had never expected to see it brought to life with quite such extravagance. She felt she wanted to laugh out loud with the sheer unexpected gaiety of it all, and the mood of depression which had been gripping her lately lifted perceptibly.

All she needed now was someone to share it with, but Antonia had already made it patently clear that the rugged beauty of their surroundings had not the slightest appeal as far as she was concerned. Nor was she suited with the narrowness of the road they were now travelling on, or the frequency of its bends. She had grumbled constantly since leaving the motorway, and Rowan felt wryly that her attitude augured ill for what lay ahead of them.

It had been a difficult few weeks. Rowan had informed the college principal that she would not be returning after the Easter break, and he had not been pleased at the news. He had tried hard to persuade her to stay on and complete her course, but she had merely said that her family circumstances made it impossible at the moment, and left him to draw his own conclusions.

Rowan had not seen Carne Maitland again, although she had no doubt that he had visited the flat in her absence. There was occasionally the faint aroma of cigar smoke in the air when she returned. From odd remarks that Antonia let fall, she guessed that he had been as good as his word in settling her debts at cards, yet her stepmother seemed to have very little notion of what was going to be demanded of her in return. When Rowan asked the size of the house they were going to, and if any local help was employed, Antonia appeared vague to the point of indifference.

'But you must have some idea,' Rowan said at last. 'Do

you know whether you're expected to cook as well as organ-
ise the housework?'

Antonia shrugged. 'I haven't the least idea. I'll worry
about that when it happens.'

'But you can't cook,' Rowan pointed out. 'The whole
thing is utterly ludicrous! Does your cousin realise this?'

'I don't know whether he does or not.' Antonia sounded
bored. 'This was his idea, not mine, if you remember.
Anyway, if dreary old Sybilla has managed all this time,
I'm sure we can.'

'We?' Rowan raised her eyebrows. 'Just leave me out of
the reckoning, Antonia. I'm going to Ravensmere strictly
under protest, to safeguard your income from the estate.'

Antonia smiled lazily and leaned across to pat her cheek.
'I know, sweetie, but all the same, you wouldn't leave me
in the lurch. And you can hardly live under Carne's roof
without doing something to earn your bed and board. By
the way——' she reached for her handbag and fumbled in
it, 'this is for you.'

It was a cheque, and when Rowan looked at the amount
it was made out for and the uncompromising signature at
the bottom, she felt her brain reel.

'What's this for?' she demanded huskily.

'To enable you to do some shopping,' Antonia said
calmly. 'Carne will be doing quite a lot of entertaining, I
imagine, and he won't want you to be lurking round in
corners looking as if you've been dressed by War on Want.'

Rowan's face was burning. 'I see.'

For a moment she looked as if she was going to crumple
the cheque up in her hand, and Antonia, alarmed, reached
forward and snatched it away.

'Don't be stupid,' she said sharply. 'Not even you can
pretend it isn't nice to have something to spend on yourself.
You can't spend the rest of your life in jeans and sweaters.
Get your hair done. Find someone to do a rescue job on
those nails.'

'Look my age, you mean?' Rowan enquired ironically,
and Antonia had the grace to look embarrassed.

'Not exactly,' she said shortly. 'But you could try and get
away from this waif and stray image. For heaven's sake,
Rowan, there must be something you want to buy for
yourself!'

And there was, of course, though Rowan doubted whether the sturdy portable typewriter in its carrying case was exactly what the donor of the cheque had intended. She had expected a further tussle with Antonia too, but her stepmother seemed to have retreated into some private world of discontent, and would hardly have noticed, Rowan thought, if she had shaved her head and painted her skin with woad.

Antonia offered no explanation for her glumness, but Rowan suspected the fact that they were travelling to Ravensmere without Carne Maitland's personal escort might have something to do with it. The estate car they were travelling in was a new one, and had been bought for Antonia's use, although she did not seem particularly impressed by the fact. Rowan guessed she would have preferred to travel in the sleek sports model she had glimpsed at the flat that first evening. She was thankful that they had been given something less powerful. Antonia was not a bad driver, but she was inclined to be reckless and impatient when conditions did not suit her, and Rowan grimaced inwardly as she contemplated what these latter stages of their journey could have been like.

'Well, here's Ravensmere at last,' Antonia commented petulantly. 'What a dead and alive hole! How much farther now, for heaven's sake?'

Rowan shrugged. 'Your guess is as good as mine.'

She thought Ravensmere was an attractive village. It was very small—a few houses built of the inevitable slate, a pub with shuttered windows and creeper-hung walls, and a combined village store and post office—but it was clean and well kept and the cottage gardens burgeoned with spring flowers.

Rowan leaned forward and stared around her. 'Is your cousin's house actually in the village?' She felt a twinge of nervousness assail her at the knowledge that they had nearly arrived at their destination. The palms of her hands felt damp and she wiped them surreptitiously on her denim-clad thighs. She wished very much that she was safely back in London, and that she had ignored all Antonia's pleas and arguments. Oh, why had she ever agreed to come all this way to take part in what amounted to little more than a charade? And at the same moment it occurred to her that she knew exactly why and she felt a sudden warmth invade her body that had nothing to do with the spring sunlight. Fool, she castigated herself silently.

'The house is called Raven's Crag,' Antonia was saying impatiently. 'Wind your window down and ask someone. It's getting late and I don't want to be driving around in these mountains once the sun has gone down.'

There didn't seem to be anyone about that they could ask, and eventually Antonia stopped outside the shop, and told Rowan brusquely to enquire there. 'And get me some cigarettes while you're about it,' she added.

The shop was small, but its proprietor had clearly decided not to let that stand in his way. Rowan thought she had never seen such a wide range of goods or so many different brand names. Every surface, every nook and cranny carried its full complement, and even the grille over the Post Office counter in the corner was plastered with posters and notices.

There was a young girl wearing a white overall behind the counter, transferring toffee bars from a box on to a plastic display tray, and she smiled when she saw Rowan. 'Yes, please?'

In spite of the range, they didn't have the exact brand of cigarettes that Antonia wanted, so Rowan bought the next best thing, knowing that she would be faced with more complaints when she returned to the car. Then she asked where Raven's Crag was.

There was open curiosity in the girl's eyes as she studied Rowan. 'You mean Mr Maitland's house? You want to take the back road, and bear to the right. It's a good climb, mind.'

The shop bell tinkled behind Rowan as she closed the door and walked back to the car. Something made her turn and look over her shoulder and she saw that the girl was peering through the crowded window watching her go, and that an older woman had joined her.

Rowan frowned slightly. It was true that Ravensmere was off the beaten tourist track, but surely the local inhabitants weren't so unused to the sight of strangers? She had intended to mention it to Antonia as she got back into the car, but the fuss her stepmother kicked up over the cigarettes drove it out of her mind.

'God, what a dump!' Antonia stormed, putting the car in gear with a hideous screech. 'It wouldn't take much for me to turn right round and go back to London!'

'Well, why don't we?' Rowan said quickly. 'This is never going to work, Antonia, and you know it. You've never had to look after a house in your life. Someone else has always done it for you.'

Antonia swung the car on to the back road with a frank disregard for its tyres. 'No, my dear simpleton, we're staying. My clever Cousin Carne may have the upper hand at the moment, but that won't last for ever.' She gave a small provocative smile. 'From housekeeper to lady of the house isn't that great a step.'

'You intend to marry him?' Rowan asked dazedly.

Antonia shrugged. 'I haven't been able to work out yet whether he's the marrying kind. But it makes very little difference these days. And there's always been a—rapport between Carne and me. There are too many other distractions in London, but up here in the back of beyond he shouldn't be too difficult to manipulate.'

'I see,' Rowan managed.

Antonia shot her a sideways glance. 'I hope you do, sweetie. I'm sure you'll know when and how to be diplomatic, and I'm relying on you to keep Sybilla out of the way too.'

The gradient was increasing sharply all the time, and there were frequent bends, so Antonia had to concentrate all her attention on her driving while Rowan sat silently beside her. So much, she told herself wryly, for being tempted into the realms of fantasy. From now on she would reserve her romantic dreams for her stories where they belonged.

What had she been hoping for anyway? A scene like something from an old Hollywood film where Carne would have seen behind the façade of the skinny sixteen-year-old and murmured, 'My God, but you're beautiful?' And even if he had done, what then? She might be three years older than he had been led to believe, but even so she was a lifetime behind him in experience and sophistication.

When he wanted a woman, it was obvious that his choice would be someone like Antonia, voluptuous and more than capable of catering to all of a man's needs. Well, not quite all. Rowan's sense of the ridiculous came to her rescue. Antonia couldn't keep house or cook, but what would that matter in the light of her other eminently desirable attributes? She had called herself a fool, but she was worse than a fool, she was pitiful. And here she was in a situation where she was going to be hurt—a situation entirely of her own making. She could have stood out against Antonia. After all, if her stepmother's plans came to fruition she would be in no need of the allowance from the Winslow estate. And Rowan herself could have found a grant to support her through her degree course. Other students survived; she could have been one of them. And now she had burned her boats behind her, it seemed. Once this strange summer was over she would have to pick up the threads of her life and start over again. It was a bleak prospect, and it was no comfort to realise that she had brought it all upon herself.

'What a road!' Antonia's derisive comment focussed her attention on the immediate present. 'It's more like a track. And do you see that notice?'

Rowan did indeed. It informed travellers quite unequivocally that the road was unsuitable for traffic in winter conditions.

Antonia shuddered. 'Thank God I intend to be well away from here before the winter!'

'But you said . . .'

'None of my plans include settling down in this backwater,' Antonia said dismissively. 'Why, Carne doesn't even spend that much time here himself.' She changed down again. 'Where the devil is this house?'

'It's right ahead of us,' Rowan said almost laconically. No other house, she supposed, would have six-foot stone gateposts each surmounted by a carved stone raven.

Antonia turned the car cautiously into the gateway and up a steep gravelled drive, bordered on each side by a rocky wall supporting a mass of rhododendron bushes just coming into bud.

They seemed to be literally on the side of the mountain

and still climbing, and as they turned the last curving bend, it was obvious why. Raven's Crag seemed to have been built as an extension of the rock itself. It was starkly modern in concept and yet seemed to blend in better with its surroundings than a more traditional design might have done.

Above them, a large stone platform jutted out, supporting a covered terrace with glass roof and walls, with a view, Rowan realised, of the whole valley beneath. Beside this, a flight of stone steps led upwards to an entrance at present hidden from view at the side of the house. Below the terrace, and facing them, a row of wide workmanlike doors concealed garages and stores.

'What a marvellous place!' Rowan got out and stood drinking in her surroundings.

'For mountain goats,' Antonia said sourly as she joined her. 'I hope there's someone to carry our cases up those steps.'

Rowan looked about her. 'There doesn't seem to be anyone about at all,' she said doubtfully. 'Shall I go up and ring?'

Antonia leaned back against the car and lit one of the despised cigarettes.

'What a splendid idea,' she approved rather mockingly. 'I can see you're going to be a tower of strength, my dear.'

Rowan went up the steps two at a time, glad of the opportunity to stretch her legs after the hours of travelling. At the top, a massive door confronted her. There didn't seem to be a bell, but there was a massive wrought iron door-knocker in the shape of a raven's beaked head and Rowan used it without hesitation. The noise seemed to echo and re-echo through the house, and was followed by a long and deep silence.

It seemed an eternity before Rowan heard a shuffling footstep approaching. The door swung open and she was confronted by a small slender woman with very white hair. Her face was lined and she leaned heavily on a stick, but her eyes were blue and clear.

'The door,' she said in a quiet precise voice, 'was not locked. You were expected.' She looked Rowan up and down, missing nothing from the brown hair parted in the middle today and tied into two bunches to the denim-clad legs. 'You must be the child Rowan,' she commented. 'Where is Antonia? Why is she not with you?'

'She's down by the garages. We were wondering whether there was anyone to help with the luggage,' Rowan said rather helplessly.

The woman raised her eyebrows. 'There's myself.'

'That isn't exactly what I meant,' Rowan said uncomfortably.

'Then I'm afraid you must manage as best you can,' the other one said with finality. 'There's no one else. Now you must forgive me if I don't await your return, but I find it difficult to stand for any length of time. I shall be in the drawing room—the door on the right. Perhaps you and Antonia would care to join me for tea.' She gave Rowan a cool rather remote smile and limped away.

Rowan returned back down the steps rather more slowly. Antonia looked up as she approached and threw away her half-smoked cigarette with an impatient gesture.

'You've taken your time,' she said. 'Where is everyone?'

Rowan lifted one shoulder. 'There's no one—except for an elderly woman who I gather is Sybilla.'

'No one at all?' Antonia's lips parted disbelievingly. 'But where's Carne? He must be around somewhere.'

Rowan turned towards the boot of the car.' Apparently not,' she said shortly. 'If you'll give me the keys I'll start getting the stuff out. There's some tea waiting for us.'

'Tea?' Antonia gave a strident laugh. 'I'll need something stronger than tea after a day like this!'

She picked the smallest case and started up the steps with it, leaving Rowan to follow with the rest of the luggage as best she could. Rowan was panting by the time she reached the top again. The front door was standing open and she walked through and dumped the cases and the typewriter down on the gleaming honey-coloured parquet floor with a feeling of relief.

She straightened herself, moving her shoulders ruefully, and took stock of her surroundings. It was a large square hall, and very light. When she looked up, Rowan realised that she could see right up to the roof of the house, which at this point seemed to consist of a massive skylight. The upper floors were reached by a wrought iron spiral stair-case. A table stood against one wall, its antique surface glimmering with polish and reflecting back the lines and colours of the great pottery bowl filled with spring flowers that it bore. This and an old oak settle standing beside the stone fireplace which, though empty now, was obviously used to complement the central heating, was the only fur-niture.

The door on the right that the elderly woman had re-ferred to was standing ajar, and feeling rather selfconsci-ous, Rowan walked across and pushed it open. Again, her most immediate impression was one of space and light. One entire wall of the drawing room was glass—enorm-ous sliding doors giving way to the terrace. The floor was covered by a magnificent Persian rug, and seating was provided by three luxuriously padded tweed-covered sofas in shades of cream and oatmeal and placed to form a large square with the fireplace. A small table had been set in front of one of them and a tray with a teapot and delicate-looking cups and saucers had been placed on it. Antonia was lounging on one of the adjoining sofas, her face set in discontented lines.

'Oh, there you are,' she said ungraciously. 'I hope you want some of this tea. I'm already in Sybilla's black books because I asked for a gin and tonic instead.'

'She walks very badly.' Rowan came forward and sat down wearily. 'Couldn't you have fetched it yourself?'

Antonia gave her a surprised look as she lit another cigarette. 'Yes—if I knew where dear Cousin Carne kept his booze. I did enquire, as a matter of fact, but it appears to be a closely guarded secret. One of a number as far as I can gather.'

'What do you mean?' Rowan lifted the teapot and poured herself some of the fragrant brew, adding a slice of lemon.

Antonia gave a slight shrug. 'Sybilla's being very odd—although heaven knows I should have expected that. But when I asked her about staff—because no one will ever convince me that she's solely responsible for all this spit and polish—she became extremely cagey and pretended that she didn't know what I meant.' She leaned forward

and irritably tapped a breath of ash from her cigarette into
the enormous carved stone ashtray on the table. 'I only
hope she means to be co-operative. This whole business is
quite hellish enough without having to battle with her all
the time.'

'Oh, do hush!' Rowan felt most uncomfortable. 'She'll
hear you.'

'Probably. But I can assure you that nothing I've said
will come as any great surprise to her. We never got on, not
even when I was a child.' Antonia gave a faintly satisfied
smile. 'Frankly, she's never approved of me wholly.'

The sound of Sybilla's stick tapping on the parquet was
clearly heard and Antonia relapsed into silence. Rowan
jumped up as the older woman entered.

'Let me take that for you.' She reached for the tray that
Sybilla was carrying with some difficulty.

'Thank you, child.' Sybilla looked quite through her.
'But I'm not yet in my dotage.' She set the tray down in
front of Antonia and directed a quelling glance at her.
'When you've finished your refreshment, I'll show you the
house.'

Rowan sat down again, feeling rather limp. It was clear
that as far as Sybilla was concerned, they were not welcome. Could it be that she felt they were depriving her of a
home, she wondered?

Yet Sybilla's own words soon disabused her of this
notion. 'No doubt it will take you a day or two to become
familiar with the layout of the house,' she was saying.
'You'll find it's been designed to take advantage of the light
wherever possible. On the first floor there's a central gal-
lery and two wings opening from it. You and Rowan will
occupy rooms in the East Wing, and share a bathroom.
Carne's rooms are in the West Wing, and his studio is
directly above them. That's one area where your services
are not required. Carne looks after the studio himself, and
no one else enters it without his express invitation. When
he's not here, it's kept locked.'

'And the remaining rooms?' Antonia drew deeply on her
cigarette.

'Guest rooms and bathrooms. Carne entertains widely,
as I expect he has mentioned to you.'

'He hasn't mentioned very much at all. And while we're on the subject of Carne, where is he? I was expecting him to be here to meet us.'

'Carne is in Barbados,' Sybilla said blightingly. 'And even if he were not, I doubt very much whether he would concern himself in staffing matters. I understood the position had been made clear to you.'

There were two bright spots of colour glowing in Antonia's face. 'Oh, it's clear enough,' she said. 'You may choose to consider yourself as staff here, Sybilla, but I don't. I've come here because it happens to suit us both for the time being. If it amuses Carne to pretend to you that I'm only the housekeeper, then I'll play along for a while. Why not? But please don't imagine you have to remain to oversee my efforts. I'm sure that's the last thing either of us want.'

'I have no intention of being any kind of overseer,' Sybilla said. 'But I'm afraid you've been misled about my continuing presence in this house. I have a small self-contained flat at the rear of the ground floor. This is my home and will always remain so. But you need have no fears—I value my privacy and have no intention of undertaking any supervisory role where you are concerned.'

Antonia ground her cigarette butt savagely into the ashtray. 'How utterly delightful.' Her voice was brittle. 'It's a deal, then, Sybilla. You keep out of my way, and I promise to keep out of yours.'

'Just as you wish.' Sybilla turned to Rowan. 'Would you like some tea, child? I'm afraid this hasn't been much of a welcome for you, after your long journey. There are some freshly baked scones in the kitchen if you would like to fetch them.'

Rowan moistened dry lips with the tip of her tongue. 'I'm not hungry, thank you, but another cup of tea would be lovely.' As Sybilla poured the tea, she searched frantically for another topic of conversation. 'We—we came through the village. It's very pretty.'

'It is,' Sybilla agreed as she handed her the cup. 'It's also very quiet, and this house is very remote. What will you find to do with yourself all day long? I understand you're sixteen. Should arrangements be made for you to continue your schooling?'

Rowan felt herself crimson, and managed to stop herself shooting a recriminatory glance at Antonia.

'I'm nearly seventeen, actually,' she said improvising desperately, 'I've left school.'

'Did you sit the public examination?'

'Yes. I passed in nine subjects.'

'I see. Yet you didn't feel it was worthwhile continuing with some form of further education. That seems a pity.' There was a reproving note in Sybilla's voice. She turned to Antonia. 'Could you not have persuaded the child to continue with her training.'

'Oh, Rowan does as she wants. She was never terribly devoted to school, were you, sweetie?' Antonia lit another cigarette, her face bland as she looked at Rowan.

Rowan said grimly, 'No, never,' and took another sip of tea to fortify herself.

'But you really don't have to worry about her, either, Sybilla. She'll keep herself occupied somehow. Youngsters these days always seem to be busy doing comparatively nothing.'

'Hmm.' Sybilla's back was rigid with disapproval. 'Then I daresay she'll be able to help you with the housework. I presume she's capable of that at least. Now, I'd better show you to your rooms.'

Rowan hastily swallowed the remainder of her tea and rose as Sybilla struggled to her feet. She would have liked to have proffered some assistance, but realised the kind of rebuff she was risking.

The rooms turned out to be the best part of the day. Rowan found hers quite charming with its green and white sprigged wallpaper, and the plain dark green cover on the continental quilt. Curtains in paler green hung at the window, which looked out over the valley, and the glint of water in the distance. With its white-painted furniture, it was very much a young girl's room, not unlike the one she had occupied in Surrey, and Rowan felt a pang of nostalgia as she looked around her.

Antonia's room was an altogether more opulent affair in brown and gold, and she was standing looking round her in evident satisfaction when Rowan came in search of her.

'Carne doesn't stint himself,' she remarked.

'No.' Rowan came straight to the point. 'What's the idea of giving Sybilla the impression that I'm some kind of slob?'

Antonia shrugged casually. 'If she disapproves of you, then she's less likely to start asking awkward questions, and I thought you'd prefer that. She can be like the Grand Inquisitor when she gets going. That's one of the things I've always disliked about her.'

Rowan gave her a long look. 'I don't mind her questions. I've got nothing to hide. The three years discrepancy in my age was your idea, not mine, although I'll never understand what possessed you to say such a thing.'

'Can't you?' Antonia sat down on her silk-covered dressing stool and took her lipstick out of her bag. She began to outline the full curves of her mouth with elaborate care. 'It's quite simple really. I've been saddled with this stepmother bit, but I don't have to like it. And while a child is one thing, a grown woman's quite another. Besides, Carne doesn't know everything about the terms of Vic's will. I had to tell him you were in my care. He wouldn't have swallowed that if I'd told him your correct age—so——' she shrugged again.

Rowan said softly, 'Just as long as we're not still here in two years' time when I become twenty-one, because then I shall be off, Antonia, and you'll have to tell your Cousin Carne any story you please.'

'Don't worry, darling.' Antonia replaced the lipstick in its gold case. 'If I'm still here in two years' time, it will be because I'm Carne's wife, and you'll be free to go, just as soon as that joyous day arrives.'

'Then I have a vested interest in making sure it does arrive,' Rowan said bitterly. 'You can count on my support, Antonia.'

'I'm delighted to hear it. It seems there's cold chicken and a salad waiting for us in the refrigerator this evening, but from tomorrow we're on our own—literally. Just before Sybilla left me, she informed me that no other help is kept. It seems there used to be, but now there isn't—illness in the family or some such thing. So we have this great barracks of a house to look after between us, honey child.' A glint of rare humour appeared in Antonia's eyes.

'I'm beginning to think bankruptcy might have been easier after all.'

Perhaps it might at that, Rowan thought soberly as she went back to her own room. Antonia seemed confident that she could ultimately wind Carne Maitland round her little finger, but he was calling all the shots at the moment. Her heart sank. All the cleaning, and the cooking as well! There would be no end to it, and she did not even dare contemplate what would happen if the guest rooms Sybilla had mentioned began to fill up.

That blasted boutique, she thought crossly. I wonder how much money Antonia owes him altogether? Surely she could have repaid him in some other way than this. I've a feeling he's going to expect his pound of flesh and some over.

Rowan saw no reason to change her opinion as the first fortnight at Raven's Crag pursued its tedious way. The house was as labour-saving as the ingenuity of twentieth-century man could make it, but it was large, with vast expanses of glass and pale surfaces which needed constant attention. Antonia's constant grumbling did not help either, and nor, for that matter did Antonia herself for much of the time. She talked a lot about how much there was to do, and she was quick to notice if anything had been overlooked, but her activities were largely confined to a little desultory dusting and flower arranging in between sporadic visits to Keswick, the nearest large town to Ravensmere.

One of the more obvious disadvantages of the deception over Rowan's age was that she was unable to drive the car, even though she had passed her driving test while she was in the Sixth Form. She had assumed, of course, in the circumstances that she would accompany Antonia on her visits to Keswick, but this was far from being the case. There always seemed more perfectly good reason why her stepmother preferred to go alone. Rowan was disappointed. She would have liked to have a look round Keswick, and seize the opportunity of buying some fresh food while she was there too. Antonia seemed hellbent on filling the large freezer in the walk-in pantry which led off the kitchen with convenience foods, and she ignored Rowan's protests.

'I don't intend to do any more cooking than I have to,' she declared disdainfully.

Rowan could have replied that Antonia did the minimum as it was, but she bit back the reply. It would only lead to a quarrel, after which Antonia would sulk, and as they had no company but each other that would be a disaster.

Sybilla had kept her word about not intruding upon them. Indeed, she kept almost religiously out of the way, which made Rowan feel uncomfortable. She doubted whether Sybilla had confined herself so rigorously to her own quarters prior to their arrival on the scene. And after all, this was her home.

But it will never be mine, Rowan thought sometimes as she prowled restlessly through the immaculate rooms, waiting for Antonia to come back from one of her shopping expeditions. I'm only here for a few months, just passing through.

Sometimes she was tempted to go and knock on Sybilla's door and ask if she could talk to her, but she had the uneasy feeling she would not be very welcome. She had encountered Sybilla a few times in the garden, and the older woman's greeting, although courteous, had been distant. Rowan knew why, of course. Antonia's careless words had done their work well, and she had to bear the burden of Sybilla's unspoken disapproval as a consequence.

Rowan supposed she was a fool to allow it to matter. Sybilla was a complete stranger, not even a relation, so her opinion shouldn't really bear any weight, and yet the realisation that Sybilla regarded her as an awkward teenager, even a drop-out, was oddly hurtful, and at the same time it was part of the ring of deceit which Antonia had deliberately enclosed her in.

Again she asked herself, why? She had always known that Antonia was touchy about her age, and had never liked being saddled with an adolescent stepdaughter, but she had never dreamed that she was prepared to go to such lengths to preserve her image of eternal youth. If it was as simple as that, Rowan thought, but what other explanation could there be? She was under no illusion that physically she could be any threat to Antonia's plans for her future.

The future. Whenever she thought of that, a small sick feeling began to well up in Rowan. If everything worked out for Antonia eventually, Rowan would be quite alone in the world, her last tenuous links with the happier past severed totally, and it was a daunting prospect even for someone older and more mature than Rowan. She had always been sheltered in a way, she supposed. Her father's money had taken care of everything for most of her life, and then there had been boarding school. Perhaps Victor Winslow had thought he was extending that protection until his only daughter was safely launched on adult life. Maybe he had even imagined that his wife and daughter would draw together in mutual need after the sorrow of his death. Looking back, Rowan thought ruefully that her father had never been one to take a very practical view of relationships. Antonia had been coldly furious when she heard the terms of the will, but although she had recovered herself swiftly, Rowan had never been left in any doubt that she was simply making the best of things. Antonia had always made the best of things, or at least the best for Antonia. That was really why they were here. After all, her stepmother could have got a job of some kind and arranged to repay Carne any money that was owing to him out of her earnings, but instead she had chosen what she hoped would be a softer option. Rowan could only hope for Antonia's sake that she had chosen correctly. She couldn't imagine Carne Maitland being soft in any way.

And certainly he had upset all Antonia's preconceptions by absenting himself without a word. Rowan knew what her stepmother had been daily expecting a letter, or even a card, but the postman's visit brought only mail addressed to Carne, and the usual bills and circulars. The telephone remained silent too, although occasionally they heard the sound of a distant bell ringing, and guessed that Sybilla had her own private telephone in the flat. But if Carne was among her unknown callers, then there were no messages for the newcomers in his house, and Antonia was becoming increasingly restive. She had evidently been expecting a very different reception.

Perhaps Antonia had made a mistake when she had regarded Carne as the young man who had once been in love with her. Had she forgotten how people could change? Rowan could not imagine Carne as any woman's slave. She remembered the cool, silver eyes, and the small scar which twisted his mouth when he smiled. He was no one's idea of a lovesick swain, she thought wryly. He was hard and sexy and diabolically attractive, and he would take anything and everything life had to offer with both hands.

Rowan thought suddenly, 'I was mad to come here. I should have stayed in London and shared a bed-sitter with someone. I'd have managed somehow. I could have worked as a waitress in the evening and studied during the day. I could have done *something*. But I'm no better than Antonia. I decided to come here too for all the wrong reasons, and now I have to live with it, and perhaps I should be glad that Antonia has told him I'm only a child, whatever her motives were.'

Her discomfiting reverie was interrupted by the arrival of Antonia herself, elegant in an Italian hand-knitted two-piece, a reminder of the boutique's heyday.

'I'm going into Keswick to do some shopping,' she announced. 'Is there anything you want?'

'Into Keswick again?' Rowan felt impelled to remonstrate. 'But I thought you'd done the shopping on Tuesday when you went in to cash the housekeeping cheque. And we were supposed to be tackling the bedrooms today.'

'All right, so I'm going to have my hair done,' Antonia said petulantly. 'You don't grudge me that little luxury, I hope.'

Rowan held on to her patience. 'I hope I don't grudge you anything. I've certainly no right to do so.'

'Then what's the argument?'

'There isn't one,' Rowan said defeatedly. 'I'll do the bedrooms. You don't have to worry about them.'

Antonia shrugged. 'I shan't, sweetie. The last thing I try to think about is this benighted hole, believe me.'

'Don't you like the house?' In spite of herself Rowan was curious.

'If it were elsewhere, it might be tolerable. But I don't like being perched halfway up a mountain, and I certainly don't care for the climate. Do you realise that it's rained every day that we've been here?'

'I suppose it has, but everything's so green and beautiful here. And we've had a lot of sunshine as well.'

'You sound as if you're trying to sell me the place.' Antonia checked through the contents of her handbag, looking slightly amused. 'It won't work, you know. When Carne and I are married, I shall persuade him to sell this place and move to somewhere more civilised and accessible. God knows what possessed him to buy this site, when he could have lived anywhere.'

Rowan thought of the morning sun touching the remaining patches of snow on the crowding fells with pink and gold. She thought of the glimpse of turquoise which was Ravensmere far below them, and the moist cool scent of the garden where plants were showing green spikes through the rich dark earth, and she thought she could understand why anyone would choose to live here.

But not Antonia, of course, who thought anywhere more than a taxi ride from Harrods was the beginnings of outer darkness. And possibly not Carne Maitland either. The house had an untouched, unlived-in air about it, for all its shining luxury, as if its worldly, sophisticated owner had thought better of the whim which had brought it into being.

She heard Antonia's car drive away, and with a sigh went along to the utility room which opened off the kitchen to fetch dusters and polish and the vacuum cleaner before commencing her onslaught on the bedrooms. It was a day when the outdoors beckoned. Early rain had given way to puffs of white cloud scudding across a pale blue sky, and although Rowan knew perfectly well that the weather could change in a moment with mist and heavy cloud coming down like a blanket, she wished she was out somewhere on a hillside lifting her face to the soft wind.

She began on their own rooms. Hers was relatively tidy, except for the small table which she had moved under the window and which held her typewriter and papers. She had started another story, and for her the creative process demanded a kind of organised chaos in the immediate environment.

She remade the bed, shaking up the quilt with deft flicks

of her wrist, and changed the fitted sheets with their matching pillowcase for another set brought from the first floor linen room, where all the bedding, towels and table linen needed for the household were kept.

Antonia's room was a different story, and Rowan gave a soundless sigh as she looked about her. Cosmetics, many with their tops and lids off, were strewn across the vanitory unit, which was coated with a faint film of spilled powder. Soiled tights and undies were draped across the dressing stool and the bedroom floor, and the dress Antonia had worn the previous evening was flung in a crumpled heap across the bed.

She thought, 'I hope Carne Maitland can afford a lady's maid for her, because she surely needs one!'

She was hot, sticky and cross by the time she had restored order, and was ready to move on to the guestrooms. These fortunately only needed a light dusting, and she opened the windows to let in some of the spring sun and air and get rid of the unused smell. She would take her lunch into the garden, she thought, and find a patch of sunlight to sit in. She wasn't sure exactly how much of the land belonged to the house, and much of the garden was overgrown and in need of attention. It needs someone to live here and care about it, just like the house, she thought sadly.

She took her crispbread and lettuce and cottage cheese and found a flat stone under a tree which seemed dry and moderately sheltered. The April wind still held a nip, reminding her that there was still snow on the surrounding hills, and could be more, even this late in a golden spring. When she had finished her brief meal, she leaned back against the tree and let the sun warm her face. She felt wearied by her rather tedious morning's work, and disinclined to start again, especially as her next port of call was Carne Maitland's luxurious suite of rooms in the other wing of the house. Today was a day for working in the garden, she thought, for cutting back briars, and uprooting nettles and dandelions and dockweeds, and pulling away handfuls of the goosegrass which seemed to be encroaching everywhere under the roses and shrubs. Not that she knew a great deal about gardening. The garden of the cottage in

Surrey had been very different from this one, with herbaceous borders alive with colour, and smooth lawns to the front and rear, and Mr Pettigrew from the village to look after it.

There was nothing smooth or ironed out about the garden at Raven's Crag. Apart from the clumps of ubiquitous daffodils, any colour was planned for later in the season, and the general effect was bleak and rather stark, like its surroundings. You couldn't transplant the pretty traditional cottagey flowers they had grown in Surrey to this place, Rowan thought, but you could create a setting for the house which would be equally satisfying. But at the moment, the wilderness seemed to be taking over again.

She brushed the crumbs from her jeans and rose reluctantly. She probably didn't need to clean Carne's rooms. No one had so much as set foot in them since she had cleaned them last time, nor would do until she cleaned them next time, but she was determined that Carne Maitland should have no cause for complaint whenever he chose to honour them with his presence.

The door from the corridor led straight into a dressing room, and his bathroom and bedroom both opened off from this. It was a reasonably sized room, with one wall entirely occupied by fitted wardrobes and drawers, yet he didn't have a lot of clothes, because she had looked. What there were, of course, were gorgeous—silk shirts and cashmere sweaters, and a leather coat as soft and supple as velvet. There were few toiletries in the bathroom, but those few were expensive and Rowan, sampling them out of curiosity the first time she had cleaned the bathroom, approved his taste.

The bedroom was something else again, with a carpet so thick that her feet sank into it as she walked across the room, and a king-sized bed, which was invariably made up with brown silk sheets. When they had first inspected the room Rowan had seen Antonia give the bed a long look, before she turned away without comment, and Rowan herself had felt hot with inexplicable embarrassment. Antonia, of course, was used to a bedroom of her own, and not merely since becoming a widow; however, Rowan doubted whether she would find the man she had chosen to be her second husband as mildly acquiescent to this as her first had been. There was a narrow divan in the dressing room, but Rowan could not imagine Carne Maitland being tamely dismissed there. Besides, a bed the size of the one in the master bedroom was for sharing, not for solitude.

There were blankets on this bed, instead of the duvets used in all the other rooms, and a dark brown satin quilted cover, all very restrained and masculine. The bed faced the windows which reached from floor to ceiling, giving a panoramic view over the valley to the fells beyond.

The sunsets would be fantastic, Rowan thought, and grinned to herself, in self-mockery. Anyone using this bed that early in the evening would probably not be staring at the sunsets, unless they'd used the ploy 'Come and see my sunset' instead of 'Come and see my etchings'. Carne, she decided, could probably use either line and make it a winner. Probably had, as well, and very likely was at this very minute, whatever time it was in Barbados.

There was a full-length mirror on the wall, and she gave its surface a brisk rub with a clean duster, viewing herself with detachment as she did so, and deciding that she looked totally out of place in this room with her faded jeans and elderly sweater shirt with the sleeves pushed up. A satin dressing gown is what I need, she thought, the corners of her mouth lifting in derision, one that fastens at the waist and nowhere else, in a colour to harmonise with the dusters. She gave the mirror's frame a final, cheerful flick and turned away, moving her shoulders wearily. She had worked hard, and she was tired. She deserved a shower and a rest before Antonia returned and it was time to start preparing the evening meal. She pushed the sandals off her aching feet and walked across the carpet relishing its softness. She leaned across the bed, straightening its already immaculate cover, testing the firmness of the mattress with a tentative hand. Then she said, 'Oh, to hell with it!' and jumped into the middle of the bed as she had been longing to do since she first entered the room. Forbidden ecstasy, she thought, bouncing up and down on other people's beds, and how many years was it since she'd done so? She had been seven and not enjoying a stiff tea-party at Sally Armitage's, until, when tea was over, she and Sally had

discovered that the double bed in Mrs Armitage's bedroom
made a superb trampoline, and they'd bounced and leapt
with undiminished energy until the arrival of a scandalised
nanny had put a premature end to their game. A childhood
incident she had not even given a moment's thought to
until now. And the Armitages' bed had not been nearly as
wide and opulent as this one. That's what this house needs,
she thought. It needs children, to fill up the empty rooms
and climb the trees in the garden, and even bounce on the
beds. But it wouldn't get them. Even if Antonia was willing
to have a child, which Rowan doubted, she couldn't imagine Carne Maitland opting for that sort of family life.

'So you'll have to put up with me pretending,' she announced, twisting over on to her back and staring up at the
ceiling. The stillness of the house closed round her. All the
faint sounds she could hear came from outside—the
rustle of the breeze which lifted the creamy folds of the
curtains at the open window, the startled scolding of a
blackbird, the distant cry of a sheep. Rowan yawned, and
watched the clouds drifting past. They looked meek and
innocent, the merest puffs of cottonwool, but they could
mass more quickly than it took to tell, and the most smiling
day could relapse into sullenness as the mist and rain de-
scended. But not today, she thought, and I ought to be out
under that sunlit sky. Yet it was somehow easier to remain
where she was, her body limp and relaxed as if she was
supported by one of those drifting clouds. Presently she
would get up and take the shower she had promised herself.
Presently, but not yet, she thought, as the pictures in her
mind blurred at the edges and became oddly fragmented.
Just for now, she was taking a well-earned rest on her own
private cloud, and her mouth smiled as she drifted on the
edges of sleep.

But her dreams were not comfortable ones. Her cloud
changed from a puffball to the colour of a storm, and in the
distance she heard thunder rumble. The clouds were gathering around her, and she was swallowed up in them, and
there was no safety for her in the angry sky, steel-grey, the
colour of a man's eyes. Then the rain began, splashing
around her in long drops like needles, and she was as cold
as ice even though none of the drops seemed to be touching

her, only the sound of the splashing water was getting louder all the time.

She came awake with a start which shook her body and sat up stiffly, her eyes going to the window. It was raining, and she would need to close the window to stop the water blowing in. She would need to close all the windows she had opened that day, she thought, and stopped in disbelief. There wasn't a sign of rain. There was only the blue sky and the soft clouds, and the shimmer of the fells across the valley. But the sound of splashing water was louder than ever.

She swung her legs to the floor. It was the bathroom, that was the only explanation. She must have left a tap running without realising it, or a pipe might have burst, although heaven only knew why it should have done, and all she could do was go and investigate and pray there wasn't too much damage.

She shook her head slightly as she stepped into the dressing room, trying to drive the remaining fuzziness of interrupted sleep out of her mind, gearing herself up to cope with a potential flood in the bathroom, wondering about stop taps, and how to contact a plumber.

She pushed open the bathroom door and walked in, expecting to see the escaping water coming to meet her across the tiled floor. But the floor was dry, and even the sound of the water seemed to have stopped suddenly, and as she realised that she registered something else—that there was a dark shadow in the shower cabinet—a shadow which moved, and Rowan put up a hand to muffle her scream because the glass door was moving, opening, and she was still too befuddled with drowsiness to make any sense of it.

Carne Maitland stepped out of the shower, his hair, his skin glistening with water, his hand reaching casually for one of the towels on the rail. He saw her at once, of course. She couldn't have moved. She was frozen to the spot with shock and sheer embarrassment, her hand still covering her mouth. For a second, his eyes were incredulous as they registered her, then he moved, grabbing for a towel now and winding it round him, and his voice was like ice as he said 'Out, darling. Now!'

Her face burned, and she was so mortified she could have died, but at least she didn't feel like a graven image, and she turned and fled, back to the bedroom to collect the dusters and the tin of polish.

She bit back a cry of dismay as she saw the crumpled bed, the wrinkled cover showing clearly the outline of her body. It was obvious even to the meanest intelligence that she had been lying there, and Carne Maitland certainly didn't come into that category. She dropped the polish and the dusters and bent frantically to pull the covers straight, but it was too late, of course.

He was standing in the doorway, the towel safely secured round his waist, and drying himself with another. And he was looking at the bed, and if Rowan had been embarrassed to have him walk naked out of the shower in front of her, that was nothing to the way she was feeling now. The blush was all over her body from her toes to her hairline.

His mouth twisted unpleasantly, and the scar beside it made him look like a devil.

He said, 'And what are you? My welcome home present? I'm flattered, of course, but aren't you a little young for games of this sort?'

CHAPTER THREE

THEY said ice could burn, and every word seemed to scorch along her skin.

She said, babbling, 'I'm not—I mean, it isn't how you think.'

'I suppose I'm relieved to hear it.' He began to towel his hair. 'Perhaps you'd like to tell me just how it is—and what the hell you're doing in my room.'

Mutely she bent to retrieve the polish and the dusters.

'I see,' he said after a moment. 'And where is Antonia?'

'In Keswick, shopping. I—I said I'd do the bedrooms. I'm sorry.'

'Does she often leave you here like this?' He was frowning.

Expediency warred with honesty and won. 'Of course not. She works very hard, and I don't mind helping.'

'When will she be back?'

'I don't know.' Rowan lifted her shoulders helplessly. 'Is there something I can get you?'

'I was hoping there might be some food—something light, preferably. I had a hell of a flight, and the motorway was murder. Eggs would be fine.'

'Eggs it is,' Rowan agreed with false brightness, looking round for her sandals, and finding them on the other side of the room. She wished Carne would return to the bathroom and leave her with a clear exit out of the room, but he didn't seem to be particularly disposed to move. He watched her as she crossed the bedroom and slid her narrow feet back into the sandals.

'Do you always do the housework in your bare feet, or do you regard my rooms as some kind of Holy of Holies?' he enquired sarcastically.

'Neither. It was an impulse,' she mumbled.

'Was it now?' His eyes went reflectively back to the crumpled bed. 'I think we're going to have to do something to curb these impulses of yours, Miss Winslow, before someone misunderstands too drastically.'

She nodded, biting her lip, her eyes unable to meet his. He wasn't going to move out of the doorway, and she was going to have to talk past him with what rags of dignity she had left.

'And one more thing,' he said softly as she reached the door. 'Coffee with the eggs. Black and strong with no sugar. I'll be down in ten minutes.'

Rowan was breathless when she reached the kitchen, and it wasn't because she'd been hurrying. She spooned coffee into the percolator bearing Carne's instructions in mind, then sliced mushrooms and tomatoes and put them to grill, while she broke eggs into a basin for an omelette, before sinking down rather limply on to one of the benches which flanked the stripped pine kitchen table. She had just made a complete and utter fool of herself in every way possible. There would be no difficulty now in convincing Carne Maitland she was only sixteen; in fact, he might even doubt that she had that much maturity. She groaned

inwardly. Antonia's view of the situation didn't bear thinking about, however amused she might have to pretend to
be. And it would be a poor defence to say she hadn't
intended to go to sleep, when she had had no right to be
lolling around on Carne's bed anyway.

'I think my Freudian slip must be showing,' she muttered, attacking her basin of eggs with a fork.

Omelettes were one of her specialities, and in spite of her
agitation, this one was no exception. It was light, fluffy and
golden brown, and she was just sliding it on to a warm
plate and arranging the grilled mushrooms and tomatoes
round it when Carne walked in.

'Would you rather eat in the dining room?' she asked as
he slid on to the bench.

'No, I wouldn't. Didn't you set this place for me?'

'Well—yes, but . . .'

'No buts,' he said. 'Or do you just intend to tantalise me
with that food?'

'I'm sorry.' She put the plate down hastily on the mat in
front of him, and went to switch off the percolator.

'This is fantastic,' he said after the first mouthful. 'Aren't
you joining me?'

'No, I ate earlier.' She set the coffee cup down beside
him.

'Then have some coffee with me. Bring another cup,' he
said in a tone which brooked no refusal.

After the briefest of hesitations she obeyed, sitting
down on the bench opposite and clasping her hands
round the pottery beaker, grateful for the comfort of its
warmth.

'Whatever your shortcomings as a chambermaid, you
can certainly cook,' he commented. 'Perhaps you'd better
limit your activities, such as they are, to the kitchen from
now on.'

'What do you mean?' Rowan stared at him.

He sighed. 'Do I really have to spell it out? I have no
pyjamas, nor have I ever owned a dressing gown. And if
the expression on your face just now was anything to go by,
close encounters of the bathroom kind aren't exactly your
scene, so I think it would be better if Antonia dealt with the
upstairs rooms from now on.' He paused, his eyes studying

her, then he said rather more gently, 'Don't look so stricken, love. I'm only trying to spare your blushes, charming though they may be. To be frank, I'd forgotten that girls still could blush.'

She said, 'Oh.' And then, 'That means I'll have to tell Antonia.'

'Tell her what?'

'Why I can't help with the bedrooms any more.' She sighed. 'I'd hoped I wouldn't have to do that.'

'Why in the world not?' Carne was grinning. 'Has she lost what little sense of humour she used to have?'

Rowan shrugged, recognising the need to become evasive. 'No—but I don't think she'll see much humour in that particular situation.'

It was true. Antonia would not want any mishaps to mar Carne's return home—nothing that would reflect on the efficient image she wanted to project. And she wouldn't find the fact that Rowan had curled up on Carne's bed for an afternoon nap amusing in the slightest. She might indeed find it uncomfortably significant, and Rowan could foresee difficulties enough in the weeks ahead without arousing her stepmother's jealous suspicions, or laying herself open to the kind of barbed remark in which Antonia excelled.

Carne, fortunately, read none of this into her words. 'I can't really see Antonia as the protective stepmother,' he said with a slight shrug. 'But perhaps you know her better than I do.'

'I doubt that very much,' she said unthinkingly, then seeing his brows rise, and the cool silver eyes fixed on her with a kind of hauteur, she stammered, 'I mean, you were close—very close—at one time. Antonia said so.'

'We saw quite a bit of each other when we were younger. Our contacts in recent years have been rather more limited, for reasons I'd prefer not to go into.'

He means because she was married to my father, Rowan thought with a little pang. She remembered Antonia saying, '*Your father, to speak plainly, sweetie, was jealous of him.*'

She said rather stiffly, 'I expect I can guess.'

'If you've been living with Antonia, then I expect you can. Is there any more coffee?'

'Yes, of course.' She took the cup he passed to her, and his empty plate. 'Would you like anything else to eat? There's some cheese and fruit, I think. If we'd known you were coming . . .'

'I barely knew myself.' Carne sounded vaguely irritable, as he flexed his shoulder muscles. Rowan remembered that in their earlier encounter he had mentioned his journey, and now that she had the courage to look him in the face a little more she could see the signs of travel fatigue in the lines of weariness about his mouth and the shadows under his eyes. 'Yes, I'll have some cheese, and an apple, please.'

She served his dessert, then refilled his coffee cup and brought it to him.

'Five-star attention,' he approved lazily. 'Keep up the good work, Rowan, and I may even start to feel like a human being again.' He smiled up at her, his fingers brushing hers as he took the cup from her, and she felt the compulsion of his attraction so strongly that it took all the self-control of which she was capable for her not to snatch her hand away and run out of the room.

And this is when he isn't even trying, she told herself in rueful desperation.

'How do you like Ravensmere?' He cut off a piece of apple and offered it to her on the blade of the knife.

'I like what I've seen very much,' she said, declining the apple with a prim shake of the head.

'It seems to have missed out on the tourist boom, which is all to the good as far as I'm concerned,' he said. 'We get our share of serious climbers, of course, but they tend to concentrate on the other side of the valley. Raven's Crag hasn't a great deal of excitement to offer. It's a scramble in places, but no more than that.'

'It's possible to get to the top, then?'

'Oh, yes, there's even a track for walkers to use, but you still need to exercise a reasonable amount of care. As you're living in my house, I suppose I'm responsible for you to a certain extent, and I'm warning you now, Rowan, not to regard any of the fells as an afternoon stroll in the park. The weather can change in minutes, and you certainly haven't lived here long enough to recognise the signs. So you never go out without the proper gear, and we'll make that a rule, please. I don't want the mountain rescue team being called out because you've behaved irresponsibly.'

It was hard to bite her lip and attempt to look suitably chastened, when she was longing to tell him that she had not the slightest intention of behaving without responsibility, and that she was fully aware of the dangers as well as the delights of her new surroundings. After all, you could hardly pick up a newspaper during the summer months without reading of someone who had come to grief, sometimes with fatal consequences, because they hadn't taken the mountains of Britain seriously enough.

She said quietly, 'You really don't have to worry about me. I don't think fell-walking is my scene particularly.'

'Then perhaps you'd like to give some thought to what is.' Carne finished the last of his apple. 'I'll be honest, Rowan. I didn't really take you into account when I arranged for Antonia to come here, and if she hadn't assured me it was imperative that you remain in her custody, I'd have made some kind of alternative arrangements for you. This is a very isolated spot for someone of your age.'

'You can be just as isolated in London.'

'But in a different way,' he said with a shade of impatience. 'At least there you have all kinds of opportunities. Here there's very little. I don't know how you're going to fill in your time.'

'Well, I shouldn't worry about it,' she said with thinly-veiled sarcasm, thinking of the hours of cleaning and polishing she had put in since she arrived. 'I'm sure I'll think of something. I'm sorry if you feel I'm going to be a burden to you. I'll do my best not to get in the way.'

'That isn't what I meant at all, you prickly child,' he said wearily. 'God, I don't grudge you a roof, but I didn't intend that you should sweat it out here with Antonia while she repaid her debt, one way or another.'

'You make it sound like a prison sentence,' she said tartly. 'Repaying her debt to society.'

'I've no doubt that's exactly how she regards it,' he said drily, glancing at his wristwatch. 'And I presume this trip to Keswick is time off for good behaviour.'

Rowan flushed slightly. 'I—suppose so.'

'You didn't want to go with her?' he asked casually. 'Or have you already exhausted its pleasures?'

'Something like that,' she mumbled. 'I'd better wash these dishes.'

'Leave them.' It was quite definitely an order, and she glanced at him in some surprise. He smiled rather tightly. 'Wrong fairy tale, love. You're Goldilocks, not Cinderella.'

'Goldilocks?' In spite of herself, her hand strayed up to touch a strand of her hair which had never, even in her most optimistic moments, been better than light brown.

'Why, yes.' He quoted softly, *'Who's been sleeping in my bed?'* and grinned maliciously as her colour deepened. 'But don't fear, fair maiden, your secret is safe with me. I won't mention it to Antonia, if you feel it's so important.' He stood up. 'And now I must go and pay my respects to Sybilla. How has she been?'

'I think she's well. We—we don't see a great deal of her.'

'That's a pity, but something else I failed to take into account—the fact that she and Antonia never got on together.' He gave her a quick glance. 'I take it time hasn't mellowed the situation?'

'Not really,' Rowan admitted, and he grimaced swiftly. 'The trouble is Sybilla isn't prepared to admit how bad her arthritis really is. That's one of the main reasons I wanted someone else living in the house for all the times I couldn't be here to keep an eye on her.'

'You're very fond of her?'

'My mother died when I was small. Sybilla damned near brought me up,' he said briefly. 'I intend to look after her.' He gave Rowan a wry glance. 'Don't look so surprised, love. I'm not entirely devoid of all decent feelings, whatever Antonia may have implied.'

'Oh, but she hasn't,' Rowan interpolated hastily.

'No?' His smile was cynical. 'Then she must have said something to cause this unease I sense in you when I'm around.'

Rowan shrugged. 'Perhaps I'm just not very used to men.'

'At your age no one would expect you to have vast experience, but you're not an early Victorian either.' He sounded amused. 'As we're going to be sharing the same roof for some considerable time, you're going to have to become used to me, I'm afraid.'

She stared at him. 'You mean—you're staying here? You're not going away again?'

'Yes, I'm staying,' he said. 'And you, Rowan Winslow, will just have to make the best of it.'

As he passed her, he ran a careless finger down the curve of her cheek and every nerve-ending in her body leapt in response to the casual caress.

'Thanks for the meal, love, and remember what I said. If you want to contribute, stick to the kitchen, and stay clear of my bedroom, if you know what's good for you.'

Shaken to the core, Rowan watched him go, and her hand stole up to touch her cheek. She thought, 'My God, I'll stay so clear I'll be invisible. And if I'd known what was good for me, I would never have come here at all.'

Antonia seemed in a high good humour when she arrived home an hour later, but her smile faded rapidly when Rowan told her that Carne was back.

'He could have given us some advance warning,' she complained, dumping two laden shopping bags down on the kitchen table. 'Thank God the house looks reasonable. I hope you remembered to do his room.'

'I think I remembered to do everything,' Rowan said a little coolly, and Antonia gave her a placatory smile.

'I'm sure you did, sweetie. Put this food away for me, will you, while I go and find his lordship.'

'He's talking to Sybilla still, I think,' Rowan called after her, and Antonia turned and came back again.

'In that case I'll wait for him to find me. He'll have heard the car by now. Make me some tea, will you, Rowan. Standing in queues at the butcher's is my least favourite occupation.'

'Oh, you've brought some fresh meat,' said Rowan, relieved. 'I'll make a goulash or something for this evening.'

'Make whatever you like,' Antonia's voice was frankly uninterested. 'I wonder why he's come back so suddenly?'

'He didn't say,' Rowan admitted. 'But he did tell me that he's come to stay for quite some time.'

'Good.' Antonia's smile was cat-like. 'That's fantastic news.'

'What's so fantastic?' Carne spoke coolly from the door-way, and Antonia turned towards him, her smile widening quite enchantingly.

'Why—darling!' She held out both hands to him. 'The fact that you've come home, of course.'

'If I'd known the kind of welcome awaiting me,' he said as he came across the kitchen to her, 'I'd have been home much sooner.'

She gave a little throaty laugh and lifted her face as his arms went round her.

Rowan murmured something and made her escape. Preparations for the evening meal would have to wait until she had the kitchen to herself. She had not the slightest desire to hang around watching Carne kissing Antonia, especially after what she suspected was the deliberate ambiguity of his last remark.

Antonia's bag and gloves and the camelhair jacket she wore while driving were flung down in an untidy heap in the hall, and Rowan sighed soundlessly as she bent to retrieve them. She went slowly up the stairs and turned towards the East Wing. She left Antonia's things on her bed with no great hopes that they would be put away, then went into her own room. She was glad it was so attractive because she had a feeling she would be spending a good deal of her time there. She went over to her table and looked down at the sheet of paper protruding from the typewriter. She had been trying her hand at a love story for a woman's magazine, and had been quite pleased with her efforts, but now the characters seemed cardboard, and the storyline ludicrously thin. She found she wanted to cry, but without knowing the exact cause of her depression. After all, things were turning out exactly as she had expected. There was no reason for her to have hoped for anything different.

Yet she supposed that in her most secret heart she allowed all kinds of little hopes to take root. Like the garden, they also wanted weeding out before too much harm was done, she thought, smiling a little ruefully at her own fancies.

The breeze from the open window suddenly struck a chill and she went across to close it. She heard the sound of voices below, and looking down she saw Carne and Antonia walking through the garden. Antonia's arm was through his, and she was smiling up at him.

A handsome couple, Rowan told herself, closing the window with exaggerated care. Whatever Carne's motives for inviting her here, she had no doubt that everything would work out to Antonia's ultimate advantage. Looking back, Rowan realised with a pang that her father had been able to refuse her nothing. But that was the kind of tribute which beauty like Antonia's would always be able to exact, she supposed.

And if they were in the garden, it meant the kitchen was empty and she could start preparations for dinner. On your way, Cinderella, she thought with a tiny grimace. Carne had been mistaken. That was a far more appropriate fairy tale for her, if one could have such a thing without the usual happy ending. Perhaps she ought to write an updated version of one where the stepmother walked off with the prince and the woodcutter's youngest daughter went in for social work. Now try laughing at that, she told herself grimly, and went downstairs.

She took time and trouble over her goulash, and it was in the oven and smelling delectable when Antonia reappeared.

'Can you amuse yourself this evening, sweetie?' she asked casually. 'Carne's taking me out to dinner.'

'But I've cooked dinner,' Rowan protested. 'I told you I was going to.'

Antonia shrugged. 'Then you'll be able to eat it, won't you? Don't try and impress Carne with home cooking, darling, it won't work. He's used to an international cuisine, as I thought you'd have had enough sense to guess.'

'He seemed tired. I didn't think he'd want to go out tonight,' Rowan said doggedly.

'Then you thought wrongly.' Antonia's voice was acid. 'He needs reviving, not mothering, thank you, so there's no need to wait up for us—with cocoa,' she added contemptuously.

Rowan flushed. 'I've no intention of waiting up at all. I hope you enjoy your evening.'

'I shall.' Antonia smiled and turned to the door, then paused and looked back at Rowan. 'You know, darling, if I didn't know you better, I'd swear you were a teeny bit jealous—and that would never do, would it?' She smiled again and left the room.

Rowan was sorely tempted to take the food and throw it in the kitchen bin, but apart from such an action being thoroughly wasteful, she was hungry in spite of her disappointment. She had intended to lay the dining room table, and find candles for the tall silver candlesticks, turning the meal into a small celebration. She supposed she should have guessed that Carne would want to celebrate in his own way, and in the company of his choice. After all, he had admitted earlier that he hadn't taken her presence into account when arranging for Antonia to come to Raven's Crag.

She looked down at her jeans and shirt in sudden dissatisfaction. She might be going to dine alone, but she could at least do so in a little style. She'd change into a dress, do her hair, put on some make-up.

When she went upstairs there was steam on the mirrors and tiled surfaces in the bathroom she shared with her stepmother, and the air was heavy with Antonia's perfume. She stripped and took a leisurely shower, then went back into her bedroom and put on a dark green dress with long sleeves, and a deep square neckline. It was too sophisticated for a sixteen-year-old, but if she was alone in the house she did not have to continue with that charade at least, she thought rather bitterly.

She hung around in her room until she heard the subdued roar of Carne's car engine leaving, and realised that must have been the distant thunder she had heard in her dream. But she resisted the impulse to go to the window and watch them leave.

As soon as everything was quiet she made her way downstairs again and went into the kitchen. Opening the oven door, she peered rather disconsolately at the simmering meat. She supposed she should have realised that Antonia would have made her plans as soon as she found out Carne was at home, and that it was too much to hope that her stepmother would have bothered to acquaint her with them.

And why should she? Rowan was forced to acknowledge. After all, Antonia had never made any secret of her intentions where Carne was concerned. And she, Rowan, had no right to feel any sense of resentment or isolation as Antonia pursued her objectives.

And of course she wasn't really alone in the house. It only seemed like that.

With sudden decision, she shut the oven door and went out of the kitchen. Feeling oddly nervous, she knocked at the door of Sybilla's flat. After a few minutes it opened, and Sybilla stood there leaning slightly on a stick and eyeing her gravely.

'Did you want something, child?' Her voice was not unfriendly, but it wasn't particularly encouraging either.

'It's nothing really. Just that I've made a goulash for supper, thinking there would be three of us, and Carne has gone out with Antonia, and there's far too much food for me alone, and I wondered if—if you'd like to have dinner with me.' Rowan could feel a slight flush rising in her cheeks as she stumbled to the end of her stilted little speech. It no longer seemed quite such a good idea, and she was regretting the impulse which had brought her here. It seemed more than likely that Sybilla would thank her politely, and shut the door. After all, she had never shown the slightest desire to seek their company after admitting them to the house two weeks before.

There was a marked silence, and she could feel Sybilla's eyes studying her appraisingly. Then a faint smile touched the corners of her mouth.

'Thank you, Rowan, I should be delighted. I had intended to have some cold meat and salad, but that will keep. Am I to infer that you've cooked this meal yourself?'

'Yes. I like cooking.'

'That is perhaps fortunate,' Sybilla remarked drily. 'I'll lay another place for you.' She accorded Rowan another small smile, then turned and went rather painfully back into the flat.

Rowan loaded a tray with plates, the tureen of meat, and a platter of crusty bread, then made her way back. This time the door was standing invitingly open, and after a quick knock she went in.

Sybilla's flat was situated in an extension to the house, and the entrance gave on to a narrow passage with doors on each side, and at the far end. Rowan found herself in a large living room, comfortably furnished in a more old-fashioned style than the rest of the house. There were a number of pictures on the walls, and every gleaming surface had its complement of ornaments and curios.

A circular rosewood dining table was set at one end of the room, laid with linen place mats and well-polished rather heavy-looking silver cutlery, with a bowl of white narcissus in the centre, their subtle scent pervading the atmosphere. A small woodfire crackled on the hearth, and beside it Sybilla was sitting in a high-backed wing chair.

'What a lovely room,' said Rowan, looking about her.

'I enjoy it,' Sybilla agreed. 'I'm very fortunate to be able to have all my own things around me. But that was something Carne insisted on when he had this house built.' Something warmed in her face as she spoke. 'And is that your goulash, my dear? It smells delicious. We'd better eat it before it gets cold.'

It was the most enjoyable meal Rowan had had since she arrived at Raven's Crag. She still found Sybilla a little formidable, but the older woman was obviously going out of her way to be approachable without being patronising. But occasionally, when there was a silence, Rowan was aware that Sybilla was watching her, her delicate brows drawn together in a little frown. Yet she knew she had been careful, steering the conversation away from the subject of school, and other danger zones which might inadvertently give away her correct age. She hadn't realised until then how many no-go areas in ordinary conversation Antonia's airy deception could create, and it annoyed her.

The subject of Antonia herself, when Sybilla broached it over coffee, seemed much safer ground. Sybilla asked about Rowan's father, and sympathised with her over the suddenness of his death.

'And he made Antonia your guardian, I understand,' she said, adding cream to her cup.

Rowan moved uncomfortably. 'Something like that,' she agreed cautiously. 'I don't really understand these legal terms.'

'Indeed?' Sybilla looked at her with lifted eyebrows. 'You don't seem to me to be devoid of understanding in any way, child. Perhaps you would like Carne to obtain details of your father's will and explain them to you.'

'Oh—no, thank you.' Rowan was secretly aghast. 'I—I know that Antonia and I have to live together until I'm twenty-one.' She gave an awkward smile. 'Unless I marry before then—or she marries again.'

'And if she should marry before you came of age, what would happen then?'

Rowan took a sip of too-hot coffee. 'I—really don't know. She—she may not want to get married again.'

'I can't imagine the widowed state holding much appeal for Antonia,' Sybilla said rather repressively. 'If she had been left a wealthy widow, that might have been different.'

Rowan bent her head. 'I suppose so. And she ought to get married again. She—she's very beautiful.'

'I tend to agree with Shakespeare, who said that beauty lives with kindness.' Sybilla drank her coffee. 'Therefore, although I agree your stepmother has great physical attraction, I would not, I fear, call her beautiful.'

As she spoke, her eyes wandered round the room lovingly, and Rowan thought with sudden intuition, 'She knows that if Carne marries Antonia she'll try to get rid of her. That's if Sybilla would even want to stay.'

Sybilla's eyes focussed on Rowan once more. She said gently, 'I should apologise to you, my dear, for speaking in such terms of your stepmother. I wouldn't wish to impose any kind of strain on your loyalty.' She frowned as she saw Rowan's hand go up to her mouth. 'And please don't bite your nails—it's an ugly and distressing habit. Years ago, bitter aloes would have been applied as a prevention. Has Antonia never thought of it?'

'I don't think Antonia notices that I bite my nails.' Rowan regarded them ruefully. 'I don't do it as often these days—only when I'm upset or nervous about something.'

'Dear me,' Sybilla said drily. 'I'm sorry to have had such an unhappy effect on you.'

'Oh, it isn't that.' Rowan gave a little sigh. 'It's been quite a day, what with Carne coming home unexpectedly like that.'

She looked up and surprised an odd flicker of expression in Sybilla's eyes and wondered if his return had in fact been quite so unexpected where one member of his household was concerned. And if so, why hadn't Sybilla warned them? Rowan couldn't imagine her guilty of petty spite, and the only other answer was that she had been acting under Carne's instructions.

She said carefully, 'It was a good job we were prepared anyway.'

'Yes,' Sybilla agreed with a kind of grim amusement. 'A very good job. Carne, I think, was impressed.'

And no doubt, Rowan thought dismally, the dinner tonight was thanks for services rendered. Carne, naturally, would assume the state of readiness he had found was Antonia's doing. And yet, if the truth were told, over the past two weeks she had barely lifted a finger.

She said, 'He told me he intended to stay for a while.'

'You sound surprised. After all, child, this is his home.'

'Yes.' Rowan cleared her throat. 'But it hasn't been, has it—up to now. He travels the world.'

'He has been very successful in his chosen profession, even though some members of his family were against it at first,' said Sybilla. 'His kind of life may seem very glamorous and exotic to someone of your age, but it can pall in the end, you know. Carne bought this land and built this house in order to put down roots. Perhaps the time has come for him to do that.' Her eyes surveyed Rowan calmly.

And that's why he's invited Antonia here, Rowan thought. He must still love her if he wants her after so many years, and knowing her as he does, there won't be any shocks or disappointments as there were for Daddy.

She stopped, realising this was the first time she had openly acknowledged to herself that all had not been well in her father's second marriage. A much younger Rowan had tried to mask her own feeling with the litany, 'But Daddy loves her. Daddy thinks she's wonderful.' But as she had approached adult life, she had no longer seen their relationship with the eyes of a child. She had absorbed the lack of caring on one side and the disillusionment on the other almost without knowing it.

She looked back at Sybilla with stricken eyes, but that lady was calmly collecting up the coffee things. 'Come, my dear. It's getting late. We'd better do the washing up.' She gave Rowan a tranquil smile. 'And don't worry. Things have a way of working out for the best which you may not have discovered yet.'

Later, as she lay sleepless in her green-sprigged room, Rowan tried to tell herself it would be for the best if Antonia and Carne were married. But the only advantage she could think of was that she herself would obtain her independence. I could go away, she thought, and never to see either of them again. But it was a pitiful effort at self-consolation, when she knew in her heart that simply not seeing Carne would do nothing to erase him from her memory.

It was very late when she saw headlights rake the window and heard the sound of the engine. She lay, every nerve of her body tense, listening, and hating herself for doing so, and eventually she heard Antonia's heels click past her room, and her door open and close quietly. She had been alone. No heavier masculine tread had accompanied her, or even followed later. But that, Rowan told herself wryly, trying to find a cool place for her cheek on the pillow, was a very small mercy for which to be thankful.

CHAPTER FOUR

WHEN Rowan got down to the kitchen the next morning, there were signs that someone had breakfasted and gone, but she did not somehow think it had been Antonia, who rarely rose before nine-thirty.

She made herself some toast and brewed a fresh pot of coffee, but she had barely sat down at the table before Antonia drifted in looking ravishing in a peignoir of pale green chiffon.

'Is that coffee?' she demanded, sinking down on to the bench. 'Really, Rowan, you might have brought me some.

No, I won't have any toast, I've never been able to understand this passion for scorched bread at breakfast. Croissants would be nice if we could get some.'

'Wonderful,' Rowan agreed ironically. 'Where do you suggest we start looking?'

'Well, of course there isn't anywhere in this benighted hole, I know that.' Antonia stirred her coffee moodily.

'How is your campaign to get Carne to move going?'

'It isn't yet. I thought I'd give him a few weeks to find out for himself how stultifyingly boring the rural life is.' She gave a satisfied little smile. 'It shouldn't take long. Carne's far too used to the high life to take kindly to isolation. Although I must admit I was impressed with the restaurant he took me to last night. It was just like a theatrical production, sweetie. They even lowered the lights between courses and . . .' Her voice went on outlining the food they had eaten, but Rowan had switched off. Her sleepless night had done nothing for her looks, and, she discovered, even less for her temper.

Antonia relapsed into silence after a while, her enthusiasm apparently quenched by her companion's lack of response, and Rowan, glancing across the table at her, saw that her lovely face was setting in lines of petulance, as if her present thoughts were not nearly as pleasing as her reminiscences of the previous night's pleasures. Rowan sighed inwardly. She knew that look. She had seen it before on a number of occasions—when her father's will had been read, for one, and when the boutique finally closed its doors for another. It was a look which said that Antonia had suddenly been brought face to face with some form of unwelcome reality, and Rowan found herself wondering whether last night's food and wine had in fact been the sugar-coating on a somewhat unacceptable pill.

But whatever had happened, or been said, she knew Antonia would tell her sooner or later. It was not in her stepmother's nature to keep bad news to herself for long.

Eventually Antonia said abruptly, pouring herself more coffee, 'Carne wanted to send you back to school. I had a hell of a job to dissuade him.'

'I can imagine.' Rowan drank some of her own coffee, but it was lukewarm and bitter and she grimaced slightly as she set the beaker back on the table. 'What did you say to him?'

Antonia shrugged. 'Oh, that you'd had a belated reaction to your father's death, and you needed careful handling,' she said, avoiding Rowan's gaze.

'That's almost disgusting under the circumstances,' Rowan said at last. 'Wouldn't the truth have been easier, and cleaner?'

'Perhaps, but I'm committed to the fact that you're an adolescent now,' Antonia said moodily. 'Frankly I hadn't bargained for Carne's sense of family responsibility. It certainly wasn't so evident in his early years. He practically put me through an inquisition last night on the subject of you. God knows what Sybilla's been telling him.' She gave a long-suffering sigh.

'Why should she have been telling him anything?' Rowan stared at her.

'Because she loves to interfere, and nothing would please her more than to put a spoke in my wheel,' Antonia replied sharply.

'Perhaps she recognises that you plan to put a spoke in hers,' said Rowan, remembering Sybilla's loving glance round her home last night.

'Hm, well that's something else which isn't going to be as easy as I thought,' Antonia said tartly. 'Carne's changed. He was always the outsider, the rebel in the family, but at times he can display signs of typical Maitland stubbornness. This business of Sybilla is a case in point. It seems inevitable that she's going to become a virtual cripple, and a suitable nursing home is the obvious answer.'

'But it's not obvious to Carne?'

'No, it isn't. And it's going to create an impossible situation.' Antonia's mouth hardened. 'I'm sure that Sybilla has as little wish to have me waiting on her as I have to do the waiting.'

'Is that what he's suggesting?'

Antonia made an impatient gesture. 'Oh, not in so many words, but that's the way the wind's blowing. It has to be if she's to go on living here as he intends.'

'It is her home, and he is worried about her,' Rowan said pacifically, and Antonia stared at her.

'You seem to know a great deal about it.'

Rowan shrugged awkwardly. 'He—mentioned it yesterday. And he's gone to a great deal of trouble over the flat.'

'Did he mention that too?'

'No, I saw that for myself. I—I had supper with Sybilla last night.'

'Really?' Antonia gave a small completely unamused laugh. 'You've been a busy girl! And what did the old bitch have to say about me?'

'Not a great deal,' Rowan replied evasively.

'I bet.' Antonia's gaze narrowed. 'Well, you can't fight on both sides in this battle, sweetie, so you'd better make up your mind now which of us you're supporting.'

'You're being ridiculous,' Rowan said wearily. 'There's no battle, and I'm taking no sides. I'd simply cooked a lot of food, and it seemed silly to waste it, that's all.'

'That precious meal you laboured over still rankles, doesn't it, darling?' Antonia drawled. 'Well, just in case you were beginning to get ideas above your station, I dropped Carne a delicate hint last night that you might make him the subject of a father fixation if we weren't very careful.' She smiled. 'The idea didn't seem to have much appeal for him at all.'

'My own view entirely,' Rowan said calmly. She was trembling inside with controlled anger. 'Is there anything else you've said or insinuated that I should know about?'

Antonia considered for a moment, her eyelids drooping. 'No, I think that about covers it,' she replied eventually with insouciance. 'And don't look at me like that, sweetie. You'd have done exactly the same thing in my place.'

'Would I?' Rowan queried ironically.

'You would, if it meant as much to you as it does to me,' Antonia said moodily. 'Do you really think I've enjoyed the kind of hand-to-mouth existence we've had since Vic died? I never want to live like that again, and I'll do anything—anything, do you understand?—to make sure that I never have to.'

'Oh, I understand.' Rowan sighed. 'I just wish that you hadn't involved me.'

Antonia shrugged. 'As if I had a choice! Like Sybilla,

you've been taken under Carne's newly protective wing.'
She frowned. 'It's a development I don't particularly care
for. The Carne I knew never wanted that sort of responsibility. That's what was always so attractive about
him. There was the family firm in the City with its seat on
the board all ready for him, and Carne turning his back on
it to go to art school.' She laughed. 'Whole generations of
Maitlands must have spun round in their graves at the very
idea!'

'And was that all that appealed to you—the fact that he
wasn't a typical member of the family?' Rowan asked,
startled.

'Of course not!' Antonia's sudden smile was catlike.
'Even you, darling, can't be that naïve. No, he was always
tremendously—imaginative, and satisfying—to be with.'
The little pauses, and the slight breathlessness with which
she uttered the last words, left her listener in no doubt at all
as to her meaning—as if there had ever been any, Rowan
thought bitterly. Antonia smiled again. 'And I'm sure his
repertoire will have increased since then.'

'Very probably.' Rowan's distaste for the turn the conversation had taken showed in her voice.

'Don't be so prim, sweetie. It doesn't suit your genera-
tion at all, especially as I suspect you're just the teeniest bit
smitten with dear Cousin Carne yourself. You do know
you're wasting your time, don't you?'

Rowan lifted her shoulders wearily. 'I don't really have
to answer that, do I?'

'Not really,' Antonia admitted complacently. 'Just remember that Carne regards you as a troublesome adolescent with a father complex, and you should have no difficulty in keeping your distance.'

'If that's what you want,' Rowan said coldly, 'I'm surprised you didn't encourage him in the school idea—or did
the possible repercussions give even you pause for thought?'

Antonia smoothed back her hair. 'But I don't want you
to go away, darling. I just don't want you to get any funny
ideas about Carne. After all, what would I do without
you?'

'I've no idea,' shrugged Rowan. 'But perhaps it would
be a good idea to find out. Shall we do it, Antonia? Shall

we say to hell with the allowance from the estate? Neither of us is likely to starve, after all. You'll have Carne, and I'll have the Welfare State. We'd manage, and I'm sure you could make up one of your convincing stories to explain my disappearance.'

'No.' Antonia slammed her empty coffee cup down on the table. 'You said you'd come here. You promised you'd help me. You can't leave me, Rowan—you know you can't!'

The complacency had gone completely. Under her make-up Antonia's face was strained, and the violet eyes had widened, and begun to fill with tears. She said again, 'Darling, you can't leave me—please!'

No, Rowan thought, bitterly, she could not leave. Although it had never been acknowledged openly, and this admittance of dependence was as close as Antonia would ever be able to bring herself to the truth, she had to stay and look after Antonia because this was the way her father had wanted it. She looked across at her stepmother with resignation and pity and saw that some of the tears had begun to fall.

'I shan't be able to manage without you.' Antonia's voice was shaking. 'Carne's planning all kinds of things—house parties, dinners, and he expects me to cope single-handed. And I can't, Rowan, you know that. Not without proper staff. I—I tried to tell him, really I did, and he started talking about our bargain, and the terms we'd made. If I make a mess of this job, he'll find some other way of making me repay that money, I know he will. You've got to help me! He still might have me made bankrupt. The Maitlands can be terribly unforgiving sometimes.'

'In spite of their sense of family responsibility, I suppose,' Rowan said ironically. 'But don't worry, Antonia, I'll stay—for as long as it takes.'

'Bless you, darling.' Antonia gave her a watery smile. 'I—I realise I haven't been pulling my weight up to now, but I will—you'll see.'

'I think you'll have to,' Rowan agreed wryly. She carried the beakers over to the sink and rinsed them out. When she turned to put them away, she found she was

alone. Antonia had left silently, to repair the ravages in her
appearance that her bout of tears had caused, and, with
any luck, to get dressed. No matter how decorative she
might look, Rowan doubted whether chiffon peignoirs
gave Antonia the air of hard-working efficiency she
needed.

She felt wretched, like a fly trapped in a jar who knows
the only means of escape is through an impenetrable barrier. But my barrier is of my own devising, she thought,
because I could walk out of here tomorrow. Only I won't,
and the fact that Daddy has hung Antonia round my neck
like some glamorous albatross is only part of the reason,
and I know that only too well.

Everything in her head was telling her that flight was the
only answer, and everything in her heart was whispering,
'Stay—because although there'll be pain and heartache
and jealousy and confusion, if you go you'll only be half
alive.'

If I go, she thought, then I'll have to live with the might-
have-been. I'm going to wonder for the rest of my life
whether my staying might have made any difference.
If I stay, and I see him loving Antonia—or what passes for
love between two people like them—and marrying her
perhaps, then I'll be able to walk away and not look back.
It isn't a lifetime. It may only be for this summer, and then
I'll be able to get my head together and my life together,
and it will be a good life without regrets because it has to
be.

But just then, as she looked round the kitchen with its
shining surfaces and stainless steel reflecting back a dozen
white-faced, unhappy Rowans, she knew she had to escape
the glass jar and its confines if only for a little while.

There was a real warmth in the air when she got outside,
and the grass and earth smelt fresh and raw after the
night's showers. Rowan took a long deep breath and felt
better, as if the sun was some kind of reassurance which was
patently ridiculous. The gardens lay at the side of the house
stretching back for some considerable way, as she had
already discovered on her tentative explorations. They
were bordered by a dry stone wall, and at the farthest limit
there was a gate which led out on to the side of the fell itself,

and it was this that Rowan made for, going up the steeply sloping path almost at a run. Not that it could really be called a garden, she thought, glancing around her. It was still unclaimed, still almost wilderness, and it would never transplant into the kind of formal garden Antonia had been used to. There were too many trees and tall shrubs, full of the argument of birds, too many reminders of the brooding hillside beyond the wall.

The catch of the gate was stiff and heavy with unuse, and she stood struggling with it rather breathlessly. It gave eventually, and rather suddenly, and the gate swung towards her creaking violently on its hinges.

Carne's voice from behind her said drily, 'You have a short memory.'

Rowan gasped out loud and her grip on the heavy gate slackened, causing it to swing even further, almost carrying her with it. Carne stepped forward, taking hold of it, pushing it shut and dropping the catch again with a kind of finality.

He said quite pleasantly, 'I thought we'd agreed no trips on to the fells without proper equipment.'

His eyes went over her, making it clear that he did not consider jeans, a cream jersey shirt and flat-heeled leather sandals to fall into the category of proper equipment, and Rowan flushed.

'I—I wasn't going far. I needed a stroll—some air. Exercise.' She looked back at him defiantly. 'Surely that isn't against the rules?'

'I spelled out the only rule,' he said with an edge to his voice. 'I'm going to become very bored if I have to keep doing so. If you want to go out on the fell, then you change into some reasonable gear. Better still, you wait until I can go with you.'

'I hardly think that's necessary.' Rowan felt resentment stab at her. 'I may be every bit the nuisance Antonia has claimed, but I'm not on parole, nor do I need a keeper.'

Hands on hips, he stared back at her, the silver eyes cold as ice. 'I think Antonia understated your nuisance value,' he said grimly. 'While you're living under my roof, you follow the guidelines that I set down. Let that be understood as of now.' He paused. 'Well?'

Rowan said shakily, 'Oh, I understand. I won't even ask what the alternative is. I'm sure it's something I wouldn't want to know about.'

'Right,' he agreed. 'But at the moment, if it's exercise that you need, you can give me a hand with some gardening.'

'Do you trust me not to swing from the trees?' she asked sweetly, then held up a hand hastily as she saw his face darken. 'I'm sorry, it was a bad joke. I'm just not used to the heavy hand.'

'That's more than obvious.' His voice was dry. 'And it explains a great deal. Well, are you going to help me or not?'

She hesitated, the sudden lift of her heart warring with her sense of self-preservation.

'I don't know very much about gardening,' she temporised.

'But I imagine you can recognise nettles and dandelions when you see them,' said Carne with a trace of impatience. 'That's the kind of level you'll be operating at.'

She shrugged rather helplessly, the thought of Antonia's possible reactions in the forefront of her mind. 'All right, then.'

'Your enthusiasm overwhelms me.' His mouth curled a little. 'Look, Rowan, this may not be a situation that either of us would have chosen, but things will become a great deal easier with just a little ordinary co-operation from you.'

'The inference being that I haven't co-operated up to now,' she said in a low voice, feeling all the bitterness of hurt in her throat. Antonia, it seemed, had done her work all too well.

'Infer anything you wish. I'm quite prepared to turn the page, and wipe out anything that's happened in the past. It's the immediate future which concerns me. Antonia won't be able to carry out her duties here in a way which will satisfy either of us if she's in a perpetual state of turmoil about you and your behaviour—surely you see that?'

'Yes, I see,' she said defeatedly. 'Perhaps you'd better show me this gardening you want me to do.'

He gave her a long look before turning on his heel and

leading the way back down the slope of the path, and she realised that he must have been working in the tangle of shrubs that she had passed. There was a spade sticking out of the newly turned earth, and a hoe and other implements lying on the path.

'Do you want some gloves to protect your hands?'

Rowan looked ruefully down at her fingers. 'I don't really think it matters.'

'You're probably right.' His glance followed hers. 'That's another habit it would do you no harm to break.'

She felt her cheeks redden. 'Don't rush me,' she said rather tightly. 'I can only take so many adjustments at one time.'

The slanting smile he sent her contained a measure of appreciation. They worked in silence for a while, Carne digging, and Rowan on her knees, tugging out handfuls of groundsel and goosegrass, and probing down with a trowel to find the endless dandelion roots. The earlier breeze had dropped and the sun shone down in unseasonable warmth. After a while Carne stripped off the sweater he was wearing, hanging it on the branch of a convenient bush. His body was deeply tanned, proving, Rowan thought, that it had been a long time since he had been forced to winter in a hostile climate, and the tan extended to every inch of his lean, muscular body, as she hadn't been able to help noticing in that paralysed moment when he had come out of the shower. The memory brought hot colour into her face, and she bent forward to tug at a particularly recalcitrant weed, letting her hair fall forward like a curtain to conceal her flushed cheeks.

So the rich, the all-conquering Carne Maitland, portrait painter to the famous, sunbathed in the nude. There was nothing very significant in that. In the cosmopolitan circles in which he moved, nudity on the beach or at the poolside was probably the accepted thing—no big deal at all. And she was no throwback to the Victorian age or candidate for a convent to be shocked because he chose to lead his life on less conventional grounds than her own. And she knew how men were made, for heaven's sake, so why all this big mental fuss? She bit back a sigh. Life at Raven's Crag was going to be difficult enough without an endless struggle against her physical awareness of Carne. It was something she was going to have to keep under tight control, because if he ever realised or even suspected, it would be hideously embarrassing. Already, thanks to Antonia's carefully worded hints, he thought she was some kind of drop-out, and that was bad enough. But it would be infinitely worse if the label of sexual precocity were also to be attached to her, and earn even more contempt.

She was a fool to care what Carne thought, she knew, but if Antonia's schemes all came to fruition this summer, then she wanted to leave Raven's Crag knowing that Carne thought well of her. It shouldn't matter, yet it did—terribly.

She snatched at another handful of weeds and recoiled with a little cry as she saw too late the stinging nettles among the grass. She sat back on her heels rubbing ruefully at the white rash on her wrist and arm.

'What have you done?' Carne came across and squatted beside her. His fingers encircled her wrist and tension welled up inside her at his touch. He said drily, 'Relax—you'll live. They say the thing to do with nettles is to grasp them firmly, then they don't sting.'

'And other bits of homespun philosophy,' she retorted, rubbing her arm. 'I didn't even see the beastly things until it was too late.'

His mouth twisted. He said, 'Make sure that isn't the story of your life, Rowan,' and released her, standing up as he did so.

Rowan said, knowing that she sounded childish, 'It's—criminal to have let the garden get into this state.'

'What are you suggesting—that I should have sent Sybilla out here, hoe in hand?'

'No, of course not. But you could have employed someone, surely?' She moistened her lips slightly. 'Just as I can't really believe Sybilla looked after a house that size all by herself, even before her arthritis worsened.'

'No, she didn't.' His eyes narrowed a little. 'But if you imagine I'm going to provide the same facilities now so that you and Antonia can put your feet up, then you can think again. As for the garden, the last man who worked it took the money and didn't do the job, and I promised myself that wouldn't happen again. Besides, I want to do it myself.'

'But for how long?' she muttered. 'A garden is a—a continuous process, not something you can pick up and discard when you want.'

'And who says I have any intention of doing that? You take a lot for granted.' There was a warning note of anger beneath his level voice.

She shrugged defensively. 'It's obvious, isn't it? You have your own life to lead—your commissions. Or are people so keen to have their portraits painted by you that they'll come all the way here instead?'

'You could be nearer the mark than you think in a number of cases,' Carne said coolly. 'But it wouldn't make any difference if they did. My enthusiasm for portrait painting has waned. I doubt if I'll be accepting any more commissions—at least none of the kind I've been offered recently.'

'But why not? You're a great success. You're famous.'

'Perhaps I've decided to become a famous gardener instead,' he said, his voice faintly amused at her vehemence.

Rowan pushed a strand of hair back from her face and stared at him. Then she said flatly, 'I don't believe a word of it. I don't believe you've the slightest intention of burying yourself up here for the rest of your life.'

'Is that how you look on Raven's Crag? As somewhere to be buried?' he asked rather harshly, and she flushed.

'No—but from the point of view of someone like you . . .'

'And what in the world does a child of your age know about the point of view of someone like me?' The silver eyes were as cold as winter as they stared down at her, and she shivered a little as her own gaze encountered them.

'I'm—sorry. Perhaps I was being presumptuous, but . . .'

'There's no perhaps about it,' he said crisply. 'I'm here at Raven's Crag and I intend to stay here until someone can show me an excellent reason for leaving, even temporarily. This is my home, remember.'

'Yet you haven't spent a great deal of your time here up to now.'

'That's something I intend to remedy. I'm sorry if that

interferes with your own plans,' he added sardonically.

'I haven't any plans.' Rowan picked up her trowel again.

'And that's something else I intend to remedy,' Carne remarked rather too pleasantly. 'I'm not altogether taken with Antonia's theory that you're still too weighed down by the past to have much interest in the future. It simply sounds like an excuse for inaction.'

She couldn't deny it. She had no idea what Antonia could have been thinking to suggest such a thing. No one in their right mind would believe that a young girl however devoted to her father's memory would be still too crushed by grief two years after his death to make any plans for her own life. But then, she thought ironically, Carne hadn't been expected to believe it. Antonia had intended it to sound just as it did—a specious excuse for her stepdaughter's shortcomings. She dug viciously at the roots of a persistent dandelion with her trowel.

'And what's your excuse?' she asked coolly after a moment. She did not have to look up to know he was frowning.

'For what?'

'For your inaction. You've just told me you're giving up your career.'

'That isn't true. Portrait painting has never been my whole life, whatever you may have been led to think.'

'No, of course not. You're—something in the City as well.'

'You make it sound like a black mark against me,' he said wryly. 'I suppose I can hardly blame you for that. For some years I held similar feelings.'

'But not any more?'

'Let's just say that I've become increasingly aware lately that I have responsibilities beyond those to myself,' he said flatly. 'There's been pressure on me for some time to do more than occupy a nominal seat on the Board.' He gave a slight shrug. 'Perhaps the time has come for me to yield to that pressure. Once, I'd have thought it was a sacrifice.'

'You don't feel that now?'

'I'm not sure what I feel. I know I've been growing increasingly disenchanted with my portrait work. This last commission was pretty much the final straw. An acquaintance with more money than sense wanted a portrait of his wife. I was half way through the sittings when I realised I was thinking what a farce it all was, and not for the first time either. I've always painted because I enjoyed it, and not simply because I could. But the enjoyment has been growing less and less lately, and Marcella was the final straw.'

'Was she beautiful?' asked Rowan.

'On the surface, I suppose. But when you looked deeper, which you must do if the finished work is to have any kind of relevance, the bone structure was wrong, and there was a mean little soul behind that too.'

'Did you finish the portrait?'

'Oh, yes,' his lip curled, emphasising the scar. 'She had some exquisite jewellery, presented by the doting Jack, so I painted that instead. Fortunately neither they nor any of their friends had the wit to realise. They thought it was a wonderful likeness, when all it was was a vast emptiness.' He smiled faintly. 'It was a salutary experience, and it helped me crystallise some of the thoughts I'd been having for several months.'

'But you don't intend to give up altogether?' Rowan said quickly.

'I shall paint for my own amusement. Living in surroundings like this I could hardly do otherwise.'

'But—surely—you'll want to paint Antonia?'

Carne lifted an eyebrow. 'I wasn't aware Antonia wished to be painted. And I don't think she could afford my fee,' he added drily.

He was being deliberately obtuse, Rowan thought angrily. It stood to reason that when he married Antonia, he would paint her. She could even visualise the spot where the portrait would hang in that big sunlit sitting room. Then she remembered that it was Antonia's declared intention to get Carne to leave Raven's Crag.

Carne said abruptly, 'You seem to be fighting a losing battle with that dandelion. Suppose you go and make us some coffee, and I'll deal with it. When you come back we'll have an in-depth probe on your motivation—or lack of it.'

She scrambled to her feet, dusting off the legs of her jeans.

'There's nothing to discuss,' she said defensively. 'I've left school, and I haven't got a job. There are thousands like me.'

'I'm not convinced of that. From what I can gather, you've made no attempt to find work, and yet you don't appear to be without ability.'

'Thank you, kind sir, she said.' Rowan's voice was bitter.

He sighed impatiently. 'Your attitude doesn't help. Do you intend to sponge off Antonia for the rest of your life?'

The unfairness of it—the deliberate cruelty—made her gasp for a moment, and there was a dazed look in the eyes she turned on him.

'I'll leave,' she said in a voice she didn't recognise. 'I'll go . . .'

'Where? To the dole queue? I think not,' he said grimly. 'I'm not trying to get rid of you, Rowan. I'm not even saying the situation is wholly of your making—although I never reckoned Antonia for the clinging type. What I'm trying to get you to face is the fact that you have a future for which you should be planning. If you need a breathing space—advice—help, then we'll try to give them to you.'

'Don't patronise me,' she said rather wildly. 'Isn't there a saying that there's no one as virtuous as a reformed rake? No one ever told you what you were going to do with your life. And you've left it pretty late to discover this sudden sense of responsibility, haven't you? And probably you wouldn't have done anything about it if your last sitter had been different—if she'd been beautiful and you'd fancied her—wanted to make love to her,' she finished breathlessly.

There was a silence. Then he said, 'You have a tongue like a wasp, darling, and a temperament to match. Wasps seem to spend most of their time living off the fat of the land in summer and being neither use nor ornament. And they often come to a sticky end at the end of it, as you will, if you venture any more wild speculations on my private life or morals. My relationships with any of my sitters, past, present or future, are no bloody business of yours, and you'd better remember that.'

'Yes, sir.' She threw her head back defiantly, her small breasts rising and falling under the urgency of her breathing. 'Will there be anything else?'

'Don't tempt me,' he tossed back at her contemptuously. 'For your health's sake I advise you to get out of my sight, and keep out of it.'

'I only wish I could do so permanently!' Tears of anger tasted bitter in her throat.

'Unfortunately for us both, you have a measure of growing up to do before that happy day.' Carne gave her a long look before turning away and reaching for his discarded spade. When he spoke again, he sounded weary. 'Run away, Rowan, and play—if that's all you have a taste for.'

Her anger, her sense of outrage seemed to drain out of her as she stood there. It was good advice he was giving her—better, in fact, than he knew. For her own sake, she should keep well out of his way. It was safer. At least she wouldn't be tempted to enjoy the sense of companionship that this brief time working beside him had given her. For a few moments, he even seemed to have forgotten that she was an irresponsible sixteen-year-old. He'd talked to her as if she was a woman. Of course it hadn't lasted, and if she was honest, she should be glad that it hadn't. Any relationship with Carne would be like one of those ancient maps bounded by uncharted seas and the warning legend 'Here be dragons.'

But it wasn't going to be easy playing this part which Antonia had so carelessly assigned to her. Especially as no definite limit had been set to their stay at Raven's Crag. She'd thought it would be weeks, but now it seemed as if it could be months. Months of living under the same roof, of sharing, even in a small part, his life—rather like a Victorian waif with her nose pressed against a baker's shop window.

The ache in her throat seemed to increase, and her mouth felt dry as she looked at him, all his attention concentrated on the spade he was thrusting into the dark earth. She could see the play of muscles in his back and arms, and knew instinctively that he was a man who relished physical activity, whether it was manual work, or sport, or making love—a thought which made her catch her breath.

Whether it was the tiny sound she had made which alerted him, she didn't know. But he turned abruptly and their eyes met, before she could school her features or wipe the hunger from her eyes. The sudden heat she felt in her body had nothing to do with the sun, and her eyes left his to move over the harsh planes of his face down to his mouth, where the little scar was vividly white against his tan. Her tongue crept out to moisten the dryness of her lips, and Carne moved with savage abruptness, or perhaps she was already moving, on her way to him. His skin was warm and imbued with the scent of fresh sweat, and she breathed him through her open mouth, through the tips of her fingers as they spread across his chest. Then his own hand came up, tangling in her hair, dragging her head back so that her face was lifted, rapt with longing, for his kiss.

He made no concessions. There was still anger flaring between them, and his kiss was in many ways a punishment. The world seemed to darken around her as she clung to him, something wild and untried within her leaping to meet the roughness of his passion as she tasted her own blood on her mouth. She was afraid—of course she was. The dragons she had sensed were here, all around her, as much a part of her as they were of Carne.

From the moment she had seen him, standing in Antonia's sitting room, she had been drawn by some barely understood compulsion, and nothing in her strictly limited experience to date had prepared her for the bruising demand of his hands and mouth. Yet with some barely coherent corner of her mind she knew she was glad that no one had ever kissed her with the same harsh, dizzying intensity, that no one's hands had ever begun the same heart-racing journey of discovery.

And then, as suddenly as it had started, it was over. Carne put her away from him so abruptly and completely that she stumbled and almost fell to her knees. She threw out a hand to steady herself, and he stepped back, away from her, out of reach. His face was taut, and he whispered an obscenity half under his breath as he looked at her, the scar giving his mouth a satanic twist.

Rowan tried to control her breathing, to drag together the remnants of her shattered poise, to say something to dispel the tension between them, but all the things she wanted to say were those that could never be uttered—those that he wouldn't want to hear anyway. She had already betrayed too much in that unguarded moment when he had looked into her eyes, and later by her naïve response to his brutality.

When he spoke, his voice was soft, but there was a note in it which grated along her nerve-endings. 'If you're waiting for me to apologise, Rowan, then you'll wait for ever. When I told you to run and play, I didn't have games like that in mind. But you——' he laughed harshly—'you're nothing but trouble through and through, are you? I won't ask where you learned your sex kitten's tricks. I don't think I want to know. But I warn you—you won't catch me off guard again.'

Wincing, she knew she had to make some kind of protest—find some justification for the way she had behaved.

She said in a low voice, 'Carne, I'm not a child . . .'

The silver eyes blazed at her, and she took an involuntary step backwards.

'Why? Because you've reached the age of consent? God, what do they teach girls in boarding schools these days? There are light years between us, baby doll, and don't you forget it, because I shan't.' He paused, his gaze raking her. 'So—get out of the garden, Eve,' he added savagely. 'I've had all the temptation I can stomach. And to think that I imagined our encounter in my shower was an accident!'

'It was—it was!' She bit her lip. 'Oh, Carne, please listen. I . . .'

'I've heard too much already,' he said coldly. 'What a pity that demure exterior was only skin deep. Now, get out of here, Rowan, if you know what's good for you—and from now on keep out of my way.'

'Oh, I shall.' She had to salvage some dregs of pride from somewhere. 'You can't imagine I want to risk a repetition of that—nauseating performance?'

'There's no risk,' he said. 'And you're fooling only yourself with your claim of nausea. If I hadn't called a halt, we'd be doing more than just kissing, and you know it.'

'You're a savage,' she said huskily.

'I'm a man—but you're far from being a woman, so

spare me your sexual experiments from now on. It's a
brand of curiosity I've no interest in satisfying.'

His words fell like a lash across her heated skin. Mortifi-
cation seemed uppermost in the jumble of emotions which
assailed her, and impulsively she lifted her hand and struck
him hard across the face. He hadn't been expecting such a
retaliation because he made no effort to intercept the blow,
and with a kind of horror Rowan saw the marks of her
fingers across his cheek. With a little gasp she turned and
fled, heedless of the branches and twigs that dragged at her,
impeding her headlong progress. And even as she ran, she
knew that her flight was futile, and much, much too late.

CHAPTER FIVE

SAFE in her room, Rowan managed to regain a measure of
her self-control. She flung herself across her bed and lay
there, too stunned by the swift passage of events and her
own emotional turmoil even to cry.

So much, she thought ironically, when she could think,
for all her good intentions. Carne had spoken bitterly of
temptation, of being caught off his guard, but the failure
had been hers. And she had known, she had gauged almost
perfectly what his reaction would be if she ever let him see
how she felt. But the knowledge of how right she had been
was no balm to her wounded spirit.

But at least it was an end to all her foolish dreams and
fantasies. There was nothing for her to hope for now—as if
there had ever been, she thought, burying her flushed face
in the pillow. She had behaved like a fool, and the fact that
her provocation had been innocent was no excuse. Innocent, or deliberate as Carne had contemptuously believed,
the result had been the same, and she writhed inwardly as
she remembered it.

In some strange way it might make life a little easier, in
time, she told herself, because at least from now on their
avoidance would be mutual. There would be no resump-

tion of the companionship she had glimpsed earlier, no
tête-à-tête meals when Antonia wasn't around, and she
had already been forbidden to clean his rooms so there
would be few occasions when they would meet, and even
fewer when they would be alone together.

She rolled on to her back, staring sightlessly at the ceiling. And if Carne had not unexpectedly decided to take a
rest from portrait painting, life would be easier still. It had
been a shock to know that he intended to spend the whole
summer at Raven's Crag, and she wondered if Antonia
fully realised his intentions. Knowing her stepmother,
Rowan knew that Antonia would much prefer Carne was a
visitor to the house to be dazzled on not-too-frequent
occasions by her charm and apparent efficiency. With him
living permanently in the same house, there would be little
opportunity for her to relapse into the easy-going régime
she had enjoyed before his arrival. Easy for her, that was,
Rowan thought, her lips twisting ironically.

As if the thought of Antonia had conjured her up, footsteps came along the passage outside, and Rowan's door
handle rattled imperatively. She was glad she had had the
forethought to turn the key in the lock.

'Rowan, are you there? What about lunch?' Antonia
demanded.

Rowan lifted herself up on one elbow, staring across at
the door. 'I'm not hungry, thanks,' she called. 'I—I have a
headache.'

She knew quite well that her stepmother had not come
upstairs to ask after her appetite, but in the hope she would
offer to prepare the meal, but nothing was going to get her
down to the kitchen. There was plenty of bread and cheese,
and several cartons of home-made soup she had made the
week before in the freezer. A simple snack along those lines
wasn't beyond even Antonia's capabilities.

'A headache?' Antonia sounded baffled. 'But you don't
get headaches.'

'Well, I've got one now,' Rowan returned mendaci-
ously.

'Well, you will be better this evening, won't you?' Her
stepmother's voice was anxious. 'I can't be expected to
cope with everything, you know.'

By everything, Rowan supposed she meant dinner. 'Won't you be eating out again?' she asked.

'Nothing's been said,' Antonia said petulantly. 'Carne came in for coffee in a hell of a mood. If he hates gardening that much, why doesn't he hire someone to do it for him?'

Rowan bit back the reply that Carne had found outside help unsatisfactory. Obviously Antonia knew nothing about the confrontation in the garden, and it was better that way, otherwise she was quite capable of adding Carne's foul mood to Rowan's headache and arriving at all kinds of totals. Rowan found herself hoping that her finger-marks had faded from Carne's face before he came into the house, or she might still have some explaining to do.

She said placatingly, 'Look—I'll make sure there's food on the table this evening, even if I don't want any myself.'

'Bless you, sweetie!' There was real relief in Antonia's voice, and after a moment Rowan heard her move away. Her mouth twisted ruefully. While domestic problems remained paramount in Antonia's mind, emotional under-currents might escape her notice at least for the time being. Until her wounds had a chance to heal, or at least form scar tissue, she thought mordantly.

Ultimately, of course, she would have Carne to face, and she turned cold and sick inside at the thought. Her only comfort was that he would probably be as reluctant to give Antonia any hint of what had passed between them as she was. All she could do was rely on whatever scraps of dignity she had left, and take her lead from him, hoping that her slap on the face hadn't made him vindictive. Somehow she couldn't imagine it, but then what did she really know about him—about his character. Her response to him from that earliest meeting had been purely emotional. It had contained neither reason nor rationality, and although she wasn't the child in years that he thought, she certainly hadn't enough maturity or experience to handle the situa-tion as she'd made so blatantly obvious.

With a muffled groan she swung her legs off the bed and stood up, walking across to the dressing chest to study her reflection in the mirror. If there were no visible marks left on Carne, then her own face bore enough incriminating evidence to convict her with Antonia. Her eyes looked twice their normal size, and her mouth looked flushed and swollen from Carne's practised assault on it. She supposed she should be grateful she didn't bruise all that easily, or her arms, and back and ribcage would have suffered from his rough handling.

No one had ever told her that making love could be more like making war, she thought, pressing her fingers lightly to her tender lips, and wondering whether it was his teeth or hers which had done the most damage. And he had accused her of playing games. She gave a brief mirthless laugh and turned away.

Ironically, her white lie was becoming all too true. She was developing a rare headache. She went into the shared bathroom and took some of the aspirin in the small medicine cabinet before returning to lie down again on the bed, but this time removing her shoes and stripping off her jeans and shirt. They were soiled anyway, and not merely from the earth she had knelt on. As she had removed the shirt she had been conscious that the fibres still retained a hint of Carne, of the warm male scent of his body. It was all too painfully reminiscent, she thought, kicking the clothes away from her almost violently before she slid under the covers. She lay still for a few moments, practising the relaxation techniques she had learned on a brief meditation course a girl at college had persuaded her to try—a lifetime ago, it seemed.

'I'd like to be that Rowan Winslow again,' she thought. 'With not a problem in the world except tomorrow's lecture and yesterday's essay.' She hadn't been particularly happy, but there had been a kind of contentment in doing her work well and conscientiously. She had been well thought of as a student. But that Rowan Winslow no longer existed. Even if she got the opportunity in the autumn, she wasn't sure that she would try to resume her course. After all, the ultimate intention was to become a social worker, and a fat cheek she had planning to help other people with their lives when she couldn't even manage her own!

Almost to her surprise, the relaxation worked, in spite of her emotional confusion, and she found herself drifting into sleep, and a dream where she stood in Carne's arms in a garden, and his mouth on hers was as gentle as a petal falling from a flower, and she awoke to find tears on her face.

She was calm, with all traces of grief or passion smoothed away, by the time she presented herself in the kitchen to cook the dinner. Antonia, clearly fearful that she would have to handle the meal herself, had already taken some lamb chops out of the freezer to defrost and was prepared to take the line of least resistance by grilling them with chips. But Rowan decided she could do better than that. She'd bake them à la Provençale, she thought, with potatoes and onions and garlic and layers of tomatoes. And she'd make an Eve pudding to follow, and if Carne read any significance into that, he was more than welcome!

The meal was in the oven sending out tantalisingly savoury aromas by the time he appeared, and no evidence to show who had made all the preparations, Rowan thought with a sudden satisfaction as she looked up wood-enly from the kitchen table and the paperback novel she was making a pretence of reading.

'Where's your stepmother?' he asked bleakly, his eyes skimming over her dismissively.

'Changing for dinner, I expect.' Rowan kept her own tone level.

'Clearly it doesn't occur to you to do the same.'

She was tempted to retort that the jeans and shirt she was wearing now were not those she had had on earlier in the day, but she bit her tongue.

'Did you want Antonia for something?' she asked.

'I wanted to tell her that some friends are coming over for a drink after dinner—the Listers. Perhaps you'd let her know. I presume the drinks cabinet is reasonably stocked?'

Anyone would think we'd been swigging the stuff in buckets, Rowan thought in sudden irritation. Aloud she said sweetly, 'I think there'll still be enough for your needs.'

Carne nodded abruptly, and left the kitchen. Rowan released her pent-up breath on a little sigh. So that was how he wanted to play it—the master of the house with a less than bright member of the staff. Well, it would do, and perhaps when sufficient time had passed, and especially if he reached an understanding with Antonia, then they could get back on a more normal footing.

Antonia was less than pleased with Rowan's news.

'Who are these Listers?' she demanded. 'Some dreary local people, no doubt. What a bore!'

Rowan shrugged. 'Carne simply said they were friends. Shall I check on the glasses?'

'Yes—fine.' Antonia frowned a little. 'A married couple, did he say?'

'No, but I presume so. Why don't you ask him?'

'Because that would be just a little too obvious,' said Antonia, patting Rowan's cheek as she went past in a little wave of *Calèche*. She was looking particularly glamorous in a draped dress in white and amber jersey, and her hair and nails were immaculate. Rowan thought of her own hair, looped back into two bunches and secured by elastic bands, and her nails, bitten down to the quick again during her morning soul-searching. In spite of Carne's acid comment, she wasn't going to change, she thought defiantly. If she looked scruffy and rebellious, that was all in keeping with the image he had of her anyway. And even if she spent an hour in the bathroom and put on the most attractive dress in her wardrobe, she still couldn't compete with Antonia.

The Listers arrived in time for coffee, which Rowan started and Antonia completed with something of a flourish. They were married, and both were slightly older than Carne, because it transpired that they had grown-up children—a girl of twenty who was working in Paris, and a teenage son, David, a year younger than Rowan. Grace Lister was wearing a caftan in muted shades of brown and gold, and an assortment of attractive rings containing semi-precious stones on her square capable-looking hands. Rowan wasn't surprised to learn that they ran a successful local pottery and gift shop. And they were far from being the local drears Antonia had grumbled about. Both Grace and her husband Clive, who was about a head shorter than she was, with a balding head and a neatly trimmed beard, had a lively line in conversation, and it was clear from the most casual observation that they and Carne were old friends.

It was also clear that while they seemed to know all about Antonia, Rowan was an unknown quantity. Carne introduced her to them, his voice expressionless, and after they had made a few conventional enquiries about how she liked her new home, she was left pretty much to her own devices. When drinks were being offered she refused Carne's somewhat pointed suggestion of a fruit juice and retired to a seat by the window, leaving Antonia to play the role of the hostess with considerable verve. Even to Rowan's rather jaundiced eye, it was a notable performance. Antonia made quite sure that the Listers knew that she and Carne were cousins, provided ash-trays and smiling small talk, saw that everyone's glass was kept filled, and deferred prettily to Carne on almost every topic, at the same time allowing a faintly proprietorial tone to enter her voice whenever plans for the house and garden were discussed.

'Carne and I think' was a phrase which seemed to rise with the utmost readiness to her lips. Watching Carne beneath her lashes, secure in the knowledge he was too engrossed with his guests to notice, Rowan thought he looked faintly amused at times, but he made no effort to contradict Antonia, or dispel the impression of togetherness she was so eager to foster.

She's making quite sure that the return invitation includes her too, Rowan thought cynically.

She was just returning with more ice which she had been despatched to the kitchen to fetch when she realised Grace Lister was bemoaning a shortage of staff for the new season.

'Lynne was wonderful, of course, a born saleswoman, but she's having a baby, and she's been told to take it easy for a couple of months,' she was saying. 'I coped over Easter, but in a couple of weeks' time it's going to start getting silly, and I can't serve in the shop and do the demonstrations as well.'

'What about David?' Carne asked.

Grace flung up her hands in mock horror. 'Worse than useless, darling. Never knows the price of anything and breaks more than he sells. Besides, just at the moment, work—especially in the family business—is a dirty word.'

'Is it now?' Carne said drily, and his eyes met Rowan as she stood in the doorway, holding the bowl of ice. 'Here's another one with similar views.'

'Oh, I can hardly believe that,' Clive Lister said jovially, smiling across at her.

Rowan bit her lip. Then she said slowly and clearly, 'I know nothing about selling pots, Mrs Lister, but if you need a salesgirl, I'd be more than willing to learn. Would you consider giving me a trial?'

'My dear child,' Grace Lister was half laughing, half embarrassed, 'I really wasn't hinting—I didn't mean to give the impression ...'

'But I did,' said Rowan. 'I need work, and there can't be many convenient local vacancies. If you're looking for staff, then I'd like to be considered.'

'Mrs Winslow,' Grace turned to Antonia, 'how do you feel about this? Do you mind the thought of your stepdaughter serving in the gift shop?'

Antonia shrugged smilingly. 'It really has very little to do with me. Rowan does as she pleases,' she said, and Rowan knew instinctively that she was inwardly simmering with anger.

Grace Lister's warm eyes studied Rowan with faint puzzlement for a moment or two, then she said briskly, 'Well, I do need someone, and you need a job, so it all fits. Shall we say a week's trial to see how we all get on together? It's very much a family atmosphere and we need to keep it harmonious.'

Rowan nodded. 'Shall I start tomorrow?' she asked politely. 'What time would you like me to be there?'

Grace Lister made a little helpless gesture as if events were moving too fast for her. 'Shall we say nine-thirty? Don't worry about overalls. I supplied Lynne's—rather pretty ones. You and she are much of a height. They should fit you ...'

'Well, how nice to have it all settled,' Antonia said brightly, and spuriously. 'Mr Lister—Clive—may I top up your drink for you?'

Rowan was standing brushing her hair in front of the mirror that night when Antonia came in without ceremony.

'What the hell are you playing at?' she demanded accusingly. 'Your job is to help me here, not to stand about all day in some crummy gift shop flogging souvenirs to trippers!'

'Then perhaps you'd better explain your point of view to Carne,' Rowan said calmly. 'He has the impression that I'm work-shy.'

Antonia's eyes flashed. 'If you think you're going to make a different impression by sliming round his friends, then you're mistaken!'

'There are times, Antonia,' Rowan said steadily, 'when you are impossibly vulgar. Now, if you don't mind, I'd like to go to bed.'

'I'm sorry, I didn't mean it—but what am I going to do?' Antonia burst out. 'You know I can't manage without you, especially with Carne prowling around like some revolting overseer all the time. I keep expecting him to inspect the ledges for dust. How am I going to manage the cooking as well as the housework?'

Rowan sighed. 'I'll cook for the freezer in my spare time, then all you'll have to do is warm the stuff up. You can do that much, surely?'

'But you didn't have to volunteer to do this awful job. It'll be terribly tiring, and I expect she'll pay you starvation wages. Those sort of places always do.'

'It's no sinecure here, and I get paid nothing at all,' Rowan reminded her levelly. 'Besides, I like Mrs Lister, and I think I'll enjoy working for her. Potteries are interesting places.'

'Well, I don't understand you,' Antonia's voice was sullen. 'If I were to explain to Carne . . .'

'No,' Rowan interrupted swiftly. 'No more explanations, please. I've had as much as I can take as it is. And it's not the end of the world. I'm only on a week's trial. Mrs Lister may decide I'm unsuitable.'

'That's hardly likely. You heard her saying how difficult it was to get anyone.' Antonia sighed deeply. 'Well, on your own head be it,' she announced magisterially, and went off to her own own room.

It was decidedly cooler the following day with a hint of rain in the air. Rowan put on a simple dark red button-through skirt and teamed it with a polo-necked cream sweater in fine wool. She also decided to wear tights and a pair of comfortable shoes instead of her usual sandals.

She had hoped to find the kitchen empty, but to her dismay Carne was sitting at the table eating a piece of toast and reading a newspaper. He glanced up as she came in, and his mouth curled sardonically.

'The gallant volunteer,' he remarked. 'At least you've dressed for the part.'

'I'll be wearing an overall anyway.' Rowan could have done with some toast and coffee herself, but she didn't want to have to eat it under Carne's caustic gaze.

'So you will. Do you think you'll be able to stand it? You'll work long hours, and the shop gets very busy during the high season.'

Rowan shrugged. 'We'll have to see.'

'That's just what we won't do,' Carne said sharply. 'Grace is a friend of mine, and I don't want you letting her down just when the shop's at its busiest because you've decided it's too much like hard work. I'd rather ring her now and tell her you've changed your mind.'

'But I haven't. Nor shall I,' Rowan said equably, although inwardly she was seething. 'I intend to do my best.'

'Whatever that is,' he said satirically. 'Well, you'd better get going. You don't want to be late and make a bad impression on your first day—whatever may happen in the future. Oh, and another thing,' he added, as Rowan slid her arms into the sleeves of her shabby cream trench coat and tied the belt round her slim waist. 'If you must try out your embryo wiles on someone, make sure it's David, and not Clive. If that's not asking too much, of course.'

She said on a little breath, 'My God.' And then, 'You bastard!'

'Harsh words, sweetheart,' he said coldly. 'But the warning stands. One hint from Grace, and I'll give you the thrashing of your young life.'

Rowan hadn't the slightest desire to go to the pottery and start work. All she wanted to do was go up to her room and cry until her heart broke, but Grace Lister was expecting her at nine-thirty, which in its way was a kind of salvation, because it meant she had to swallow her misery and her rage and go.

A persistent misty drizzle was falling as she made her way down the drive. How very appropriate, Rowan muttered to herself, winding a dark red silk scarf round her hair

and securing the ends at the nape of her neck. Grace had
given her fairly explicit directions how to find them. ('Not,'
she'd said, laughing, 'that you could actually miss us.
Ravensmere isn't your bustling metropolis.')

Rowan's step became brisker once she had walked
through the gates and out on to the road, as if some invisible burden had suddenly been lifted from her. And the
fact that the road wound downhill to the village helped
too. When she finally emerged into the main street, she
paused for a minute to get her bearings, then took the
turning which Grace had mentioned.

The pottery was housed in an adjoining pair of converted cottages. The workshops and display rooms
occupied the ground floor, and the upper floor, coupled
with an extension at the rear provided the Listers with their
living accommodation. The whole building had been
painted white, and a small hand-made sign swung from a
wrought iron support.

Grace must have been looking out for her, because as
Rowan approached she flung open the door, and Rowan
heard the welcoming tinkle of a bell.

'You're early,' she greeted her smilingly. 'That's a good
start.'

As Grace showed her where to hang her raincoat,
Rowan found herself wondering if her new employer had
really expected her to arrive at all. There had been a note
of—surprise?—in Grace's voice when she greeted her, and
Rowan thought that probably hints had been dropped
after she had gone to her room the previous night. She
could have ground her teeth in rage, but she forced herself to stay cool. Whatever had or had not been said—and
maybe she was just being over-sensitive—Grace was hardly
likely to discuss it with her, so the best thing she could
do was put it out of her mind. And for the next hour or two
she was kept so busy as Grace took her round the show-
rooms, showing her the range of pots they produced and
their prices, that she had little time to worry about any
possible impression which might have been given in her
disfavour.

The Listers, she discovered, were more than competent
potters. They dealt mainly in stoneware and ceramics, and

the goods which crowded the shelves and display tables had been conceived and executed with real flair and imagination. Their use of glazes, Rowan thought appreciatively, was clever, and often inspired, and she loved the chunky peasant shapes of much of their cookware.

She turned regretfully to Grace. 'It's a pity you have to put up notices asking people not to touch. Most of these things are aching to be picked up and handled.'

Grace looked pleased. 'Do you feel that too? I always feel that's the mark of a successful pot. After all, it only comes into shape because of the potter's handling originally. But it's a rule we've had to make, otherwise the breakages would be more horrendous than they are. Later on, we'll show you the process itself—you can have a go at throwing a pot yourself if you like—and you'll see the time and the effort which goes into each item, and know why it breaks my heart every time someone bungs one of them on to the ground and blitherly says "Sorry".' She paused and then laughed. 'Speech over for today! To return to basics—everything is priced before it's put on display—we use small stickers on the base of each item. But as a general guide, we put up one or two lists as well so that people can decide whether what we're offering is within their price range without being put to the embarrassment of asking. Generally speaking, you'll be on your own in here—unless there's an emergency, say, a couple of coach parties arriving together—and it can happen, and then you holler for Clive or me.'

'Are there generally a lot of visitors in the summer?' asked Rowan.

'Quite enough,' Grace admitted. 'The local pub specialises in bar snacks and has got itself into a couple of the eating guides on the strength of it, so we benefit indirectly from that. But we don't just sell to passing trade. We also supply gift shops in Keswick and Windermere with a range of ceramic plaques, souvenir mugs—that kind of thing.' She sighed. 'Never a dull moment!'

She waited for a moment, then said, 'Well, what about it, Rowan? Do you think you'll be able to cope? You're rather younger than any of the other assistants we've had—Lynne, for instance, was nearly twenty.'

Rowan felt a dull flush rise in her cheeks. Antonia's deception was reaching beyond the select little group at Raven's Crag, she thought bitterly, and wished she could tell this friendly woman the truth. Yet how could she? To do so would involve an explanation of Antonia's motives, and Grace Lister was a friend of Carne's. Besides, to a stranger, Antonia's plotting and planning would sound totally incredible, she thought unhappily.

'I've always been used to responsibility—since my father died,' she said at last, rather awkwardly, and Grace's brows drew together in a swift, sympathetic frown.

'You poor kid! What a sad way to have to learn to grow up,' she said softly. 'Come with me now, and I'll show you the overalls—you'll have to shout up if you'd rather die than wear them—and also where that other essential process, the coffee making, takes place. It's no one's particular job, by the way—just whoever is least busy and most parched.'

The overalls were delightful, Rowan thought, fashioned on the style of a Victorian pinafore in a small flower print on a brown background. She wandered round the show-room, examining the pots with care and trying to fam-iliarise herself with the prices, just in case she suddenly had to cope with an influx of tourists. Not that it seemed likely, she thought. It was still a little early in the season, and it was raining harder than ever.

She had had a look round the workroom and received a cheerful wave from Clive who was working away at his wheel, swathed in a voluminous, clay-spattered smock. She had drunk some excellent coffee out of a creamy mug, speckled with brown like a thrush's breast. She had dusted the display tables, holding her breath as she did so. Now she needed a customer—her first, she thought, as she perched on the stool beside the cash register.

Nevertheless when the shop bell tinkled, she started vio-lently, and had to slide one foot to the floor to steady herself. The newcomer looked at her and grinned, and involuntarily she found herself returning his smile. He was tall, with dark curly hair and rather cherubic brown eyes.

'Hi,' he said, looking round. 'And where's Lumpy

Lynne, the Pregnant Potter's Mate?'

'If you're a friend of hers, perhaps Mrs Lister might know.' Rowan moved to descend from her stool, but the young man—he was little more than a boy, she now realised—halted her with an upraised hand.

'Forget it. Just idle curiosity on my part, and as Mum will no doubt tell you, more idle than curious at that. I'm David Lister, returned to do my duty and study for blasted exams, even though something tells me that two years' work into six weeks won't go.'

'I shouldn't think it will,' said Rowan, smiling faintly. 'I'm Rowan Winslow, and I'm the new shop assistant.'

He bowed gallantly, clicking his heels together. 'And a great improvement on the old one, if I may say so. May I say so? For one thing, you're neither married nor pregnant—or at least I hope not. Who knows what grisly secrets those shrouds of Mum's conceal?'

'The usual standard equipment, I hope,' Rowan retorted, tongue in cheek. 'But neither of the fates you've mentioned have befallen me yet.'

'Then this is clearly my lucky day, and Thursdays are usually hell on wheels.' He swung the rucksack he was carrying to the ground, narrowly missing a display of tall pottery vases, and Rowan gave a cry of alarm.

'For heaven's sake, watch out! You'll smash something.'

'That's genuine Lumpy Lynne terminology if ever I heard it,' he said, grinning. 'Did she leave you her phrase book, by any chance?'

The bead curtain which separated the showroom from the other part of the cottage swung aside and Grace Lister appeared.

'Oh, my God,' she said in a tone of deep suffering. 'No wonder it's raining! I thought you were still halfway up some frightful mountain. Rowan, this is my younger child, whom I do not recommend. I heard you yell out. I suppose he was doing his normal mass destruction bit.'

'Mother, you wrong me.' David put an arm round her and kissed her resoundingly on the cheek. 'Is there any lunch? Mountaineering is hungry work, you know.'

'And naturally you've been starved all the time you've been at the Masons',' his mother scoffed. 'Lunch will be in an hour, and if you can't hold out until then I suggest you go and concoct yourself a sandwich, and stop bothering our new assistant. I don't want Rowan handing her notice in as soon as she's begun.'

'Nor do I.' David's face assumed an expression of mock horror. 'Where did you find her, by the way—if it's not a secret?'

'None at all,' Grace said blandly. 'She's a distant relation of Carne Maitland's, staying at Raven's Crag for the summer, and she needed a job.'

'Oh—so Carne's back is he?' David's tone held indifference, and something more, and Rowan saw Grace give him a sharp look. He bent and picked up his rucksack. 'Right, I'll go and make that sandwich, and have a bath, I think.' He smiled at Rowan, a cheerful grin lifting the corners of his mouth. 'See you later, Rowan, I hope. Things are looking up round here at last!'

'I apologise for my embryo Casanova,' Grace said drily when he had gone. 'Don't hesitate to slap him down if he steps out of line in any way. As you've probably found out for yourself, there aren't a great many young people in the immediate vicinity, and David's a social animal, if ever there was one.' She sighed. 'That's why I agreed to let him go on this rock-climbing course with some of his school friends, when I suppose he really should be buckling down. Fortunately, he's reasonably bright—one of these lucky people who can skim through with the minimum effort. What about you, Rowan? Didn't you want to continue your education, and perhaps go on to university or art college?'

Rowan smiled rather tightly. 'That's a sore point at the moment,' she said after a pause. 'I—I haven't decided what I want to do with my life yet. But it certainly wouldn't be art college,' she added hastily.

'No?' Grace's brows rose. 'Yet why should you? I suppose it's just because my mind always tends that way, and knowing you're related to Carne . . .'

'But I'm not. Not in any way,' Rowan said hastily. 'My stepmother is his distant cousin, that's all.'

'I see.' By her tone, Grace obviously saw nothing at all. 'I'm sorry, dear. I got the impression last night that it was

Carne who was responsible for you, and I assumed . . .' She broke off. 'My family will tell you I'm always jumping to the wrong conclusions,' she added ruefully. 'I'd better get back to my pot before I drop any more bricks!' She gave Rowan another, rather uncertain smile and vanished.

Rowan sat down on her stool again, with a little sigh. Grace, she thought, must be mistaken. The last thing Carne Maitland wanted was the kind of responsibility that she represented. He had made that more than clear already, she told herself, wincing.

And David's arrival could present a fresh complication. Rowan had little doubt that he would ask her to go out with him, and refusal would be difficult without hurting his feelings, yet he was too young for her in every way, and not merely in years.

And besides, she thought, staring out through the rain-washed windows at the deserted street, even if David happened to be a more than eligible bachelor, it would still make no difference when there was only one man in the world that she wanted – and he was totally out of reach.

CHAPTER SIX

IN spite of Rowan's forebodings, the next few weeks passed more swiftly and peacefully than she had dared hope. April gave way to May, and warmer weather, bringing the arrival of the tourists in increasing numbers.

She found she was enjoying her work at the pottery, even though it was hardly intellectually demanding. She liked sharing the customers' obvious pleasure in their purchases, and the craftmanship they represented. She had even made a tentative attempt at throwing a pot herself, warmly encouraged by Grace, and when business in the showroom permitted she watched, fascinated, the practical afternoon demonstrations they staged.

And David was too busy making up for lost time with his

studies to provide any real embarrassment, even though he made a point of coming down to the showroom for a brief chat on most days when he returned from school. It disturbed Rowan a little to realise that Clive and Grace were prepared quite benevolently for David to start dating her once his exams were over in June. From remarks Grace had made Rowan gathered that David had at one time been paying a lot of attention to the girl in the village shop, Beth Wainwright, but this had not pleased his parents.

'They're a strange family,' she had commented frankly one day when she and Rowan were having coffee together during a quiet spell in the shop. 'They seem to have an inbuilt chip on their shoulders which goes back generations according to the locals. Beth's a nice enough girl in her way, but her brother Jeff is a nasty piece of work. Never has a steady job, but always seems to have plenty of money. I was afraid that David's friendship with Beth might bring him into rather too much contact with Jeff, who's a couple of years older and has all a ne'er-do-well's questionable glamour.'

'There's a funny atmosphere when you go into the shop,' Rowan said slowly. 'Not the busy, gossipy one you'd expect from a small village store, but rather secretive and withdrawn. They're never friendly.'

'Well, there could be a reason for that,' Grace said briskly. 'Jeff persuaded your—Carne to give him a part-time gardening job at Raven's Crag, but it didn't work out for some reason, and Jeff was fired. And Mr Wainwright's sister Maggie used to help Sybilla with the housework until your stepmother's arrival—so there would be a little over-spill of bad feeling as there've been two jobs lost at the house.'

'Oh, lord!' Rowan was dismayed. 'I had no idea. And yet the day we arrived they were odd.'

Grace laughed. 'Well, it could be that, or it could be just the Wainwrights. They're fools to themselves. They could have a marvellous business if their attitude was just a little more congenial.'

Reflecting on this conversation later, Rowan thought it was too easy when she was chatting to Grace to forget that she was only supposed to be sixteen.

Grace had already commented more than once that Rowan had an old head on young shoulders, and Rowan herself almost gave the game away by practically volunteering to drive the van to Windermere with a rush order of plaques which no one really had time to deliver.

As the point was being argued over by Grace and Clive, she had said eagerly and unthinkingly, 'But I'd love to go . . .' and then seeing their surprised looks, she had hastily corrected herself, 'If only I were old enough to drive.'

'Even if you were, you'd have to have a qualified driver sitting with you,' Grace said kindly. 'We went through all that with David. Fortunately, he passed first time—God knows how. We reckoned the examiner was so amazed to find he was still alive at the end of it that he passed him in gratitude.'

Rowan was furious with herself for the near-slip, and even angrier over the situation which had provoked it. She arrived back at the house that evening in no very good temper. Even the lush beauty of the rhododendrons towering above her on both sides of the drive failed to soothe her, and the sight of Antonia sitting at the kitchen table reading a magazine with not a sign or a smell of dinner anywhere brought her to simmering point.

'Aren't we going to eat this evening?' she demanded, dumping her shoulder bag down on the table.

Antonia yawned. 'Carne's taking me out. I'm absolutely exhausted! I've been working all day.'

Rowan looked caustically around her before she moved to the freezer to find something for herself. Antonia was constantly complaining of being dog-tired and overworked, but however she occupied herself during the day, there were few signs of her activities in the house. Raven's Crag was losing that pristine quality it had enjoyed when they arrrived. The gloss was noticeably wearing off, because preserving it took more time and energy than Antonia was prepared to devote to it.

I suppose she'll let it deteriorate to a certain point and then present Carne with an ultimatum that she must have help, Rowan thought.

'Did you get paid today?' Antonia asked, as Rowan filled a saucepan with water and put it on the hob to boil.

'Pay-day is tomorrow. Why do you ask?' Rowan checked in the fridge that there was still some of yesterday's lemon cheesecake left.

Antonia shrugged. 'It occurred to me that it was about time you started contributing something to your keep,' she said gently.

Rowan swung round. 'My keep?' she exclaimed. 'Good God, Antonia, look around you! There's a list of menus for the week pinned up on the wall, and the freezer is full to bursting. I thought that was my keep.'

'As you wish, of course,' Antonia shrugged again, and turned the page of her magazine. 'I thought you might be getting a conscience over living here at Carne's expense when you were earning yourself. How much do they pay you, by the way? I don't think you've ever mentioned it.'

'No, I don't think I have,' Rowan retorted coolly. 'Because I don't think it's any of your business. Has Carne suggested I should start contributing to the household budget?'

'Not in so many words,' Antonia said softly. 'But I imagine he's a little—surprised, shall we say, that you haven't even offered to do so. I can't imagine what you do with your wages. You never go anywhere or buy anything.'

'I save it,' Rowan said pleasantly. 'In a bank account in Keswick, which Clive very kindly drove me in there to open when I started work. He was a little—surprised, shall we say, that you hadn't already done so.'

A slight flush rose in Antonia's face. 'Perhaps you'd like to inform him that I'm not your keeper.'

'But that's exactly what you've made yourself—remember?' Rowan flashed. 'I'm sixteen, stepmother dear, according to your little fabrication, so you can't complain when people treat me as if I was really that age, and expect you to do the same. Why, I can't even use my driving licence, and Clive and Grace needed a driver badly today. I could have helped out, but because of your stupid lie I had to keep quiet.'

'Well, three cheers for the little friend of all the world!' The line of Antonia's mouth was suddenly ugly under her make-up. 'You needn't be so bloody sanctimonious about my fib. Lying should be second nature to you. Your father did enough of it towards the end of his career. He even made me believe he was a rich man.'

Rowan said, her voice shaking, 'You—unutterable bitch!' and started round the table towards her. She had some crazy idea of taking Antonia by the shoulders and shaking her until her teeth rattled, and she was almost choking with grief and rage.

Antonia leapt up with a squeal of alarm, dropping her magazine. 'Keep away from me, Rowan! Carne—oh, darling, help me! Keep her off me. I think she's gone mad!'

Rowan felt a hand grip her shoulder. She swung round and glared up at him through eyes hazed with tears.

He demanded coldly and furiously, 'What the hell do you think you're playing at?'

Antonia said hysterically, 'I mentioned poor darling Vic, and she suddenly went berserk. She hates my talking about him. She's never been able to accept what we were to each other.'

Rowan said in weary disgust, 'Oh, my God!' and sank down on the bench.

Carne's voice was level. 'I think you'd better go up to your room until you can control yourself. It's time you began to grow up, Rowan, and learned that there's some behaviour that just isn't acceptable. I think making jealous scenes over your father's widow comes into that category, don't you?'

She didn't look at him. In the same weary tone she said, 'You don't really expect me to answer that.'

'I don't expect very much of you at all, Rowan, and yet I'm constantly disappointed just the same.' His voice bit. 'When are you going to start behaving like a normal human being?'

'Probably when I get away from here,' she said quietly. 'Would someone please turn off that pan before it boils dry? I was intending to heat up my supper, but I suddenly seem to have lost my appetite.' She picked up her bag and walked out of the kitchen.

She was shaking inside when she reached her room, her hands clenched into fists at her sides. Her immediate impulse was to go into Keswick somehow first thing in the morning and withdraw all her money from the bank and return to London, but calmer reflection told her that if she did this she would be letting the Listers down badly because they were counting on her to work in the shop until the end of the season. She wondered if they would be willing to accommodate her in their spare room, but had to dismiss that. Carne was their friend, and she was living under his roof. If she wanted to leave, they would want to know why—and what could she say?

Looking back, she had to admit Carne's interruption had been a timely one for all sorts of reasons, even though it had ended to her disadvantage. But she could imagine what the Listers would think if the story was repeated to them, and she also had to admit that Antonia had been pretty convincing.

Beware Antonia and her spur-of-the-moment lies, she thought bitterly. She could see now how easily the initial untruth about her age had come into being. She found herself recalling long-forgotten incidents in her childhood, when Antonia's word had been accepted above her own, and remembered her miserable bewilderment when her father rather brusquely waved aside her stumbling explanations. But she had been too young then to recognise that Antonia was lying. She had thought her stepmother was genuinely mistaken.

Men, she thought, would always want to believe Antonia, to trust her, because she was a beautiful woman. For Victor Winslow disillusionment had probably come slowly, but Rowan knew that it had come.

And now there was Carne, who had trusted Antonia enough to lend her a large sum of money, and believed what she said. How many years of marriage would it take before his disillusionment set in? Rowan wondered bitterly.

I ought to hate him, she told herself. I ought to despise him for not being able to see what she is—shallow and self-seeking. But I don't, and I can't.

But it was little comfort to tell herself that at least this time she would not have to live under the same roof and see him being made unhappy. And perhaps Antonia, married to the man she wanted, and with all the money she would ever need, would become a reformed character. And perhaps the moon was made of green cheese, Rowan thought wryly.

She would remain in her room until they were both safely off the premises, she decided, and as an extra precaution she locked her bedroom door and the door leading into the bathroom, in case Antonia took it into her head to pay her another visit.

I can face her tomorrow, because I must, but not tonight, she thought.

She kicked off her shoes and lay wearily down on the bed, and eventually she must have dozed, because when she opened her eyes it was almost dark, and the house was very still.

Rowan sat up slowly, waiting for her head to clear a little. She felt muzzy, and there was a faint throb in her temples which usually in her experience presaged a thunderstorm. She glanced apprehensively towards the window and saw that the clouds gathering over the fells were slate grey and navy, and somewhere in the distance she thought she heard the faint rumble of thunder. She groaned and swung her feet to the floor. A storm was all she needed, she thought fatalistically.

The air seemed to press down on her as she made her way downstairs to the kitchen. She scrambled a couple of eggs, piled them on to buttered toast, and made herself a strong cup of coffee.

She hadn't imagined the thunder this time. She could see the flash of lightning too, as the storm approached, and she wondered ironically what effect it would be having on Antonia, who was terrified of thunder and lightning. It would probably give her an excuse, always supposing she needed one, for clinging to Carne even more closely, confirming the impression of helpless fragility she liked to give.

A perceptible drop in the temperature indicated that it was about to pour with rain, and Rowan shivered as she cupped her hands round the comforting warmth of her beaker.

A few large drops stung the kitchen windows, and then the downpour proper began with a searing flash and roar of thunder that sounded immediately above the house. Rowan flinched instinctively, and at the same moment all the lights went out.

It wasn't completely dark, but it would be soon, and Rowan swore mildly as she made her way across the kitchen. A large torch and a number of spare batteries were kept in one of the cupboards she knew, but she doubted whether Raven's Crag boasted anything quite so prosaic as candles.

But Sybilla would have some, she thought suddenly, and wondered how she was facing up to the storm. Sybilla did not seem the nervous kind, but thunder had a habit of reducing the most stalwart souls to a jelly.

She went along to the flat door and knocked. 'It's Rowan,' she called. 'Are you all right? Can you see your way about?'

There was no reply. Listening intently, Rowan could only hear the sigh of the wind in the trees outside, and another deafening peal of thunder. She knocked again, louder.

'Sybilla? Please answer. Are you all right?'

Silence. In exasperation, Rowan tried the flat door, and to her surprise it swung open at once. She went in and called, but there was still no reply. She frowned as she stood there, uncertain of what to do next. It wasn't possible, surely, that Sybilla had gone out with Carne and Antonia?

Feeling like some guilty intruder, she began to look round the flat. Perhaps Sybilla had taken some tablets and had an early night. But the bedroom was empty, and there were signs in the living room—an empty coffee cup, a book lying open on a small table beside an armchair—that she had been there quite recently.

Could it be—was it possible that Sybilla had gone out for her usual evening stroll in the garden and had been taken unawares by the storm?

Oh, no! Rowan thought, her heart contracting in dismay. Where could she find shelter, except under a tree, which was worse than being out in the open?

She dashed to the cloakroom and found her raincoat, not bothering to pull it on, just putting it over her head. Then she went out. The rain was steady and felt like ice. Rowan switched on her torch and shone it in front of her. The light seemed feeble in the gathering murk, but it was all she had. She walked forward carefully, pausing every now and then to call Sybilla's name, but the wind seemed to carry her voice away, and she wasn't sure even now she wasn't getting soaked on a wild goose chase.

When she heard the answering cry she thought at first it was her own voice getting tossed back at her by the wind in some weird way. She stood, head bent, listening, and trying to cut out the racket around her, and heard the voice again, very small and wavering and somewhere ahead of her.

She shouted, 'Sybilla? I'm coming. Hang on!'

But Sybilla was not able to do anything else, as Rowan realised when she rounded a bend in the path and saw the crumpled heap lying there. A groan escaped her.

She ran forward and knelt down. The older woman was a pitiful sight, her face twisted with pain, her white hair and clothes plastered to her by the downpour, but she managed a wry smile for Rowan.

'My—stupid hip, dear child. It just seemed to collapse under me, and I fell, and couldn't get up again. I—think I've damaged my ankle too. It twisted, you see, as I tried to keep my balance.'

'Everything's all right now, I'm here,' Rowan said soothingly, trying to dam back the feeling of panic besetting her. She was there, but what could she do? Sybilla wasn't as fragile as she looked, which was a good thing considering the condition she was in, but could Rowan manage to lift her? Her ankle was the least of her problems. Shock, and the soaking she had received, could bring on pneumonia, and it was essential to get her into the dry and fetch medical attention without delay.

She said, trying to sound cheerful, 'I'm going to get you back in the house, Sybilla. I think the best thing is if you could link your arms round my neck while I lift you. I'll try not to hurt you.'

Sybilla shook her head. There was a pinched look round her mouth, Rowan saw apprehensively. 'I'm—too—heavy for you, my dear. Fetch Carne.'

'He's out,' Rowan explained gently. 'And so is Antonia. We're on our own. We have to manage. Now, put your arm round my shoulders and let's see how we get on. We can't stay here—you're lying in a puddle.'

'Carne has been levelling some of the ground here to make a lawn,' Sybilla said on a little gasp, as she struggled to comply. 'I came out to have a look. I tried to hurry when I heard the thunder.'

It took all Rowan's strength to get to her feet with Sybilla clinging to her like a dead weight, trying to muffle little gasps of pain as they moved with awful slowness back towards the shelter of the house. It was an endless shuffling progress and at times it seemed to Rowan, whose back and shoulders were aching almost intolerably, that some malignant force was moving the house away from them as they moved towards it.

But eventually they reached it and Rowan took Sybilla round to the kitchen entrance to avoid climbing the steps up to the front door. She deposited the older woman on the bench by the kitchen table, and went out again to find the torch which she had dropped. Fortunately it still worked, and she ran back to the house.

Sybilla was shivering violently, she saw compassionately.

Trying to sound brisk, she said, 'You must get those wet things off, Sybilla. I'll go and find your nightdress and dressing gown, then I'll phone your doctor—that's if the phone's still working.'

She fetched the dressing gown at once and left the kitchen, knowing instinctively that however difficult she found it, Sybilla would not wish to undress in front of her or want her assistance in doing so.

As she lifted the receiver, the reassuring buzz of the dialling tone came to her ears, and she breathed a sigh of relief as she dialled. The doctor was at home, and promised to come at once. Rowan flew upstairs and fetched a blanket before returning to the kitchen.

'This is probably the warmest place to be,' she remarked as she went in. 'But I've brought you some extra wrapping all the same. I'm sorry it's so dark.'

Sybilla gave her a faint smile. 'The storm is passing, dear child. Perhaps they'll be able to restore the power soon. It isn't usually off for very long.'

'I can't even make us a hot drink,' Rowan mourned,

unfolding the blanket and putting it round Sybilla's thin shoulders.

'You've done quite enough for me. Now you must go and get out of your own wet things—yes, I insist. Unlatch the front door so that Doctor Mortimer can let himself in when he comes. I shall be quite all right.'

Rowan wasn't sorry to obey. In spite of the sheltering raincoat the rain had penetrated right through to her skin, and she felt chilled and clammy. It was good to strip off her wet clothes and underwear in her room, and towel her body briskly until her circulation started to move more normally. She pulled on dry cord pants in olive green, topping them with a matching rollneck Shetland sweater. She was just making her way downstairs when the doctor's car arrived.

He was a middle-aged man, very calm and practical, and he praised Rowan for her prompt action. He examined Sybilla's ankle and diagnosed a sprain, and in spite of her protests, announced his intention of calling an ambulance.

'I'm taking her to Heatonbank for observation,' he told Rowan, deftly popping a thermometer between Sybilla's indignant lips. 'It's a private clinic and nursing home, where she can have a couple of days' cosseting. I suppose you'd like to accompany her, Miss Winslow. I'll leave a note for Carne explaining exactly what's happened.'

'This is ridiculous, George,' Sybilla said roundly when she could speak again. 'This child doesn't want to go to a nursing home.'

'Nothing very childish about her behaviour this evening,' the doctor said drily. 'Now, tell her what you want her to pack in an overnight bag for you.'

Rowan was returning with the bag, when he stopped her.

'It's her heart that I'm really worried about,' he said briefly. 'She had a couple of slight attacks about a year ago, and I had to warn her about over-exertion then, but she's proud and stubborn and doesn't relinquish her responsibilities easily, as I probably don't have to tell you. I'd hoped this idea of getting Carne's cousin here as housekeeper might help, but . . .'

He shrugged, and Rowan said slowly, 'I think it has. She

has her own flat to look after, and I don't think we could ever change that. But she and my stepmother are not very friendly, I'm afraid. There isn't much contact between them.'

He frowned slightly. 'Yet she seems very fond of you.'

Rowan said with some constraint, 'She doesn't really know me very well, but she's always been very kind.'

He nodded. 'So you'll go with her. I want her to be caused as little agitation as possible, and a familiar face . . .'

'Yes, of course,' she assured him.

The ambulance was soon there, and Sybilla was put carefully into it by two cheerful men.

'I am not ill,' she announced, looking very frail. But she was almost asleep when the journey was over, although she opened her eyes and looked at Rowan as she was being lifted out of the ambulance. 'Dear—girl, what would I have done without you?' she muttered drowsily, and Rowan guessed that Dr Mortimer who was following in his own car had administered some sort of sedative.

While Sybilla was being put to bed in a comfortable room, a young nurse took Rowan along to a waiting room furnished with easy chairs.

'The rain's easing off,' she commented, swishing chintz curtains across the windows. 'And the power's back on, thank heavens. We've been operating off our emergency generator.

'Oh, hell!' Rowan's hand went to her mouth. 'I left all sorts of things on back at the house.'

'Well, I don't expect anyone will complain,' the nurse said comfortingly. 'This was rather an emergency, you know. We had Miss Maitland in here some time ago for tests, so it's lucky you were around when this happened.'

'Yes,' Rowan agreed soberly.

She was left alone for a while, then someone brought her a cup of tea, rather too milky for her taste. She had finished it, and was wondering, rather forlornly, whether Dr Mortimer had gone, and how she was going to get back to Raven's Crag, when the door opened and Carne walked in.

Rowan said ridiculously, 'Oh, it's you,' and flushed.

'How is Sybilla?' he demanded sharply.

'She was nearly asleep when they brought her in. They

haven't told me anything yet.'

'God, what a thing to happen,' he muttered in an angry undertone. 'What was she doing in the garden, for heaven's sake?'

'She'd gone out to look at your lawn. She goes for a stroll every evening, you know she does. Apparently her bad hip—collapsed in some way, and she fell.'

His mouth twisted. 'Then from now on, she takes her stroll in company—which she'll love,' he added sardonically. He paused, then said in a slightly altered tone, 'It was a good thing you were there, Rowan.'

She made a little defensive gesture. 'You speak as if I had any real choice.'

'And you speak as if you were being kept a prisoner.' His mouth twisted. 'I thought that was Antonia's view of the situation. I didn't realise you felt the same. Of course, it must be a rather circumscribed life for you. You must miss the bright lights of London.'

'I didn't have a great deal of time for enjoying bright lights, even if I'd wanted to.' Rowan couldn't keep a slight snap out of her voice, remembering the hours at college, the endless essays and studying, the shopping and the housework. 'But you really don't have to worry about me. I've made a life for myself here.'

'Yes, you have,' he said in an odd tone. 'Perhaps I haven't given you sufficient credit for that—among other things.'

She was on guard instantly. It was safer when he thought badly of her; she was less vulnerable then.

'Let's not have any misunderstandings,' she said tightly. 'I didn't take the job at the pottery to win your good opinion, but to make some money so that I can get away as soon as possible. I don't need charity, or a surrogate father either.'

'I wasn't aware you were being offered either.' His eyes and voice were cold again. 'However, while you're under my roof there seems no reason why you can't enjoy a normal social life. At the moment you seem either to be working or mooning around the house, quarrelling with your stepmother. Not a satisfactory situation from anyone's point of view.'

'But not one that really need concern you. And I'm quite capable of organising my own social life.'

'Then I hope it's David Lister and not Jeff Wainwright that you're including in your plans,' he said caustically. 'David's a young idiot, but there's no real harm in him. You'll be reasonably safe practising your feminine wiles on him.'

'I don't need your advice or your permission!' she hit back. 'Why can't you leave me alone?'

'I wish to God I could,' he said savagely. 'But I'm responsible for you, Rowan, and I can't forget it, even if you seem determined to. I'm not used to girls of your age— the way you're a siren one moment and a hooligan the next.'

For a moment their eyes locked in challenge, and it was Rowan who looked away first, even turned away, moving over to the window, touching the curtains with nervous fingers. Even when they were at odds with each other his proximity had the power to disturb her almost unendurably, recalling to her mind and her body just how it had felt to be in his arms, to feel his mouth bruising hers. 'Siren', he had said. Well, her song was muted now, deliberately so, because wanting him could only bring her pain.

Standing with her back to him, she said with difficulty, 'I'm sorry, I don't know why I behave as I do. I—I'm not used to men of your age either.'

She heard Carne give a sharp sigh. He said, 'Then, on that note of guarded truce, I'll go and find Sybilla's room and see if there's anything she wants. Do you want to come with me?'

'Not—not if you want to speak to her privately.'

'There's nothing I wish to say that you can't hear, Rowan. Besides, she'll want to see you. I imagine she's probably quite well aware that she owes you her life.'

'That's an exaggeration.' Rowan moved uncomfortably.

'Not according to the note George Mortimer left,' he said drily. 'According to him you're the heroine of the hour.'

'That's very kind of him,' she said stiltedly. 'But I only did what anyone else would have done.'

'Did you?' His brows rose. 'Somehow I doubt that, Rowan. You give an impression of total fragility, and yet I suspect it's false—like other impressions you give.'

She stood motionless, her brain working frantically as she assimilated his words. If he suspected—if he knew the truth, then all Antonia's carefully laid plans could come crashing down round her ears like a house of cards.

She said falteringly, 'I—I don't understand.'

'Of course you don't.' There was a mocking note underlying the urbanity in his tone. 'And now let's go and see Sybilla.'

On the way down the corridor they met the Sister in charge coming in search of them. Miss Maitland was still awake, and asking for them, she told them a little reproachfully, her keen eyes taking in Rowan's flushed cheeks and the strain in her expression.

'You've had a trying time, child,' she said briskly. 'A glass of warm milk and an early night wouldn't come amiss.'

Sybilla looked very small in the bed, her white hair subdued into two neat plaits. The style made her look oddly youthful without robbing her of any of her dignity, Rowan thought.

Sybilla reached out a hand to her, and she took it.

'I'm so glad you're still here, my dear.' Her voice was a thread of sound. 'I wish to ask a favour. My flat—my plants—will you look after them? I don't want . . .' She paused as if through breathlessness, but Rowan guessed she didn't want Carne to hear her say aloud that she didn't want Antonia in her flat, among her treasures. She would know he wouldn't want to be reminded that the two women he loved shared a mutual antagonism—and yet, Rowan thought, it was something that would have to be faced eventually by all three of them.

'Of course I will,' she said gently, her fingers pressing Sybilla's. 'Don't worry about a thing, and you'll be home before you know it.'

Sybilla's eyes were heavy, but she managed a smile. 'Such a kind child—and such a foolish one. But you'll learn, my dear. You'll learn.'

Then Sister was moving forward authoritatively, saying

Miss Maitland must be allowed to rest now, and talking about visiting hours and arrangements for clean laundry. Rowan hoped that Carne was taking in all these essential details, because her mind felt suddenly heavy and thick, and she couldn't think clearly any more.

It was better when they got outside the nursing home. The storm had cleared the air, and racing clouds obscured the stars.

'But they're there all the same. It's just that I can't always see them,' she thought, and didn't realise she was speaking aloud.

'What are?' Carne's voice sounded unusually close, and she turned in surprise to find him bending over her, his eyes searching her face.

'Why, the stars,' she said stupidly, and a thousand more of them burst and glittered in front of her as, worn out by the conflicts and alarms of the past hours, she began to cry.

Somewhere, she thought she heard Carne swear softly, then his arms went round her and she let herself relax limply against him as deep rasping sobs tore at her throat under the hagridden sky.

As she began to regain some of her self-control, she realised that somehow he had got her into the car, away, she supposed, from the interested gaze of anyone who happened to be looking out of the nursing home windows. Her wet face was pressed against the silkiness of his shirt, and his hand was stroking her hair as the sobs died away into hiccuping gulps. For a moment it was agonising pleasure to stay where she was, to allow the featherlight caresses continue, but at last she made herself sit up and move away from him, using her knuckles to wipe away the last tears clinging to her lashes like the child he thought her.

'I'm sorry,' she said in a small voice.

'For what?' He produced a handkerchief and passed it to her. It smelt of his cologne, his warmth, and she touched her mouth with it.

'For crying all over you. Men hate that.'

'This man would be very ungrateful to resent any of your tears, Rowan. I think you're entitled to them,' he said quietly.

'I must look like a freak,' she muttered.

'On the contrary, you look like the surrounding land-scape—as if you'd been washed by rain,' he sounded faintly amused. 'But this car isn't the right setting. You should be in some forest glade, a dryad, peeping through leaves with a sprig of rowan berries in your hair. I'd like to paint you like that.' His hand reached out, smoothing her hair back from her face, touching the curve of her cheek.

Her mouth was dry, and breathing was difficult. A crazy impulse to snatch his hand, to drag it to her lips, to her breast, was threatening to overwhelm her, and stonily a voice inside her head was reminding her of the last time that she had so disastrously allowed herself to yield to his attraction. It means nothing, she thought. He's just being kind. He's trying to comfort me because I've been upset. But nothing—nothing has changed. And I must never let myself forget that—or hope for anything else.

She moved restlessly, a slight turn of the head but enough to indicate that she found his touch unacceptable, and after a second his hand fell away.

She said, trying to keep her voice relatively light, 'I don't think I want to be painted. Don't you have to keep awfully still? Besides, dryads don't bite their nails, do they?'

There was a long silence, then Carne said too evenly, 'Probably not. Then I'll have to look for a different model. Any suggestions?'

She said woodenly, 'I wouldn't imagine there would be any shortage of applicants.'

'How true,' he said mockingly. 'And some of them actually want their portraits painted as well.'

The implication in his words had the power to hurt her, and that was another thing she had to hide.

After a moment she asked, 'Are—are you going to start painting again?'

'It seems so,' he said wryly. 'I thought I'd given it up, but it hasn't let go of me. My bid for ultimate respectability will have to be deferred yet again.'

He pressed the ignition and the car purred into life, making its way slowly down the steep curving drive of the nursing home, and out on to the road.

Rowan stirred in her seat. She asked bewilderedly, 'Where are we going?'

'Home, of course.' Carne's hands looked relaxed on the steering wheel, but she was conscious of some tension in him which extended to her. Perhaps he too was remembering that morning in the garden when she had thrown herself at him, and was regretting creating a further opportunity for physical contact between them. She shrank farther into her corner of the car.

It began to rain again, and he switched on the windscreen wipers and turned on the heater. The swish of the wipers and the hum of the engine had a comfortingly soporific effect, and Rowan felt her eyes becoming drowsy as she huddled in her seat. A series of curious meaningless images began to pass through her mind—images of trees, bright with scarlet berries, their branches moving in a breeze which seemed to hold the echo of laughter, and a girl with brown hair who bent to scan her reflection in a pool of water—only it was a mirror, and the face which looked back at her was not her own, but Antonia's, her mouth curving in a smile of triumph and possession, and even the mirror wasn't the same, but a painting in an ornate gilded frame.

She awoke with a start and a little muffled cry to find the car had stopped, and Carne's voice was saying, 'Calm down, girl. We're home.'

She fumbled with the catch on the passenger door, but it swung open and he was there, his arms reaching in for her, and lifting her out.

'What are you doing?' Rowan began to struggle.

'Carrying you,' he replied briefly. 'And don't try to tell me you're perfectly capable of walking, because it isn't true.'

He was right, but she went on struggling, because it would be better to crawl up the steps on her hands and knees than be carried in his arms, her body crushed against his.

She gasped, 'Put me down!'

'When I'm good and ready,' he said coolly. 'This is my house, and I give the orders—remember?'

'I'm not likely to forget,' she retorted rebelliously, and heard him laugh softly. They had reached the front door, and surely he would have to put her down now, she thought wildly. The door was big and heavy, and the handle was stiff, but it swung open without the slightest protest and they were in the hall. Carne was still carrying her, moving with a long, swift stride towards the spiral staircase, and she didn't want to struggle any more—because he had brought her home, and she knew that anywhere he was, her home would be, and that what she felt for him was deeper, far, far deeper than any physical attraction, so deep that she was almost frightened by it. Her arms slid up round his neck, and his stride checked and he looked down at her. There was no amusement in his face, no mockery, only a questioning which stripped away all the pretence, all the defence. Rowan stared back at him mutely, her face naked and vulnerable under his insistent scrutiny.

Somewhere there was a noise—a door opening—and then Antonia's voice, drawling and rather higher pitched than usual. 'Cradle-snatching, darling? Your—appetites must be jaded these days!'

The dream, the spell, whatever it had been was shattered. Rowan saw Carne's face change, tauten as he turned to look at her.

He said pleasantly, 'Hardly snatching, my sweet, restoring her to her cradle. Rowan's had a tough evening.'

'And I, of course, have had a wonderful time. That bloody storm, a power cut in the restaurant, and then back here to chaos,' Antonia said petulantly. 'For goodness' sake put her down, Carne. She's not a baby, after all, and I presume you don't want to become the centre of some adolescent fantasy.'

'Oh, I don't know.' His own voice lengthened to a drawl. 'It might be rather a novelty—for a while.'

For a moment Antonia stared at him incredulously, then she turned on her heel and stormed back into the room she had left, slamming the door behind her. He stood looking after her for the space of a few heartbeats, then as if nothing had happened, he started up the staircase with Rowan, stunned and silent, in his arms.

CHAPTER SEVEN

HE did not speak or look at her as he carried her along the passage, and shouldered his way into her room. Three long strides took him across to the bed, and he was lowering her on to it and sinking down beside her, his hands pinning her to the pillow like a butterfly on a cork as she tried vainly to twist away from him.

He said softly, 'You're home, Rowan,' and she found herself realising that it was the third time he had used the word 'home' and that three was the magic number in all the fairy tales. Only, suddenly, this was no fairy tale. This was stark reality, and she was frightened alone with him in this room, on this bed. Nor was this her home. It was her cage which she had to share with him—a man who had never lived his life by conventional standards.

She said, 'No!' on a little gasp, and saw his brows lift as he bent towards her.

'You don't mean that.' His breath was warm on her face and the silver eyes seemed to glitter as he stared down at her. 'You mean yes. Don't pretend any more, Rowan. Don't pretend about anything. Like the song says *But for now, love, let's be real.*' Be real for me.'

Long fingers captured her chin, held it still, preventing her frenzied twisting on the pillow.

'Let go of me!' The room was dark, but the plea came from a deeper darkness somewhere inside her. 'You—you don't mean this, Carne. Aren't you afraid I'll make you the centre of an adolescent fantasy?' Antonia's words still stung in the repetition.

He smiled. 'Women have fantasies too. Wouldn't you like to discover how they differ?' He touched his mouth delicately to the corners of her mouth and the pulse in her throat, and every nerve in her body sang a song she had never heard before, a song she must make sure she never heard again.

'No.' She closed her eyes against the almost hypnotic effect his gaze was having on her. 'Nor do I want to be the focus for anyone's—jaded appetites.'

She felt his body tense, his hands tighten painfully on her flesh.

'Is that a fact?' he said eventually, and his voice was too pleasant. 'Then that's your misfortune, my little nymph.'

He began to kiss her, slowly and languorously, parting her lips with insistent sensuousness, while his hands moved on her, unfastening the buttons of her shirt.

She said against his mouth, 'Carne—please!' but it sounded like a moan.

He lifted his head slightly and looked down at her. There were little devils dancing in his eyes, and the scar beside his mouth emphasised its cynical twist. He said softly, 'I have every intention of pleasing you, darling, and teaching you to please me too. I'll make you drown in pleasure. Like this.'

His questing fingers had already found and dealt with the small clip which fastened her bra in the hollow between her breasts, and now his mouth followed the sensual, teasing path of his hands. His tongue made little circles on her skin, and her breath choked in her throat as she fought to retain even a semblance of control while his lips tormented the rosy tautened peaks of her aroused womanhood.

Her hands reached up involuntarily, spreading across his back, drawing him down to her, and he muttered huskily, 'For God's sake, Rowan, touch me, not my clothes.' She obeyed, her fingers fumbling with the buttons on his shirt, partly because she was shy, and partly because her whole body was trembling with the desire he had created in her. The warmth of his skin beneath the tentative exploration of her hands was a reassurance in some strange way, so that when his mouth returned to claim hers once more, her response was unguarded and innocently passionate. There was a new urgency in his caresses, a new demand in his touch which she answered willingly. Even when his fingers released the button on the waistband of her jeans and began to slide down the zip, she had no thought of protest, only an acquiescence which seemed to melt her bones.

Somewhere, she was dimly conscious of an alien sound, but it did not really impinge on her awareness until Carne thrust himself away from her with a muffled curse, looking over his shoulder at the door. And then she realised what the sound had been. There was someone at the door—someone knocking, who could only be Antonia. At any moment she might walk in and see them there together. With a little incoherent cry she sat up, dragging the edges of her shirt across her body.

'Carne? Are you there?' Antonia's voice sounded sweet and a little plaintive. 'It's the telephone, darling. I couldn't quite make it out, but I think it could be the nursing home.'

Carne muttered with a groan, 'Sybilla—oh, my God!' He almost flung himself off the bed, thrusting his shirt back into the waistband of his pants as he went. Rowan heard the door open, and his voice sharp with enquiry, then there was silence. She lay alone in the darkness feeling dizzy and a little sick. One minute she had been half way to some kind of seventh heaven, and now she was back on earth with a vengeance.

She swung her feet to the floor and stood up gingerly, wondering whether her legs would support her and rather surprised when they did. She took off the rest of her clothes and put on her nightdress, then went across to the dressing chest to brush her hair.

Her own eyes, wide and shadowed, looked back at her, and not a stranger's, and she knew she had to be glad of that. She still belonged to herself. But for the interruption she would have given herself to Carne without a second thought, and lived to regret it for the rest of her life. Because although she loved him, she would not have woken in his arms the following day to find herself beloved in return. To him, she was simply a novelty—and even that was provided by her innocence. But once she was innocent no longer, she would not even have that attraction for him.

She put the brush down with a little inward shiver. All the time she was listening for the sound of someone coming. If something had happened to Sybilla, surely one of them would tell her. The thought of having to make herself go downstairs and face Antonia was a distasteful one, yet she could not sit in her room for the rest of the night and not know what had happened.

She put on her dressing gown and belted it tightly around her, and slid her feet into slippers. Then she made her way downstairs. Halfway down the spiral staircase she paused, puzzled. The sitting room door stood ajar, and there was the sound of music coming from the lighted interior. Rowan went across the hall and pushed the door open fully. Antonia was sitting with her feet up on the sofa, smoking a cigarette. She looked towards the door as Rowan came in, and smiled, a small, triumphant smile.

'If you're looking for Carne, darling, then he's not here. His—caller had rung off by the time he got downstairs, so he's gone chasing off to the nursing home to see what's happened.' She smiled again. 'You know, if Sybilla was—say, forty years younger, I could be quite jealous. Well, don't stand there hovering like a ghost! Come in, sit down and we'll have a cosy little mother and daughter chat. I'm sorry I had to curtail your romantic little interlude, but I thought it had probably gone far enough.'

'You mean—you don't care that Carne made love to me?'

Antonia looked at her with a kind of amused tolerance. 'Oh, I don't think it got that far—certainly not in so short a time. Carne has far too much finesse for that. Don't forget how well I know him.' She stretched languidly, her arms above her head, her full breasts straining against her thin sweater. 'He was ripe for a little—mischief. I sensed that when we were together earlier, and I knew I'd have to be careful. I'm having the devil's own job to keep him out of my bed as it is.'

Rowan said quietly, 'I don't think I want to hear about your relationship with Carne, Antonia.'

Antonia shrugged. 'I just don't want you to get ideas above your station, my sweet. I thought it would be quite interesting if Carne—amused himself with you for a while. I decided I'd call a halt at an appropriate moment, always supposing your naturally virginal qualms hadn't already done so. For all his experience, I doubt if virgins are altogether to his taste.'

'You are quite vile,' Rowan said very clearly and distinctly. 'And the phone call?'

'Quite bogus, darling, as you've guessed. All a terrible mistake on my part when he returns. He won't be in the best of tempers, of course, but then what man would be? I had to fight him off earlier, and now you've been snatched away almost at the moment of truth.' She gave a little yawn. 'I'm so glad I'm not a man. Such basic creatures! A little healthy frustration will bring most of them to heel.'

'And you think playing a kind of sexual Grandmother's Footsteps with Carne will make him propose marriage eventually?' Rowan couldn't conceal the scorn in her voice.

Antonia's eyes widened. 'Oh, I think so, darling. After all, he's proposed everything else. Where are you going?'

'To bed,' Rowan retorted bitterly.

'Very wise,' Antonia approved. 'But just one thing, sweetie, don't lie awake hoping. Driving to Heatonbank and back will have cooled Carne's ardour, I imagine. But even if it hasn't, surely you don't really want to be second best?'

From the door, Rowan said wearily, 'At this moment, I don't even want to be first.'

But it was a long time before she could get to sleep, lying alone in the darkness, and telling herself over and over again that she was glad to be alone.

She managed to slip out of the house without meeting anyone the following morning, and reported for work as usual. Grace commented immediately on her wan appearance and demanded to know if she was sickening for something.

Rowan said she didn't think so, and wondered privately what Grace would say if she told her she was sick at heart.

Fortunately two coach parties arrived almost within minutes of each other, and Rowan was kept too busy finding wrapping paper and suitable boxes for the customers to bear their spoils away in to worry about her own problems. It was lunchtime before she had any time to herself. Grace and Clive were both busily absorbed in the pottery itself, so she carried her mug of homemade soup and cheese and apple sandwiches into the showroom and ate them by herself. She was sitting staring rather drearily through the window waiting for the next influx of visitors when David came into the shop.

He said, 'I've got to the stage where I think I'll scream if I see another text book.'

Rowan tried to sound brisk and encouraging. 'You'll be fine.'

He gave her a wry look. 'I wish your confidence was shared by the staff at school, or anyone—myself included.' He paused, then said swiftly, 'Look, there's a disco at Arnthwaite next week. Will you come to it with me? A sort of pre-exam binge?'

Although she had been half expecting an invitation at some time from him, Rowan was a little taken aback. David saw her hesitation and said hurriedly, 'Of course, if you're too busy . . .'

If she refused, he would be hurt, she thought. He knew as well as she did how limited the opportunities for any kind of social life were in the village.

She made herself smile. 'Thank you, David. I'd like that.'

'Great!' He returned the smile with interest. 'In fact, fantastic. I'll get Dad to lend me the van. The disco's on Friday evening, so I'll pick you up about eight.' He hesitated. 'There'll be no problem? I mean, there's no one you should ask first?'

'No one at all,' she said steadily. She could imagine the sort of barbed comment she would have to put up with from Antonia, but she would face that when it happened. She closed her mind against what Carne would think.

David seemed disposed to hang around and chat, so she was almost relieved when a car stopped outside and disgorged two elderly couples. It turned out they visited the area each year and were regular customers at the pottery, so Grace had to be fetched from the workroom to welcome them, and show them the new lines. Rowan hung about in the background, feeling surplus to requirements, and was glad to hear the shop bell tinkle again.

She turned to greet the newcomer, and paused, the words choking in her throat as she saw Carne standing in the doorway, watching her. He was wearing close-fitting black pants which emphasised the length of his legs, and a matching high-necked sweater in thin wool. A cream-coloured jacket hung from his shoulders. She had grown so accustomed to seeing him in casual jeans that she had forgotten how elegant he could look.

She stared at him, not knowing what to say or how to react, her hands twisting in the folds of her overall. Carne observed the nervous movement with an enigmatic expression, and at that moment Grace also turned and saw him.

'Hello, stranger. What brings you here?'

'I wanted a word with Rowan,' he said briefly. 'I thought this might be her lunch hour, but I can see you're busy.'

'Oh, that's all right,' Grace said blithely. 'I can manage. Take her away with you, Carne, and give her a breath of air. She's been looking peaky all morning, poor child.'

'But I've had lunch,' Rowan protested. 'I'm not entitled to . . .'

'Rubbish!' Grace declared roundly. 'We don't operate under union rules here. Run along, and don't keep Carne waiting.'

Rowan groaned inwardly, but the customers were beginning to look more interested in what was going on than they were in the pots they were examining, so she made no further protest. Her mouth set mutinously, she went across to the door and Carne stood courteously aside to allow her to precede him into the fresh air. His car was parked a little way up the street, and she looked at it a little uncertainly.

Carne's hand fastened round her arm with no uncertainty at all. 'In you get,' he ordered.

'But where are we going?' she demanded, trying to twist free of his grip and failing. 'I'm supposed to be working and . . .'

'Grace said you needed air, so I'll take you down to the lake. We'll use the car, because I haven't a lot of time.'

She sat silently beside him as he manoeuvred the car expertly through the narrow street. There were a number of cars parked near the pub, adding to the congestion.

'I ought to get back,' she said resentfully. 'Grace will be rushed off her feet in a moment.'

'Grace will cope. She's noted for it.' He shot her a side-ways glance. 'But I wouldn't say you can. In that get-up you look like Little Nell, or some equally washed-out product of a Victorian novel.'

'Thanks,' muttered Rowan, and he smiled faintly.

'At least when you're annoyed you have some colour in your cheeks.'

They were out of the village by this time, and on a road Rowan had never taken before, running along the edge of the lake. Carne swung the car on to the verge and stopped, switching off the engine and pocketing the keys. Rowan opened the passenger door and climbed out. There was a faint breeze coming from the water, and she breathed it deeply and gratefully, trying to make herself relax. She walked forward through the scatter of trees and mossy boulders to the narrow shingle beach which ran down to the water's edge. There weren't many people around—some picnickers a few hundred yards away, with children dipping cautious feet in the water, and in the middle of the lake, a boat with a solitary, hopeful fisherman.

Carne came to stand beside her. There was space be-tween them, but she was as aware of him as if she was pinned in his arms, breast to breast, thigh to thigh, and she gave a slight, involuntary shiver.

'Are you cold?' he asked.

'No—the sun's really warm today,' she returned stil-tedly. She hesitated, then said, 'How—how is Sybilla?'

'She spent a comfortable night, and is making excellent progress, or so I was told this morning. That telephone call last night——' his mouth twisted a little '—didn't come from the nursing home.'

Rowan moistened her lips with the tip of her tongue. 'Well, that's good.'

'That isn't exactly how I saw it last night,' he said wryly. 'Although now I'm inclined to think it was a blessing in disguise. I'm sure that's your view, anyway.' She made no reply, and after a brief pause, he went on, 'That's the reason—or one of them at least—that I didn't come back to the house last night. Because I guessed that by the time I'd driven to Heatonbank and made sure all was well with Sybilla and returned, saner counsels would have prevailed with you—and I wasn't in a mood for kicking down locked doors.'

'It wasn't locked,' she said without thinking, and flushed deeply at his sardonic laugh.

'No? Then perhaps that's an omission you'd do well to repair from now on. Although you'll be safe for the next few days, because I have to go to London. That's why I wanted to talk to you first.'

'It's all right,' Rowan said hurriedly. 'You—you don't have to apologise or explain. I understand.'

'I haven't the slightest intention of doing either,' he said, raising his eyebrows. 'Any regrets I may have certainly wouldn't add up to an apology, and as for an explanation—I'm male and you're female. That's all that needs to be said.'

'I see,' she said bitterly, after a pause.

'I rather doubt that, but in any case don't brood about it, Rowan. All's well, after all. I didn't succeed in my fell design, and that's something we should perhaps both be grateful for.'

'Oh, yes,' she said ironically, the image of Antonia coming into her mind. 'In other words, saner counsels prevailed with you as well.'

'You could say that.' His voice was laconic. 'Although I haven't time now to discuss the finer points of my moral dilemma. We'll save it for my return.'

'No, thank you.' Her voice shook a little. 'There's nothing to discuss. I'm under no illusions as to why you behaved as you did. In some ways, I suppose I invited it. My—juvenile crush was a little obvious. But you cured that completely, which I imagine was the purpose of the exercise.'

She paused, waiting for some kind of reaction—perhaps protest, perhaps anger, but there was only silence, so she continued, 'I—I suppose I should be grateful. Not many girls my age get a lesson in lovemaking from an expert, even if it did go rather further than you intended. But it taught me something else as well—to stay in my own league from now on.' She attempted a nervous laugh. 'I don't know if you know quite how overwhelming you can be when you want. I—I was terrified!'

'Then you hid it very well,' it was Carne's turn to be
ironic. 'Fear was about the last emotion I thought I'd
disturbed in you. Even I can learn, it seems. But one thing
we can agree on—it did go further than I intended. I
meant to kiss you goodnight, that's all.'

'A paternal gesture that went astray?'

'You know better than that,' he said rather wearily. 'If
you want the truth, I wanted to comfort you, and I also
thought you wanted to be kissed. Was I so wrong?'

'No,' she said. 'You were quite right. I did—and now I
don't any more. I'm not indulging in any more girlish
fantasies about you, Carne, they're altogether too dangerous. I may not come very high in your regard, but I think I
deserve better than to be seduced because you're bored—
or frustrated.'

Her voice faltered and died away. When she dared look
at him, she took an involuntary step backwards, catching
her foot against a loose pebble and stumbling. At once, his
arm came out to catch her and stop her falling. She
wrenched herself free.

'Don't touch me!'

'An instinctive reaction,' he bit back at her. 'It won't
happen again. My frustrations might get the better of me,
and I might give you the hiding your late father signally
failed to do.'

'You can't deny it,' Rowan said defiantly. 'It's all part of
this weird game of cat and mouse you're playing with
Antonia. You can't make love to her, and you thought
you'd punish her through me. Well, it didn't work. But
from now on I wish you'd confine your attentions to her—
and leave me out of it.'

Carne was very pale under his tan, and the silver eyes
were blazing. The scar beside his mouth seemed to throb as
he spoke.

'Thank you for your masterly summing up of the situation. From now on I promise you neither you nor Antonia
will have anything to complain of. And now I'd better get
you back to work.'

He turned away and walked back to the car, and Rowan
trailed after him. She felt as if she wanted to die. Carne was
already in the driving seat, his fingers tapping the steering

wheel when she presented herself hesitantly at the side of the car.

'If you'd rather I walked . . .' she began, and he turned on her mercilessly.

'I'd rather you got out of my life altogether, Rowan, but we can't have everything we want. Now get in the car, and I'll drive you to Grace's.'

'I want to be out of your life.' Her voice hardly rose above a whisper. 'You don't know how much I want it. But you don't have to worry. Just as soon as I can, I'll be gone. I don't care what I have to do to achieve that.'

'Then that's fine with me.' Almost before she had closed her door, he set the car in motion, reversing in a flurry of gravel, and driving back the way they had come with scant regard for safety or speed limits.

He stopped outside the pottery, and turned to her, his eyes like frozen winter, his face set grimly. 'Assuming that you'll still be here for the next week or so, perhaps you'll keep an eye on Sybilla. A daily telephone call will do. You don't have to put yourself out.'

'I shan't be,' she said tightly. 'I like Sybilla.'

'And she likes you.' His face didn't change; if anything it hardened slightly. 'Even she can be fallible, it seems.'

Long after the car had gone, Rowan stood staring sightlessly at the empty street. She thought despairingly, 'What have I done? Oh God, what have I done?'

Rowan felt physically and emotionally exhausted as she returned to the house that evening. The shop had been full when she returned, and there had been a constant influx of customers all afternoon, which had been a relief in many ways, because they had prevented her from brooding, and had also stopped Grace from asking what would have been awkward questions. But Grace had been too busy to do more than comment in a puzzled away that Rowan's lunch break hadn't seemed to have done her a great deal of good.

Somewhat to her surprise, the kitchen door was locked, and she had to fumble in her bag for her key. The house was full of silence as she let herself in, and as she glanced round, she saw a piece of paper secured by a jug of flowers in the centre of the kitchen table.

She groaned inwardly, even before she read it, knowing what it would contain. '*Expect me when you see me, Antonia.*' Well, that was short and sharp and to the point, Rowan thought, filling the kettle, and spooning instant coffee into a beaker. But how nice it would be for once when she came in tired to find a meal waiting for her, or even a friendly voice to enquire about her day.

She sat down with her coffee, and ran weary fingers round the nape of her neck. She had hoped to be able to persuade Antonia to drive her to Heatonbank so she could visit Sybilla, but she would have to be content with a phone call, it seemed. She wondered without much interest where Antonia had gone. Not out for yet another meal, because she had already eaten, as the dirty dishes stacked carelessly in the sink bore mute witness. Rowan sighed, wrinkling her nose at the thought. Relations between Antonia and herself had never been relaxed or easy, but when they were living in London, they had done better than this. But perhaps that was because Antonia had had no alternative, Rowan thought cynically. Here at Raven's Crag, poised to take over as the future mistress of the house, she did not have to try any more with a stepdaughter she had never particularly cared for anyway.

Besides, I came here for her convenience, so I can hardly complain now, Rowan told herself bitterly.

She supposed she ought to make herself a meal, but tiredness and emotionalism from the day's events had robbed her of her appetite, although the warm coffee was comforting. And presently she would make a start on Sybilla's flat—after she had phoned the nursing home.

Sister, when she spoke to her, was reassuring. Sybilla, it seemed, had enjoyed a good day and needed nothing. She had been moved into a room with another elderly lady who also had a penchant for crossword puzzles, and chess and bridge problems, and they were getting on like a house on fire, so Rowan was not to worry, Sister added firmly, and Rowan smiled rather wanly as she replaced the receiver.

She enjoyed tidying the flat, dusting the ornaments and treasures, and restoring order. The atmosphere was like a soothing hand, and almost imperceptibly she began to feel better, as if Sybilla's bracing personality was in the room with her. She stripped the bed, and took the soiled linen with her when she left to wash in the automatic machine in the laundry room.

'What on earth are you doing?'

Antonia's voice halted her as she was locking Sybilla's door.

Rowan swung round, her arms full of sheets. 'Sybilla asked me to look after the flat for her,' she answered awkwardly.

Antonia gave a short laugh. 'Rather a waste of time, isn't it?' she observed critically.

'On the contrary,' Rowan was horrified. 'Sybilla's much better today. She . . .'

'Spare me the details,' Antonia invited languidly. 'Her state of health really doesn't interest me that much— except that it solves one rather serious problem.'

'I don't understand,' said Rowan, frowning.

Antonia smiled. 'Darling, you really are very naïve! Sybilla collapsed, right? Which probably means she's going to be virtually a cripple for the rest of her life. If she was younger, and her heart was all right, she could probably have something done about her hip—as it is——' she shrugged negligently, 'one can only say that she's in the best place. And I for one am not sorry.'

'But she'll be coming home,' Rowan protested uneasily.

'Will she?' Antonia's brows rose. 'Not as far as I'm concerned, my dear. I came here to keep house for Carne, not to nurse a sick old woman. Why, she'll probably end up in a wheelchair. Carne has discharged his obligations to her very honourably, but there must come a time when even he must see that enough is enough. This house is totally unsuitable for an invalid.'

Rowan said sharply, 'Carne wouldn't do that.'

Antonia laughed. 'I think I know him better than you do, sweetie. Carne likes people who are strong and whole— beautiful people. He won't have much time for cripples, physical or emotional.' She smiled, and Rowan felt as if someone had clawed her skin, leaving long malignant weals on the flesh. 'And I think he'll do as I want,' she added casually. 'If there hadn't been this trip to London, we'd probably have reached an understanding. As it is, when he comes back I shall get him to paint me. He never would in the past.' Her smile widened. 'It's going to be a beautiful summer.' She paused, then added gently. 'So be a busy little girl, sweetie. Go and visit Sybilla, and clean her flat, and slave away behind the scenes, and see where it gets you. You and Sybilla are both going to be losers, I'm afraid.'

'I don't understand why you're being like this.' Rowan felt unutterably weary. 'Neither of us is any threat to you.'

'No,' Antonia agreed. 'And I intend to keep it that way.' She turned and walked back towards the hall and the spiral stairs. She was wearing one of her expensive Italian knit suits, and her hair in a coil on top of her head, and Rowan wondered where she had been, looking so deliberately soignée. Then she shrugged slightly. It was none of her business and Antonia obviously hadn't the slightest intention of making it so, and the best thing she could do was load these sheets into the machine.

It was a little disconcerting when she returned home the following night to find the pattern had been repeated, however, and this time Rowan fretted, because she needed Antonia to drive her to Heatonbank. She didn't get paid at the pottery until the following day, so a taxi was out of the question. If Antonia came home at the same time as the previous evening, she would have time for a hasty visit, she thought, but of course Antonia did not return home. Rowan had been in bed for over an hour when she heard the car engine.

Before she left for work the following morning, she went up to her room and tackled her.

'Are you going to be out again this evening?'

Antonia gave her an irritable look. 'Yes, as it happens, What difference does it make?'

'Every difference.' Rowan tried to sound reasonable. 'I have no transport, and I need to visit the nursing home. Sybilla will be needing clean nightdresses—a change of library books.'

'Then you'll have to make some arrangements to get there,' Antonia said coolly. 'I made no extravagant promises to visit Heatonbank, and I've no intention of acting as your chauffeur. You take far too much for granted, Rowan.'

Rowan looked at her bleakly. 'Is that your final word?'

'I'm afraid so. If you want to be the Good Samaritan, it will have to be under your own steam.' Antonia's tone revealed her profound lack of interest in the subject under discussion, and Rowan turned silently and left the room.

In spite of everything, she had never dreamed that Antonia would refuse to give up whatever her evening's entertainment was for once. And the most galling thing was that she could drive the car herself if only she had the spare set of keys. Carne wasn't around to see her and question the legality of what she was doing. And Sybilla would be expecting her. Sister had asked rather pointedly on the phone the previous evening when Rowan would be coming, and she had assured her she would be along next day. It seemed she would have to spend some of her hard-earned wages on taxi fares, which would deplete the amount she would be able to save.

It was a grey morning, the air full of fine mist-like drizzle, and customers at the pottery were few and far between. Rowan was brewing coffee when David appeared.

'You look rather blue,' he greeted her. 'Having second thoughts about our date?'

'Oh—no.' Rowan realised with compunction that she had scarcely given it a second thought since the arrangement had been made. 'I just have a slight problem, that's all. I need to get to Heatonbank Clinic this evening to visit Sybilla—and I assumed my stepmother would take me, only she can't and—and now I'm a bit stuck.'

'I see.' David chewed his lip thoughtfully. 'Does it have to be tonight? I mean, Dad and Mum are going to see her some time—I heard them say so. Perhaps they could make it tonight.'

'No, please,' Rowan broke in quickly. 'It's my own fault. I should have checked with Antonia that she was available before making the arrangement. I don't want to cause your parents any trouble.'

'Don't talk so daft.' He looked and sounded surprised. 'You got them out of a jam, didn't you? They'd be pleased to help.'

He vanished into the workroom before Rowan could say

any more, and after a few moments Grace arrived, looking severe.

'When you need help, you ask. That's what friends are for, young woman,' she said forthrightly.

'But it was all my own fault,' Rowan began, and Grace gave her an odd glance.

'Was it? I'd have thought Mrs Winslow could have spared one of her crowded hours to run you there and back, but I'm just poking my nose into what doesn't concern me,' she added cheerfully. 'So we'll pick you up this evening about half past six, and if Sybilla needs anything, you can pop into Keswick tomorrow with Clive and get it for her. And any time you want to go to Heatonbank just let us know and one of us will drive you. If Clive and I are too busy, I daresay David can be prevailed upon,' she added, grinning. 'I hear you're going to the disco with him next week.'

'Yes.' Rowan's eyes searched her face. 'You—you don't mind?'

'Why should I?' Grace gave her an amused look. 'If I thought either of you were thinking in terms of a serious relationship, then I should mind, but I know David isn't, and you . . .' she stopped suddenly, a curiously embarrassed expression crossing her face. 'Here I go again,' she muttered after a pause.

Rowan's face grew hot. There was no point in pretending she did not understand, in asking Grace what she meant. Grace was shrewd and she had looked at Rowan long and hard when she had returned after that brief drive to the lakeside with Carne.

She said with an effort, 'It's all right. I know I've made a fool of myself, and I don't mind you knowing it either. That's what friends are for as well.'

Grace's face cleared. She said warmly, 'Rowan, I won't pretend I haven't been worried. I love Carne dearly, but . . .' She hesitated, then said in a little rush, 'But if you're looking for a father figure, then he won't do, and at your age that's all it can be. You could be hurt very badly. And as for Carne—well, you're a lovely child in your own self-contained way, and he wouldn't be human if he wasn't tempted.' She smiled at Rowan. 'You don't believe me, but it's true. You have beautiful bones and a kind of—fey quality. I'd have thought the artist in him would have found it irresistible.'

Rowan thought, 'He saw me as a dryad with mountain ash berries in my hair.'

Aloud she said expressionlessly, 'He's going to paint Antonia.'

'Well, that figures.' Grace gave a little sigh. 'He's known her for a long time, after all. And he's been around. Perhaps he's ready for a relationship where there'll be no illusions to shatter.' There was a little silence, then she said briskly, 'Now, perhaps we'd better have that coffee while it's still fit to drink.'

Rowan carried hers back to the showroom. It was kind of Grace to be worried about her and to voice her concern. Tactful too to call her 'self-contained' when she knew ruefully she was transparent as glass. But no longer, she thought. All that was going to change, and by the time this summer was ended she would have her own façade to hide behind, her own wall around her emotions to shelter her while she licked her emotional wounds.

Perhaps one day she would even be as cynical as Carne, settling for the known, the predictable even if not particularly admirable, because where there were no illusions there could be no hurt, not any more.

She thought of Carne as he must have been when he was young, before the scar on his face, before the private inner scars which no one could see. He'd loved Antonia then, wanted her passionately. Now the wheel had turned, and she was going to be his, even though neither of them were the same people. He had opted for the life of a wealthy vagabond, jet-setting from one commission to the next, taking his pleasures as he found them, while Antonia had settled for marriage to a rich widower, and what had seemed at the time to be comfortable inertia, and probably that was what she intended to settle for the second time around as well, and Carne would continue in his own way too, and if that was what they wanted, she hoped they would be happy.

To her, it sounded like a recipe for certain misery, but then if Carne was hers, she would want him in every way there was—as husband, as lover, as friend. No limitations, or half-measures.

And that, she thought staring into the misty street, was how she did want him and always would, long after this strange summer was over.

CHAPTER EIGHT

THE Listers were as good as their word. Rowan had no problems getting to see Sybilla, who was clearly making excellent progress. She and her room-mate Mrs Patterson had become firm friends, and it was obvious the relationship would continue when they had left Heatonbank, although Mrs Patterson expected to spend a few weeks of convalescence with a married daughter in Bournemouth before returning to her own home in Keswick.

Rowan saw little of Antonia. She seemed to be out most of the time, and the house was beginning to take on a neglected quality. It wasn't being used sufficiently to be really dirty, but it looked uncared for, and Rowan grieved silently when she returned there in the evenings. She kept rigorously to her own side of the bargain, looking after her own room, and, on the Monday which was the pottery's usual closing day, shopping and cooking for the freezer. David had taken her into Keswick, so that she could also go to the bank, and as they were driving out of the town Rowan thought for a moment that she saw Antonia going into one of the tall grey villas on the hill, but it was only a glimpse, and there had to be other tall redheaded women about. But when she arrived back at Raven's Crag and found the house deserted yet again, it made her wonder for a while, but she shrugged her curiosity away. If Antonia had made some friends, that was all to the good. Perhaps she would be content to stay in the area after all when Carne and she were married.

She kept reminding herself, almost grimly, at regular intervals that they were going to be married, and it was rather like pressing on an aching tooth, but one day the pain would stop. It would have to. She couldn't spend the rest of her life looking back to a house perched on a rain-swept fellside.

Antonia never asked how Rowan was managing with her visits to Sybilla. Nor had the subject of Sybilla's even-tual return to the house been raised again, except by Doctor Mortimer, who told Rowan that with ordinary care the older woman should be able to take up her former life again.

'In fact I'd like to see anyone try to stop her,' he re-marked rather obliquely, and Rowan glanced at him quickly, wondering whether he had sensed any of the undercurrents between Sybilla and Antonia.

She smiled. 'That's wonderful. Her flat's all ready and waiting for her. I only have to make up the bed.'

She didn't mention the conversation to Antonia when she saw her next. It would be better, she thought, to wait until Carne's return before broaching the subject.

As the date of the disco approached, she found she was looking forward to it more than she had dreamed possible. She had started to become accustomed to working all day and spending her evenings at the house, and a little gaiety would do her no harm at all. She even bought herself a new dress, urged on by Grace, a floating Indian cotton in shades of green and gold with heavy embroidery around the slashed neck and long full sleeves. She had had her hair trimmed too so that it swung softly towards her face, and she had some ear-rings which she had bought in London long before, Indian ear-rings with three tiers of tiny gold sequins.

She felt more cheerful than she had done for some time as she walked down to the pottery on the morning of the disco. As she went towards the village shop she noticed some youths outside tinkering with motorbikes, but there was nothing new in that. They had been there before many times as she went to and fro, and the tallest one with the studs in his black leather coat and an ear-ring in one ear was Jeff Wainwright, the erstwhile gardener at Raven's Crag.

Usually they took no notice of her, but this morning was

different. As she approached, Jeff Wainwright straightened up slowly and stood, blocking the footpath. Rowan made to step off the kerb and walk round him, disliking the long insolent look he gave her, but he moved too, and she paused, a little nonplussed and more than a little wary, although she told herself that she could come to little harm in broad daylight within a few feet of the shop where his mother and sister were both working. Not, she thought wryly as she met his gaze with a defiant lift of her chin, that she could count on much help from that quarter. Mrs Wainwright, and particularly her daughter, had given her the most perfunctory service whenever she had been in the shop, and Beth's attitude bordered on the surly. She never returned any of Rowan's tentative smiles, or replied to any of her questions or comments with more than a monosyllable.

Now Jeff Wainwright said, 'I want a word with you.'

'If it's about your job at the house, then you'll have to see Mr Maitland when he gets back,' she said quickly.

One of his companions laughed, and Jeff gave a sneering smile. 'I don't want any lousy job with 'im. No, it's you I want to talk to. Hear you're going to the disco tonight with 'im.' He jerked a thumb in the direction of the pottery.

Rowan said coolly, 'News gets around.'

'Well, that's village life, isn't it?' he said. 'Folks have nowt to talk about except each other. But you wouldn't know about that, coming from London.'

Rowan said politely, 'What I do know is that you're making me late for work. May I get past, please?'

'Presently. There's no hurry.' He looked her up and down and she forced herself to stay impassive under a glance which stripped the clothes from her. 'How do you fancy going with me instead?'

'With you?' Rowan echoed stupidly, then she rallied. 'Frankly, I don't.'

'The thing is,' he said, still watching her, 'Dave used to go with my sister, and she's still keen on him. They might have got back together if you hadn't shown up. Now, if you were to tell him you were going with me tonight, then he'd ask Beth, and everyone would be happy.'

Rowan said coldly, 'I'm afraid I wouldn't. I don't know

you, and I certainly don't want to go out with you either to a disco or anywhere else. And if David had wanted to date your sister, he would have done so. You really can't interfere in people's lives. Haven't you discovered that yet?'

One of the others imitated what she had said in a high falsetto voice, and someone else sniggered. Rowan felt herself flush. The situation was making her increasingly uneasy, yet pride forbade that she should run from it ignominiously.

Jeff said, 'Not good enough for you, am I? But I'd give you a better time than Dave, for all his classy accent.' He grinned insolently. 'Better than that hard-faced bastard up on the fell too.'

The colour in Rowan's face deepened. It was impossible that there could have been any gossip linking her name with Carne's, she knew that. It was just a spiteful barb from a young man with a grudge that had found a target.

She shrugged in an effort to be casual. 'It's a village disco, not a life partnership. I don't have exclusive rights in David. He can dance with your sister if that's what he wants. Now will you move, please? I have to go to work.'

If he detained her again, then she was going to be frightened. She might even be forced to retreat into the shop and suffer the humiliation of asking for their help, but she would do it if she had to, and perhaps Jeff Wainwright sensed something of her determination, because he stood to one side and Rowan went past him, her head high. She could hear the sounds of amusement from the others, some muttered remarks, probably ribald, and breathed deeply in relief. It had been an unpleasant little incident, but it was behind her now. All the same, she wished in a way she had refused David's invitation. Not that she thought for one minute he would have invited Beth Wainwright instead, but at least she would not have been involved in any little dramas. That was the last thing she needed, she thought ruefully, shivering a little as she remembered the final look Jeff Wainwright had given her, half sensual, half antagonistic. That was something she couldn't understand. She was the last person on earth, the last type to appeal to someone like him. There was nothing about him—his looks or his personality—which appealed to her, and she was

quite sure that he felt the same about her. Perhaps asking
her out had been a quixotic gesture to help his sister
achieve her heart's desire, but somehow she didn't think so.
He didn't look the type for quixotic gestures of any kind.

She wondered whether she should mention what had
happened to Clive, but decided against it. The imminence
of David's exams was already causing a certain amount of
tension, she had guessed, and Clive might suddenly come
the heavy father and forbid David to go to the disco at all.
And he needs to go, she thought. He's been working very
hard, and he really needs a break and some relaxation.

But Jeff Wainwright's intervention had taken the edge
off her own anticipation. And as she put on her overall and
went into the showroom, she found herself hoping that that
was the end of the matter.

There was a steady stream of customers that day, and as
it turned out she saw little of either Clive or Grace, and
certainly had no opportunity of a private word with them.
David did not put in an appearance either and she guessed
this was one of the days he had classes to attend, instead of
studying at home.

When the pottery closed for the evening, she was in no
great hurry to leave, moving round the showroom, doing
some desultory tidying. She needed to go back to the house,
of course, to have something to eat, to bath and change,
but she was afraid she would find Jeff Wainwright waiting
again, although she told herself she was being ridiculous. It
was hardly likely that he would still be hanging about, and
anyway, she would have to face him at the disco later.

She walked up the street towards the shop, and as she did
so Beth Wainwright came out and began putting some
apples in a bag from the small fruit and vegetable display
on the pavement. Rowan gave her a tentative smile, but
the look she received in response was cold and inimical.
Beth was quite a pretty girl, but hostility made her look
plain, and Rowan wished she could tell her that even if she
had been willing to break her date with David, it was
unlikely in the extreme that he would resume his relationship with Beth. He might joke about school and his
exams and hopes of a university place, but Rowan had
little doubt where his sights were set, and Beth would only

be laying herself open to more heartache if she imagined his plans for the future would ever include her.

She thought with a trace of irritation, 'Oh, why does everything have to be so difficult?'

It had been a warm sunlit day, and it was going to be a beautiful evening, she realised as she turned in through the gates and walked up the drive at Raven's Crag. The sky was the clear unsullied blue of early summer, and only the merest wisps of clouds drifted along the tops of the fells. The thought of shutting herself away from it all into a hot, heavy, smoky atmosphere shrill with noise was not particularly appealing.

Rowan turned the corner which led to the house and stopped abruptly, her eyes fixed in disbelief on the car that stood there. Carne's car. So he was back again, without a word to anyone. Even Sybilla had not known when Rowan visited her the previous evening when he intended to return. A prickle of apprehension touched her nerve endings as she stood staring at the car. There was no sign of Antonia's vehicle, she realised uneasily, and Antonia should be here to welcome Carne home to a clean house and a decent meal, because that was the least of the strange bargain they had made. Or was Antonia so sure of him now that she no longer needed to bother to keep his terms?

Forcing herself to reluctant movement, she mounted the steps and opened the front door. Inside the hall she paused for a moment, looking about her, biting the soft flesh of her inner lip, seeing the house as Carne must see it, stale, unlived-in, uncared-for, its former brightness dimmed and tarnished by neglect. Everywhere, it showed.

She listened intently for a moment for some sign, some sound of his presence, but everything was hushed and silent. If she hadn't seen the car, she would have thought the place was still unoccupied.

She went through to the kitchen. At least she could restore some order there—do the inevitable washing up which Antonia would have left for her. She pushed open the door and went in.

Carne was sitting at the table, a pot of coffee and a plate in front of him.

'Welcome home,' he said sardonically. 'Can I offer you a

drink and a cheese sandwich?'

He was smiling a little, but that didn't fool her. Underneath there was anger.

She said, faltering a little, 'I'm sorry. If you'd let us know, I'd have made sure there was a meal for you.'

'Where's Antonia?'

'I don't know.' She looked straight at him, and saw his brows lift sceptically. 'You don't believe me.'

He shrugged. His eyes held hers. 'Give me one good reason why I should.'

She tried to smile, to lighten the odd atmosphere surrounding them. 'I—I can't think of any.'

'That's what I thought,' he drawled. He picked up his cup and drained it. 'Sure I can't offer you a cup of this delicious brew?'

She shook her head. 'I—I don't want anything.'

'I'm not sure I blame you,' he said slowly, his eyes going round the kitchen, lingering on the littered untidy surfaces, and the smears of grease on the sink and cooker. His mouth curled in distaste. 'There are two of you in the house,' he said with icy precision. 'Surely between you, you can make a better job of it than this. The rest of the place is no different, with the exception of my studio, and your bedroom, because I've looked.'

'You've been in my bedroom?' She looked at him indignantly.

'The arrangement was that you should keep out of mine,' he reminded her. 'Besides, it isn't the first time, or had you forgotten?'

Her glance fell away. 'No, I hadn't forgotten,' she said in a subdued voice.

There was a silence, then Carne asked, 'Who does the typewriter belong to?'

'It's mine. I brought it with me.' Rowan moistened her lips with the tip of her tongue. 'I—I bought it with the money you gave Antonia for me—before we ever came here. I hope you don't mind.'

'Do you use it much?' The silver eyes were fixed intently on her face. 'I don't recall noticing it before, but then my mind was on other things.'

She said, 'I try to write short stories. I haven't done

much lately because I've been so busy.' She saw his derisive smile, and her voice rose defensively. 'I work long hours at the pottery, and I've been visiting Sybilla each evening. It doesn't leave a great deal of time for other things.' She flushed suddenly as she saw the mockery in his eyes and realised she had used the same words as he had done. 'And I didn't mean *that*,' she added bitingly.

'I'm relieved to hear it.' He leaned back in his chair, lacing his fingers behind his head, making her only too aware of the lean muscular length of his body. 'So—what do you write when you have the time? School stories? Tales of derring-do for tiny tots?'

Rowan's flush deepened. 'Just—stories,' she said lamely, then, fired by the growing amusement in his face, 'Well—love stories, if you must know.'

'How very precocious of you, Rowan,' he said lightly. 'You must have a vivid imagination, my child. Perhaps I should have read what was in the typewriter, after all. I might have learned something about you.'

Her heart was hammering unsteadily. 'I don't think there's a great deal to learn,' she answered at last, and his mouth twisted.

'You think not? Well, you should know.' He stood up, scraping the chair across the floor, and the sound made her flinch. He stretched lazily, then held out a commanding hand to her. 'Let's turn our backs on this mess for a while. I'll take you for a walk on the fell.'

'Now?' She was taken aback.

'Why not?'

For every reason there is, she thought feverishly as her mind searched for one that she could say aloud without betraying too much of herself.

'You—you said I wasn't to go on the fell without proper equipment—proper clothes. I still don't have them.'

'I'm proposing a short stroll, not a ten-mile hike,' Carne drawled. 'The weather's good, and even if it changes, I can undertake to get you back to the house in one piece. I made the rule because I didn't want you wandering off by yourself and getting lost, but now I'm breaking it because I'll be with you, and there'll be no danger. So come on.' He held out his hand again, and when she made no move to join him, his face darkened. 'It isn't an invitation, Rowan, it's an order. I need some company. I've had enough of my own for one day.'

'And I'm all that's available,' she could not repress the bitterness in her voice.

He shrugged, his face enigmatic. 'If that's how you want to look at it. However it is, you're coming with me. And don't tell me you couldn't do with some air and sunlight. You're far too pale. You always were.'

And walking beside you in the sunlight won't change a thing, she wanted to cry out in passionate response. It's torment to me. Surely you see that? Surely you understand? But she said nothing, and the silence began to stretch between them. Carne moved suddenly, and she was afraid he was going to take hold of her, force her to go with him, and the thought of his touch, however casual, was enough to make her body go weak. She walked forward past him, and out of the kitchen door into the sunlit garden, and after a pause he followed her. She tried to keep a space between them, without distancing herself too obviously. They moved in silence until they reached the gate that led out on to the fell, and Carne said curtly, 'Let me do it,' as Rowan went to open it. She moved back quickly, almost snatching her hand away, and he gave her a long ironic look which brought the colour surging into her face. She wouldn't have been surprised if he had suggested they called it a day and went back to the house, but he held the gate open for her silently, and she went through it and out on to the hillside.

Trees grew down almost to the boundary wall of the garden and a few steps took her amongst them, her feet moving over grass and moss. It was cool and green and sheltered there, and the air had a damp freshness which she breathed deeply. There was a track of sorts, winding upwards quite steeply, and she slowed her pace deliberately, saving her breath for the climb ahead.

It was like walking through some dim green cloister, and the silence enfolded her, so much so that she started when a blackbird flew up out of a bush just ahead of her, trumpeting its alarm call.

At a point just ahead of them a tree had fallen, its broad

trunk blocking the track. Carne swung himself over it effortlessly, and turned to help her, but she ignored his outstretched hand, reaching instead for an overhanging branch as she scrambled across the obstruction. He was watching her, his eyes narrowed, as she dropped to the ground.

He said suddenly, 'That dryad painting could work very well. Sure you won't sit for me?'

For a moment Rowan gaped at him, then she said stiffly, 'I'm quite sure. But I'm sure you could find plenty of other models.'

'How very true,' he said wryly. 'But not for this particular setting. It demands an elfin quality, which you have. Did you know your hair blazes like a chestnut when the sun catches it?'

'No,' she said baldly. 'Nor am I particularly interested.'

'Very refreshing,' he said laconically. 'A lot of girls your age are fascinated by their appearance to the exclusion of everything else. But not you. You write, and you cook, and you sell pots. What other secrets and hidden talents do you possess, I wonder?'

'Not a thing,' she assured him tightly. 'And I really don't like this sort of personal conversation.'

'Private ground. No trespassers,' he said softly. 'Why, Rowan, you change fairy tales ever time I see you. Now, you're the girl asleep behind the thorn hedge, only I hope you don't intend to remain there for a hundred years.'

'If I did, at least people would stop tormenting me,' she said wearily.

'Is that what I do? Would you prefer me to be kind? The trouble is our ideas on what constitutes kindness might not coincide.'

'And cruelty is so much easier, isn't it?' she flashed. 'I think you could find a worthier target for your edged remarks.'

'You think I'm cruel.' He frowned a little. 'Yet some people would tell you I haven't even started yet.'

'Then God help some people,' she retorted. She felt perilously close to tears. 'I think I've walked far enough.'

'Chickening out?' He stared at her. 'You really don't like to be alone with me, do you, Rowan?'

She shrugged defensively. 'Is it any wonder?'

'Perhaps not.' His tone was weary. 'Would it ease the situation if I told you that I have no ulterior motive? That I've seen the error of my ways, if you want to put it like that. It's unfair to pressure you, or to make demands on you that you're not old enough or mature enough to handle.'

'Thank you,' she said rather bitterly.

'Oh, for God's sake! You can't have it both ways.' His tone bit at her. 'I'm frankly not used to your peculiar child-woman combination—and I mean peculiar to you. By standing back, I'm trying to do us both a favour, because there's no future in it, Rowan, not for a man of my age and a girl of yours.'

She heard him with a kind of inner agony she had to suppress at all costs. She wanted to fling herself into his arms, to tell him she could manage without the future as long as there was now—that as long as what was between them was allowed to exist, it didn't matter that it couldn't last. But she held back because he might reject her, and that she would not be able to bear. This pain would pass as it had to, and there might even come a time when she would be able to remember this strange summer with a kind of tranquillity. But if she offered herself, and Carne refused, even if it was out of kindness, then there would be no peace.

She said stonily, 'You take a hell of a lot for granted. As it happens, my plans don't include you either.'

She didn't look at him, but just walked forward through the trees without waiting to see if he followed or not. But he was there, his hand on her shoulder, turning her to face him.

'What plans are you talking about?'

'Nothing that need concern you.'

'Of course I'm concerned,' he said sharply. 'Can't you get it into your head that while you're under my roof, I'm responsible for you?'

'But I don't want you to be.' That much was the truth anyway. 'I can do without a father figure in my life—and if I needed one, he wouldn't be you anyway. Nor do I particularly want to be "under your roof". It wasn't my idea ever, believe me.'

'I think I do,' said Carne in an odd voice. 'So whose roof do you want to be under? The Listers'? Do these nebulous plans of yours involve young David, by any chance?'

Rowan grasped at the implication as if it were a lifeline. 'I like David. Why shouldn't I? He is my age, after all.'

'I suspect he'll never be your age,' he said smoothly. 'Go easy on him, Rowan. He's led a comparatively sheltered life. You may be an overwhelming surprise for him.'

'You'd better ask him that tomorrow.'

'Is that a subtle way of telling me you're seeing him tonight?'

'Yes—he's taking me to the disco at Arnthwaite. Or should I have asked permission first?'

Carne was very still suddenly. 'No, you've made your views on that quite clear. I assume that you've cleared it with your stepmother. You wouldn't deny her some right to intervene in your affairs.'

No, she couldn't deny that, she thought, and a total disaster Antonia's intervention had proved.

She said quietly, 'Antonia has no objection.'

'Then there's no problem,' he said. 'And now shall we admire the view, which was the purpose of the exercise in the first place.'

They had emerged from the shelter of the trees on to a small plateau. Above them, the fell soared away—grey rocks streaked with lichen and scree, wild and desolate. To the right, a small waterfall edged its way between boulders worn smooth by its passing. Over to the left, the ground fell away and Rowan found she was looking out over the valley. Basically, she supposed it was the same view that Carne had built his house to enjoy, but because they were now so much higher, it was even more spectacular, and today the air was clear so that she felt she could see to the ends of the earth.

The encircling mountains seemed to crouch like stone animals basking in the late sunlight, and far below Ravensmere lay in its hollow like a small blue handkerchief that someone had carelessly let fall to the ground.

A movement caught her eye and she turned her head sharply, just in time to see a large blue black bird launch itself into the air and sweep down towards the valley with a harsh cry which seemed to linger on the air, echoing the rawness she felt inside.

'Did it startle you?' Carne was at her side, and she was suddenly aware of the steepness of the ground. One false move, and she could be sent tumbling and twisting to lie eventually—where? She swallowed, and the temptation to turn to him, to take his hand, to rely on the strength that she knew instinctively he was offering was almost over-whelming. Almost, but not quite, because what would it be but another false move among so many, and although her bones would be left intact, she thought her heart would break.

'A little.' She tried to steady her voice. 'What was it—a crow?'

'Hardly,' he said drily. 'Raven's Crag isn't just a name, you know. There are whole families of ravens up here. It's the end of the breeding season now, and most of the young ones will have learned to fly. That one just then was an older bird—probably a parent giving us a word of warning not to trespass too closely.'

'Oh—I wish I'd caught a closer look. The only ravens I've ever seen were at the Tower of London, and there they look like sleek City gents.'

'Yes, they do rather.' His tone was amused, and percep-tibly the tension between them relaxed a little. 'And yet the original birds were far from civilised. Legend says that they went to the Tower to guard the head of one of the mythical Celtic kings which is buried there. And of course it was ravens that fed the god Odin as he hung on the Tree of Knowledge trying to acquire wisdom.'

'And they fed Elijah too, didn't they?' Memories of Sunday school stories returned to Rowan. She smiled. 'I wonder if they'd feed stranded hikers, lost up here in the mist.'

'I doubt it very much, so I advise you not to test it out. But they're interesting birds. Last spring when I was here, I spent hours watching them, and their courtship rituals are really something to see. The males put on an aerobatic display which would put the Red Arrows to shame, while the females sit around pretending to be bored out of their

skulls.' He grinned. 'It makes them seem almost human.'
He paused. 'Keep an eye open at your disco tonight,
Rowan, and see if I'm not right.'

'Yes, I will,' she agreed, but the constraint had returned.
'I—I ought to be getting back to the house. I have to
change and . . .'

'Fine.' His tone was cool again. 'Can you find your own
way down? I'll stay here for a while.'

'Yes, of course.' Rowan turned away, trying not to
appear to be hurrying, but afraid to linger at the same
time. As she reached the trees, she ventured a glance back.
Carne was standing where she had left him, staring out
over the valley. He was so still that he seemed to have
become part of the rock around him, and there was a
loneliness about him which tore at her, but with a little
smothered sob she turned back and went on down through
the trees towards the house.

Staring at herself in the mirror, Rowan decided that the
green dress was a great success. The only pity was that she
had not the slightest desire to go to the disco with David, or
anywhere else for that matter. She picked up the lip gloss
and applied it with care, wishing there was some miracle
cosmetic which could banish the downward curve of her
mouth and the look of strain in her eyes. She sighed. No
amount of gloss and sheen could camouflage the hunger
within her, and she could only hope that David's percep-
tions were not sufficiently developed for him to notice.

The door from the adjoining bathroom opened abruptly
and Antonia came in. Rowan looked at her in mild surprise. Her stepmother hadn't sought her out in this way for
some time. She supposed Antonia wanted her to prepare a
meal for Carne. Certainly she wanted something, Rowan
knew of old that rather wary look in her eyes, and the
tightness around her mouth.

'Going out?' Antonia sat down on the edge of the bed
and lit a cigarette.

'Yes,' Rowan returned evenly. 'But you don't have to
worry. There's masses of food in the freezer and . . .'

'Why on earth should I be worried about food? Good
God, Rowan, you have the most prosaic mind! No—
rather I wanted you to do me a small favour.'

Rowan sighed. 'I thought you might—but I'm going out very soon, Antonia. I haven't time to . . .'

'I don't mean exactly at this moment.' Antonia's voice was impatient. 'You could do this at any time, although it would be best if it were sooner rather than later. The thing is——' she hesitated, then said on a little rush—'I need to borrow some money—and you must have some, Rowan. You've been squirrelling away your wages from that pottery, and you can hardly have touched your allowance. You haven't bought anything except that rag you're wearing, and that can't have cost a fortune.'

'You have such winning ways, Antonia.' Rowan swung round and faced her stepmother, and Antonia had the grace to flush a little, flicking a sliver of ash on to the carpet.

'Well, it's hardly my sort of thing, darling.' She was making a clear effort to be placatory. She too was wearing green—the softest of tweed skirts and a bloused suede jacket, and she looked down at herself with faint complacency as she spoke, smoothing an imaginary crease from the immaculately cut skirt. 'But we won't argue about our respective tastes in clothes,' she added hastily. 'The thing is can you help me out?'

'Just like that?' Rowan's mouth had a wry twist. 'What's gone wrong, Antonia? Why do you suddenly need money? You have your allowance too.'

'That!' Antonia said derisively. 'My God, there's hardly anything left. I had to have new clothes. None of my London stuff would do in this backwater.'

'Well, the next quarter's will be due very soon. Surely you can hold out until then.' Rowan was irritated. 'Whatever it is you've seen, they'll probably keep it for you if you give them a deposit. What is it this time—another dress?'

'What? No, nothing like that.' Antonia hesitated, staring at the glowing tip of her cigarette. 'If you must know, I owe some people some money. I thought I'd be able to repay them, but it hasn't worked out like that, and the whole thing is getting to be the most ghastly embarrassment.'

'You owe money?' Rowan felt as if she was reliving an old nightmare. 'But, Antonia—why? How? It's just not possible!'

'It's more than possible.' Antonia sounded sullen. 'Heavens, Rowan, I've got to have some pleasure. Carne couldn't just shut me up here and expect me to exist from one of his visits to the next, knowing no one except those dreary Listers.'

Rowan's heart sank further. When Antonia had begun, she had assumed this was some debt left over from their London days which Antonia had either forgotten at the time, or chosen to ignore, but now it seemed that she had contracted new obligations. And a chord of memory sounded faintly . . .

She said, 'It's to do with Keswick, isn't it? I thought I saw you there one day. You were going into a big house.'

Antonia nodded, her face set and hard. 'That's the one. I didn't intend to get involved this time, really I didn't. After all that unpleasantness with Celia, I'd learned my lesson, and the stakes were much lower, of course, or they were when I started playing. In recent weeks, they've gone up.'

Rowan said with a groan. 'Not bridge again? Oh, Antonia!'

'You needn't take that bloody pious tone! I'm not used to this sort of life, mouldering away on a mountainside. I need to be in the middle of things, meeting people of my own sort. I really thought I'd go mad, and then I met Louise in the hairdressers—our appointments were at the same time—and we started to chat. She invited me to her house, introduced me to her friends—it was like a lifeline. And then we started playing, I won. The first few times I was incredibly lucky, and then the run of cards turned against me, and it's been against me ever since.'

Rowan said levelly, 'How much do you owe them?'

'Somewhere in the region of five hundred pounds.'

'Oh, God!' Rowan felt sick. 'I haven't anything like that amount saved.'

'Then let me have what you've got.' Antonia's eyes were very bright as she fixed them on the younger girl's face. 'I'll pay you back—you said yourself the next quarter's allowance is nearly due. Only I must have the money now—and Carne mustn't know. It would spoil everything.'

Rowan looked down at her hands, clenched together in her lap. The words had a familiar ring, echoing other small borrowings in the past when they lived in London. Only there had never been any repayment, just a series of vague excuses whenever Rowan had tentatively broached the subject, and, wise now, Rowan knew why. Because there had always been more debt. And she knew too that however sincere Antonia's intentions might be at the moment, her promises were nebulous in the extreme. And now there was more deception. She wouldn't have been here if Antonia had not told Carne that ridiculous lie about her age, and the other lies since. Was there never to be any end to this mountain of half-truths and distortion?

She said in a low voice, 'Toni, I worked hard for this money. If these people have waited this long, surely they'll wait a little longer. And you can't go on just keeping things from Carne when you feel like it. If—if you're going to marry him, he's bound to find out what's going on anyway. Wouldn't it be better to tell him yourself than allow him to hear gossip, perhaps?'

'But if you give me the money, then there won't be any gossip.' Antonia was leaning forward, her shoulders hunched tensely. 'The other things, the accounts in the shops I can settle myself, but I must pay Louise and the others. They're treating me coolly already as it is.'

Rowan thought it was a pity they hadn't done so from the outset, but she supposed they could be excused for thinking that Antonia was in the same comfortable circumstances as themselves. Mrs Winslow of Raven's Crag, with her smart, expensive clothes and definite aura of Knightsbridge, did not give the impression of comparative poverty.

She tried a new tack. 'But if I did help you out, would you stop seeing them? Daddy always said that a good card player needed luck as well as skill, and I don't think you're lucky, Antonia.'

'Of course I'll go on seeing them. They're my friends—all that makes life here bearable. Don't you preach your bloody little sermons at me, my girl! And don't bring your father into it—not if you're going to talk about luck. If he'd been a little "luckier" in his business deals, I shouldn't be in this fix now.' Antonia's voice held a note of faint hysteria.

'Perhaps.' Rowan turned back to the dressing table, picking up the discarded glosser and putting it in her bag with fingers which shook slightly. 'Or perhaps we're just not a very lucky family. It's certainly not a star I'd be inclined to hitch my waggon to.'

In the mirror she saw Antonia make an impatient gesture with her cigarette. 'Never mind all that. Are you going to help me or not?'

'I don't think I can.' Rowan felt cold. 'The person to approach is the man you're going to marry. Try being honest with him for once, Antonia. It might work wonders.'

'If you think that,' said Antonia as she got up, 'then you're even more stupid than I gave you credit for. No man likes to have his ideals shattered, not even a cynical bastard like Carne. Perhaps you should remember that.'

'Fortunately I'm not the focus for his ideals, or lack of them,' snapped Rowan as she shut her bag.

Antonia came to stand behind her. 'So you won't help me?'

'I can't. I haven't anything like the sum you need, and I have my own future to think of. When this summer is over, I have to become self-sufficient. I shall need every penny I can get and more.' Rowan's tone was short, but she was shaking inwardly. This was the first time she had not allowed herself to be coaxed and wheedled or bullied into doing what Antonia wanted, and it was not easy. It would have been much simpler to have gone into Keswick after the weekend and drawn out her savings and handed them over, at the same time kissing them goodbye forever. But this time she couldn't do that. Antonia's future was settled with Carne. Hers was anything but secure, and it was desperately important that when this endless summer at Raven's Crag was over, she should be able to achieve a measure of independence.

There was a short, electric pause, then Antonia said venomously, 'My God, I'll make you sorry for this. I'll make you sorry you ever came here!'

Rowan bowed her head. She said, 'It's too late for that, Antonia. I'm sorry already,' but her stepmother had already gone, banging the door viciously behind her.

CHAPTER NINE

IF Rowan was rather silent on the drive to Arnthwaite, her companion did not appear to notice. In fact David seemed on top of the world, even bringing a reluctant smile to her lips with his extravagant compliments, and chattering nineteen to the dozen about his classes. Much of what he said did not demand a response, and Rowan was left in peace with her own disturbing thoughts.

She hadn't liked the implied threat in Antonia's parting words, but really there was very little her stepmother could do that she hadn't done already, she told herself ruefully, except make her miserable in even more ways. And if she did start on some kind of campaign of petty persecution, it would be an even greater incentive for Rowan to leave.

She wondered if Antonia would take her advice and go to Carne with her troubles, but doubted it. She gave a little smothered sigh. At least when they were married, Carne would take his wife on his travels with him, and there would be less opportunity for her to become bored, or seek dangerous relief from that boredom. And that was the only real advantage she could see coming from the marriage. She found herself remembering how alone Carne had looked, standing looking down over the valley he loved, and which Antonia hated. What kind of compromise would they ever reach over that—or over the problem of Sybilla? Perhaps Carne intended to learn from the ravens on the fell, she thought ironically, and was prepared to do anything to please his lady-love, even to the point of sacrificing his home and his principles.

Not that it made any difference to her, Rowan tried vainly to remind herself. By the time Carne and Antonia came to resolve their differences in whatever way seemed best to them, she would be long gone.

The small car park at the back of the village hall was filling up by the time they arrived, and David parked the

van in the shadow of an overhanging tree in the corner.
There were a number of motorcycles as well as cars parked
there, and Rowan found herself wondering, slightly
troubled, if Jeff Wainwright had arrived. It had been a day
of strange encounters from the beginning, but she hoped
she would be able to forget about most of them in the noise
and movement of the dancing.

She left her wrap in the small cloakroom and went out to
find David. A bar had been set up in the entrance hall,
selling soft drinks as well as alcohol, and he was waiting for
her here.

'Can I get you anything?' He gestured towards the counter.

She smiled at him. 'It's a bit early. Shall we dance up a
thirst?'

'Great.' He took her arm, and they went through the
swing doors into the dance. Up to then the sound had been
muffled, but now it burst upon Rowan, and instinctively
she put her hands to her ears, squinting up at David in
mock horror.

'You'll get used to it,' he bawled in her ear. 'Let's find a
table while there still is one. These discos usually get
packed out.'

Before an hour had passed he was right, and there were
still more people arriving. Rowan, on her way to the cloakroom, saw that one of them was Jeff Wainwright, but he
was standing at the bar and didn't see her as she edged
past.

She found she was enjoying the dancing. The rhythm
was irresistible, and her own natural grace did the rest,
making the music part of her. The only problem came
when the pulsing beat slackened and softened, and David
reached for her to draw her close into his arms. She didn't
want to dance held close against him, but at the same time
she didn't want to hurt his feelings, and she could tell her
lack of response bewildered him as she held him gently but
firmly away from her. At last, on the pretext that she was
tired, she persuaded him to sit down, and told him she'd
like that drink now.

'A Coke, please,' she added.

She had expected him to make a similar choice, but

when he returned, the glass he was holding unmistakably held alcohol, and she glanced at him quickly.

'It's only shandy,' he said rather defensively, putting her Coke down in front of her.

They were not alone at their table for long. David seemed to know most of the people at the disco, and they were soon joined by several other young couples, most of whom appeared to be at school with him, and were also enjoying a brief respite before the onset of the examination season. They were pleasant and cheerful about the coming ordeal, and Rowan enjoyed listening to the constant wise-cracking between them. When the music started again, someone else asked her to dance and she agreed, feeling guilty because it was such a relief not to dance with David all the time, and become established in everyone's eyes as his personal property for the evening. He was dancing too, she was glad to see, with a pretty girl wearing jeans and an enormous Snoopy tee-shirt. When eventually Rowan returned to the table, David and some of the others had disappeared to get more drinks.

'I've brought you another Coke,' he said when he returned. 'Or did you want something stronger?'

'This'll be fine.' She supposed that was another shandy he was holding. He stood beside her, but she could sense he was restless, his glance constantly shifting round the room, and she guessed her aloof attitude while they were dancing hadn't pleased him. She was sorry about it, but she couldn't help it. Allowing him to paw her on the dance floor could only lead to more embarrassing scenes later on when he took her home. She supposed it was inevitable that dating him would lead to an end of the easygoing relationship they had enjoyed up to then. He was young, virile and physically attractive, and her determination to keep him at arms' length would have been a blow to his vanity which he wasn't mature enough to cope with yet.

They danced again, but there was constraint between them, and Rowan was quite glad when they were joined on the floor by the girl in the Snoopy tee-shirt and her partner, who was called Neil. It was shortly after supper—a lavish home-made buffet served by members of the local Young Farmers' Club—that David vanished. It was dark in the hall, and the flashing lights from the disco itself didn't aid visibility, but Rowan, peering round, couldn't see him anywhere, and as the time passed she began to grow uneasy, and finally a little angry. She had plenty of partners, but David's defection had been noticed, and she saw Penny in the Snoopy shirt and a girl called Jean exchanging smug and rather pitying smiles which rankled.

She began to wonder if he had been taken ill, but as Neil and some of the others visited the cloakroom and returned without making any comment, she could only assume they hadn't seen him. She peered at her watch, then got up and went out to the bar, ostensibly to get herself another drink. People were standing at the counter three deep waiting to be served, but David was not among them, and after a brief hesitation, Rowan returned her empty glass and went out of the hall.

The night air felt chilly after the overheated atmosphere of the disco and she shivered a little as she hesitated in the porch wondering where to look first.

Then, 'Good evening, Miss High and Mighty,' said a voice, and she looked up to see Jeff Wainwright grinning at her. 'Leaving so soon? We haven't had our dance yet.'

'I haven't the slightest intention of dancing with you,' Rowan said coldly. 'I needed some fresh air, that's all.'

'Of course it is.' He stood with his hands tucked into the pockets of his leather jacket, still grinning, and after a moment she turned on her heel and went back into the village hall, not waiting to see whether he followed. When she got back to the table, there was a sudden lull in the conversation, and she guessed that David and herself had been the subject under discussion.

Rowan was beginning to feel humiliated. At any moment she expected the swing doors to open and see David come in with Beth Wainwright. In fact that might have been an improvement on the present situation. At least then she would know where he was and with whom, she thought angrily.

When another half hour had stumbled past, and there was still no sign of him, Rowan decided she had had enough. She said a brief goodnight to the other members of the party, who were now clearly as embarrassed as she was herself, and went to the cloakroom for her wrap. There was a pay telephone in the foyer, and she decided she would try and get a taxi home, although first, to satisfy her own curiosity, she would see if the van was still there. She couldn't really believe David would simply have gone home without her. Relations between them hadn't deteriorated to that point, or anywhere near it for that matter, but he might have gone joy-riding with someone more amenable to his advances.

However, the lights of another vehicle making an early departure from the hall revealed that the van was there under the tree, looking just as they had left it a few hours earlier. Puzzled, Rowan made her way carefully across the rutted ground, then paused. Inside the van she could see a shape, and a movement, and she was reluctant to go any closer. David, it seemed, had found company and was making hay while the sun, or rather the moon, shone.

She was on the point of beating an unobtrusive retreat back to the hall and the telephone, when she heard the sound of a muffled groan that stopped her in her tracks. Frowning, she went nearer the van.

'David?' Her voice was tentative. 'Look, David, are you all right?'

She waited, but there was no answer, just another groan, and, worried now, she went to the van and jerked open the driver's door. The interior light came on, and she saw David slumped behind the steering wheel. Two things struck her immediately—that he was alone, and that he looked ghastly. He was very pale, his skin had a greenish tinge, and his eyes were closed.

She said his name, and as he rolled his head round to look at her she saw that he was having difficulty focussing, and at the same time she smelt the alcohol on his breath.

She said helplessly, 'Oh, my God! What on earth have you been doing?'

'S'all ri, Ro'on,' he muttered. 'S'all ri, really.' With an immense effort he produced the keys from his pocket and began searching for the ignition.

Rowan leaned forward and snatched them smartly from his grasp. 'You're driving nowhere, my lad,' she said grimly. Her brain was whirling. Surely a couple of shandies, which was all she had seen him drink, couldn't have had this disastrous effect. Besides, it wasn't beer she could smell, it was spirits.

She took a tissue out of her bag and wiped his forehead. 'Who gave you the whisky?' She made it sound like a friendly enquiry.

He growned, concentrating with an effort. 'Jeff,' he said at last. 'Goo' ol' Jeff.'

'Good old Jeff,' Rowan echoed ironically. 'Who else?'

She remembered their encounter earlier, and the way Jeff had stood there grinning insolently at her, daring her to pass him, which of course she hadn't done. Obviously it hadn't been convenient for her to find David just then. Probably they hadn't got him quite drunk enough for their purpose. She made a little muffled sound of disgust.

Now, it seemed, the priority was to get him home to the pottery as quickly as possible. She eyed him, wondering exactly how much he had had to drink. If Jeff and his buddies had been pouring whisky down him, then there could be a possibility of alcoholic poisoning, but somehow she didn't think even they would have gone that far, she decided, crossing her fingers surreptitiously.

Her first task was to shift David out from behind the wheel and into the passenger side, and for a while she debated whether to go and call some of his friends to help, eventually deciding against this. As he was under age, the fewer people who knew about this little escapade the better, she thought, and she would only seek assistance if he proved impossible to cope with.

Her liking for David and her affection for his parents were strained to the limits over the next ten minutes or so. David accepted her presence in the van quite amenably, but refused to grasp its purpose. He showed no inclination to be moved across to the passenger seat, and every inclination to become amorous as she tugged and pulled at him.

Eventually, totally fed up, she slapped his face, and after that things happened in quick succession. First he began to cry, then he was sick, and finally he passed out—which, Rowan thought, gritting her teeth, was the best idea he'd had so far.

Once he was unconscious, she found it was easier to go

round to the passenger side and drag him from behind the steering wheel. By the time she had finished she was dripping with perspiration, and her dress had caught on the door handle and ripped quite badly, and she felt like bursting into tears or alternatively vomiting herself.

She climbed in, slamming the door, and tried to start the engine. After a lot of prevarication and a fair amount of choke, it complied sullenly with her modest demands and submitted to being backed cautiously out from under the tree. The clutch, she discovered, was fierce, and the accelerator sluggish, and between the two of them, she hiccuped her way out of the car park while David's recumbent form slid about like a rag doll beside her.

Between her anxiety for him and the problems of driving the van after months of never having been behind the wheel of a vehicle, coupled with the unfamiliarity of the road, the journey back to Ravensmere was a nightmare. Fortunately they encountered little other traffic, so her inability to find out how the headlights dipped proved of minor importance. But every garment she was wearing was sticking clammily to her body, and she felt stiff and aching with tension by the time she had rounded the final bend into the village street, and taken the turning for the pottery. She drew the van to a halt, switched off the engine, and slumped forward over the wheel, trying to calm herself and steady her erratic breathing for the next stage of the onslaught—getting David out of the van and into the house without waking or worrying Grace and Clive.

She moved wearily at last, fumbling without looking for the catch on the driver's door, when it gave way apparently of its own accord, and she nearly fell out. She gave a startled cry and clutched at the dashboard, and a hand came to steady her.

Carne's voice demanded icily, 'What the bloody hell are you supposed to be doing?'

Rowan found herself dragged without ceremony from the van. In the light of a street lamp, they regarded each other. In an oddly detached way she thought she had never seen him look so angry.

'I'd like an answer,' he said at last grimly. 'I realised a while ago that you shouldn't be judged by normal people's standards, but I never dreamed you'd go as far as breaking the law and risking killing yourself. What was David thinking of to let you do this crazy thing?'

'Not very much at all.' She wanted to sink down on to the cold and dusty road at his feet and weep. She gestured towards the van. 'See for yourself.'

It seemed a long time before he came back, but when he did he was molten with rage.

'You—let him get into that state?'

'Yes, it's my hobby, pouring booze into minors. Didn't you know?' she retorted, her voice getting perilously high. In some mad way the wheel had come full circle, she thought, remembering the first time she had seen Carne bending over Antonia's recumbent form, and her own anger and suspicion.

'Don't try to be clever. This is too damn serious,' he rapped. 'How much has he had?'

She shook her head. 'I've honestly no idea. I wasn't there when it happened. You could try asking at the village shop.'

'I could also try giving you a damned good hiding!' His hands gripped her shoulders, his fingers biting painfully into her flesh. She stifled a little cry, and he smiled grimly. 'Hurts, does it? Believe me, it's the very least I'd like to do to you. You could have been killed, you stupid, irresponsible little bitch, don't you see that? And what would have happened if the police had stopped you?'

'Very little.' She was stiff with rage now. 'I've had nothing to drink all evening except Coca-cola. I have a valid driving licence, and I imagine the van is insured for other drivers. David I would have to lie about, but I'd have done that for Grace and Clive's sake. Now for God's sake will you stop going on and endlessly on at me and help me! He needs to be indoors.'

Carne's hand fell away from her, and without another word he walked over to the van. Rowan took a long shuddering breath, then followed him. David was semi-conscious, muttering to himself and breathing stertorously, and no sooner had they lugged him out of the van into the air than he was sick again.

'God damn it, we'll have to wake his parents,' Carne said

savagely. 'We can't risk him choking in his sleep.'

It seemed a long time, waiting in the living room for Grace to come down. Carne had deposited David on the sofa, and Rowan stood by the hearth watching him. He still looked ill, she thought judiciously, but he was a slightly better colour.

Grace came in, hastily tying the sash of her dressing gown. 'David!' She bent over him anxiously. 'What on earth . . .?' Her voice died away, and slowly she straightened, looking at Rowan. Her eyes slowly assimilated Rowan's dishevelled appearance, her white face, the torn dress, and a look of unutterable contempt stole over her pleasant face.

'I don't know what part you played in all this,' she said quietly. 'But I never want to see you again, Rowan. Please leave my house, and don't come back.'

Sinking her teeth into her lower lip until she could taste blood, Rowan went to the door. She could have protested, she supposed, as she went out into the night. She might even have got Grace to listen to her eventually, but David's mother had more pressing matters on her mind. She stumbled slightly, and realised that silent tears were pouring down her face.

From behind her Carne said, 'Where are you going?'

'Back to the house.' Her voice was muffled as she pressed her hand almost convulsively to her lips. She kept her head turned away because she didn't want him to see her distress.

'The car's round the corner.'

'I'd rather walk.'

'Don't be a fool,' he said wearily. 'You'll ride back with me. And don't take Grace's parting words too seriously. She's very upset. Clive will make her see reason. He was calling the doctor when I left.'

She made no reply, and after a moment he said, 'Rowan, we have to talk. You must see that.'

'I think enough has been said already.' She brushed the tears away angrily with her fist.

'On the contrary, we haven't even begun yet.' That grim note was back in his voice, and he took her arm, urging her forward. 'I infer from a previous remark of yours that the

Wainwrights were responsible for tonight's disaster. What makes you think so?'

'David told me so. He'd been missing for over an hour and when I went to look for him, Jeff was there. He seems to have a sense of grievance over the fact that David no longer goes out with his sister, and earlier today he wanted me to break my date and go to the disco with him so that David could go with Beth. I—refused. I imagine this is his not very subtle revenge.'

They were at the car now, and he unlocked the door and put her into it, before going round and getting into the driving seat.

He said too gently, 'Unless, of course, you'd like to drive.'

There was a long silence, then Rowan shrank back in her seat and closed her eyes.

'Of course,' he said at last, 'I won't ask to see the valid driving licence. I'm sure it exists and was legally obtained—but that unfortunately invalidates a number of other points. And number one on the list is—exactly how old are you, Rowan?'

Her voice shook. 'I'm—nineteen. I shall be twenty in October. Does that satisfy you?'

'Not in the slightest.' His voice was still pleasant, but there was a note in it that made her shiver. 'The next question is, naturally, why did you feel it necessary to perpetrate this elaborate charade that you were a mere child, barely above the age of consent? Is it some kind of long-term practical joke?—because if so someone should have warned you, I'm not amused by such things.'

'It wasn't a joke,' she said at last.

'Then why?'

Rowan was in an agony of indecision. To tell the whole truth would implicate Antonia. She shrugged in the darkness inside the car. 'It—just seemed safer. Your reputation is pretty notorious, after all, and Antonia was worried about me. We—we thought if I pretended to be younger you'd leave me alone, but how mistaken can you be?'

Carne said very quietly, 'I think that should be my line.' Then he switched on the engine, and the headlights lit up the quiet street like a pair of blazing eyes.

When they stopped outside the house Rowan almost fell out of the car and ran for the steps, treading on her skirt and almost falling as she did so. Almost at the same moment as she heard his car door slam, he was beside her.

'Oh, no, sweetheart,' he said mockingly, 'you don't get away that easily, and you know it.'

His arm went round her, scooping her up, and he carried her into the house, pinned to his side like an unwieldy parcel. Rowan gasped, her fingers catching in the fine wool of the sweater he was wearing to try and maintain some sort of balance. She tried vainly to kick him, and one of her shoes fell off.

'Put me down!' she raged.

'When I'm good and ready.' He carried her into the sitting room and dropped her almost casually on one of the sofas, where she lay staring up at him in a welter of Indian cotton, her eyes enormous.

'You've torn your dress.' His voice was conversational. 'And as it's ruined already . . .' He leaned over her, his fingers parting her neckline, then wrenching at it so that the flimsy material ripped like paper down to her waist and beyond.

She said, 'No—please . . .'

'Why not?' She had been trying to shield her bared breasts with her hands, but he took her wrists and forced them away, his silver eyes beginning a long slow scrutiny which had her writhing in impotent shame. 'There's nothing to stop me now, darling. No moral or ethical considerations about your youth and innocence to give me pause. I've held you before—remember? I've had a taste of the way your mouth and your body can respond, and it's made me hungry for more—for the whole banquet in fact.'

She said desperately, 'Carne—no—I'm sorry I lied to you, but it seemed the best thing to do at the time.'

'Sorry?' He shook his head. 'You don't even know the meaning of the word, sweetheart, but you will by the morning.'

His kiss was hard and insolent, draining her of the strength to resist, even if the will was there. As her mouth parted helplessly under the pressure of his, and a long uncontrollable shiver of delight ran through her, something in her mind screamed, 'Not like this. Not when he's angry,' and she began to struggle again, to try and thrust him away.

'Don't fight.' He lifted his head and looked down at her. 'The battle's over anyway, and you know it, so why not enjoy the victory together?'

'Because I'm not your conquest,' she whispered. The world had gone dizzily, crazily awry, and she saw him through a haze of tears.

Carne shook his head. 'Don't cry.' He bent forward, licking the tears from her cheeks with swift, sensual movements of his tongue. 'Tears aren't a ploy that work with me, so you're wasting your time—and mine. Time that could be better spent.'

His hands moved restlessly, freeing her from the ruins of her dress, dragging it ruthlessly down from her shoulders and tossing it aside to lie in a crumpled heap of green and gold on the carpet.

'Dryad colours,' Carne said mockingly. 'But I think when I start my picture, I'll paint you as you are now.' His hand slid the length of her body, teasing, cajoling, arousing, and he smiled as her breath escaped on a little tormented sigh.

'I could damn your cheating little soul, only dryads don't have souls, do they, my love, only bodies. So I'll have to make do with that.' His mouth caressed the pulse in her throat, then slipped down to the hollow between her neck and shoulder, lingering there, while his fingers moved on her, exploring, discovering, making all her secrets his own. Rowan moaned helplessly, twisting her head from side to side on the softness of the cushions beneath her. His touch was magic, it was torment, it was madness.

She whispered in a voice she hardly recognised as her own, 'You must let me go.'

'Like hell I must,' he grated. 'But make your nominal protest if that's what you want. You don't sound as if you've even convinced yourself.'

She began, 'Antonia . . .'

'Is asleep,' he said briefly. 'So she won't come to your rescue this time. Not that you want to be rescued, do you, sweetheart, any more than you did last time. You want all this and more.' He bent and kissed her breasts, gentling their rosy peaks with his tongue until she felt she would dissolve into pure sensation. Her fingers tangled in his hair, drawing him nearer to her, while deep within her a slow, sweet ache welcomed the unaccustomed weight of his body above hers and beckoned him closer still.

This, she thought, had been inevitable since the first time she saw him. This was why, if she was honest with herself, she had yielded to Antonia's dubious persuasions and come to Raven's Crag, because she wanted him more than anything she had ever wanted in her life, and now he was going to be hers, so why suddenly was there this bitterness welling up inside her, this sense of loss and hopelessness?

She said aloud, 'You don't love me.'

He raised his head and looked at her, his mouth twisting cynically.

'I wasn't aware it was a prerequisite.' His voice slowed to a drawl. 'Accept the fact that I want you quite badly, Rowan, and keep your sentiment for your home-made fairy stories upstairs.'

For a moment she was stunned, then she began to push at his shoulders.

'Wanting isn't enough,' she flashed.

'Then I'll have to make it enough.' His tone hardened. 'Don't be naïve, Rowan. Don't start dressing up your needs with irrelevant emotions.'

'Emotion is never irrelevant,' she said in a low voice. 'And I can't help being naïve. This isn't a situation I'm used to.'

'And what's your next line—"I'm still a virgin?"' he asked sardonically. 'I thought I'd made it clear that the charade was over, and that it was time for more grown-up games.'

It's no game, Rowan thought desperately. It's all deadly serious, because if you take me, then I'll belong to you for ever, and that's the last thing you want. At the moment I'm a novelty with my straight hair and my small breasts, but soon I'll be an embarrassment because after tonight there's no way I'm going to be able to hide what I feel for you—if you become my lover.

She shrugged a shoulder. 'I didn't say I wasn't going to play,' she said a little petulantly. 'But surely there must be a market price on virginity. After all, it's a rare commodity these days.'

'Very rare,' he said evenly, after a pause. He was very still, poised above her like a hawk, the silver eyes hooded and a little blank as they looked into hers. 'But if we're bargaining, how about exchanging your most priceless gift for a painting—a Carne Maitland original, signed by the artist. Subject—a dryad, naturally.'

Rowan shook her head, flicking a strand of brown hair back from her face.

'I think I'd prefer cash. It takes a long time to paint a picture, and I don't intend to spend one hour longer in this house than I can help.' She saw a muscle flicker in his tanned cheek, and pressed on recklessly. 'Well, Mr Maitland, how much are you prepared to pay for your banquet? Enough, I hope, to take me back to London and keep me for a while until I find a job.'

'Oddly enough, I seem to have lost my appetite. I've never had to buy a woman yet, and I don't intend to start with you, you mercenary little bitch.' The contempt in his tone stung her, but she made herself smile at him.

'Then may I please have what's left of my dress?'

'With pleasure.' He reached down and tossed it to her. Watching her struggle into it, he added coldly, 'I hope you don't expect me to pay for a new one.'

'I don't expect anything from you,' she muttered, her hands shaking as she tugged ineffectually at the torn material. She felt sick and degraded, and close to tears again.

'That's very wise,' he said harshly. 'Tell me this—do you plan to peddle your dubious wares to anyone else?'

'I shouldn't think so.' She dared not meet his gaze. 'You're the only person I know who could afford to pay the price I want. I won't settle for anything less.'

'You'll settle for nothing at all, Rowan, because that's what you'll get from me. If you want out of here then you'll have to work and earn your way back south.'

'I'll work,' she said. 'My God, I'll work. I'll do anything I have to—anything at all to get out of this place and away from you. Do I make myself clear?'

'As daylight and crystal.' He sounded very weary. 'Now, get out.'

By the time Rowan reached the spiral staircase, she was trembling so much she could hardly move, and she had to haul herself up it painfully, step by step. She was afraid Carne would come after her, but from the half-open door of the sitting room she could hear the chink of a bottle on a glass, and as she completed her long, solitary ascent, she found herself wishing that she too could seek the oblivion of alcohol.

When she awoke the next morning, the sun was pouring through the window, and for those few confused moments between sleeping and waking she thought in exasperation that she had overslept, that she was going to be late for work—and then, as she sat up, she began to remember, and the brightness of the day slipped away from her.

She put her hands over her eyes and sat very still, trying to shut the whole disastrous day and night of her consciousness; but that, of course, was impossible, and somehow she had to get out of this bed, and take hold of the ravelled threads of her life and try and force them back into some kind of cohesive pattern.

She put on her dressing gown and went into the bathroom to wash and clean her teeth. There was no sound from Antonia's room, and after a moment's hesitation she opened the door and went in. The sheets on the bed were turned back, but at the same time it had a curiously unruffled appearance—not at all as if someone had slept the night there. Rowan looked at it for a long moment, then she backed into the bathroom and closed the door quietly again.

She dressed herself quickly in jeans and sweater and went out on to the landing. The whole house was quiet. Outside the sun danced on the leaves, and turned the azaleas in the driveway to flame, and there was movement and colour and birdsong, but inside there was silence.

Rowan walked towards the stairs, and paused as she heard the creak of an opening door. Antonia came into view. She was fastening the sash of her peignoir, and her face was closed, with a small tight smile playing about her lips. She glanced up and saw Rowan watching her, and the smile widened into triumph.

She said quite amiably, 'Good morning, sweetie. You look dreadful. Wasn't your night on what passes for a town round here a success?'

Rowan moistened her lips. She said carefully, 'It was all right.' She hesitated. 'Antonia, I'm sorry about our disagreement—about the money. If I could help, I would, only it's impossible and . . .'

'Don't worry about it,' said Antonia. She put up her hand and pushed it through her hair, lifting it luxuriously away from the back of her neck.

Rowan stared at her. 'But you said . . .'

'I was hasty,' Antonia said, and smiled again. 'The fact is the money isn't a problem any more. It really isn't, sweetie.' As she spoke, she glanced back over her shoulder towards the room she had come from. Carne's room. Then she looked back at Rowan. 'You were quite right, angel. It was the simplest solution in the end,' and her smile was ripe with reminiscent pleasure.

Rowan felt sick as if someone had just jabbed her unexpectedly and unpleasantly in the midriff, but she kept her head up and neither her gaze nor her voice faltered as she said, 'I'm very happy for you, Antonia—happy about everything. I suppose you and Carne will be getting married quite soon.'

'Quite soon,' Antonia agreed. 'It's just a question of fixing up the formalities.' She paused. 'I imagine you won't want to waste any more time around here. You'll be anxious to get back to London as soon as possible.'

'Yes,' Rowan said noncommittally. Anxious, she thought, wasn't really the word. It didn't do anything to describe the gnawing, desperate agony which had her in its grip.

'Well, there's nothing to keep you here now.' Antonia was studying her fingernails with some attention. She looked very beautiful this morning, Rowan thought detachedly, and much younger with those harsh, strained lines gone from her face. Perhaps that was what the prospect of security did for you, or maybe it was the way most women looked after fulfilment, sleek and relaxed and not caring who knew it.

Antonia went on, 'I managed to persuade him to forgive us for our little deception—eventually.' She giggled. 'But you really made him angry, sweetie. Not a sensible move. Carne's a bad man to cross.'

Rowan made herself smile back. 'So I discovered.' She managed to inject, she thought, just the right amount of ruefulness into her tone. 'All the more reason to make myself scarce as soon as possible.' She paused. 'Did—did Carne tell you that I'd lost my job at the pottery?'

'No.' Antonia's eyes flicked up sharply and fixed on Rowan's face. 'How did that happen?'

Rowan shrugged. 'It's a long and complicated story, and I won't bore you with it, but it does mean I'll have to get another job. I haven't nearly enough money saved yet to see me through college next winter.'

'But you could find work in London, surely.'

'Perhaps, but I think I'd stand a better chance in Keswick. The souvenir shops and cafés often want extra help in the holiday season. Will you be going into Keswick later on, because if so maybe I could go with you and see what was available.'

'I shan't be going in,' Antonia said almost absently, as if she was thinking about something else.

'Oh.' Rowan was taken aback. She had become used to Antonia's almost daily absences, but she should have realised that now Carne was back, there would be a change in the pattern of her stepmother's days. 'Well, it doesn't matter. Next week will do.'

There was a pause, and then Antonia seemed to re-focus on her. 'Honestly, sweetie, I think you'd do far better if you went south again. And I'd have thought that under the circumstances you'd have preferred it yourself. You'll get over your little crush on Carne much more easily at a distance.'

Rowan looked back at her steadily. 'Antonia,' she said, 'I came here for your convenience, but I'm going to leave for my own. I haven't the slightest intention of presenting myself in London with nowhere to live, no job and hardly any money. Not even you could expect me to do so. I'm sorry if my continuing presence here is inconvenient to you, but maybe I should remind you that I never wanted to come here in the first place.'

'No, you didn't,' Antonia s voice was silkily pleasant. 'What a pity I didn't leave you there to stagnate in that dreary little flat. Believe me, darling, if I could have done so, I would have.'

'Oh, I'm well aware of that.' Rowan couldn't disguise her bitterness. 'I was just a means to an end, but now you're going to be married and your allowance is safe, I've become instantly dispensable. Well, unfortunately you're going to be stuck with me for a while yet. Thanks to you, my life is in sufficient mess as it is. Next time I'm going to try and get it right.'

Antonia lifted a hand to her mouth to mask a yawn. 'Just as you please, sweetie,' she said lightly. 'I merely thought it would be less—humiliating, shall we say—if you made a tactical withdrawal. But we won't fall out about it.' And, as Rowan turned to go downstairs, 'Oh, and if you're going to make some coffee, I would love a cup. Carne, too, I dare-say.'

Rowan wanted to scream at her, 'Make it yourself!' but she controlled herself. Antonia, she thought, would now be hell-bent on making her life at Raven's Crag as difficult as possible, and she would just have to ride out the storm as best she could. And making coffee to order would probably be the least of her troubles, so it was not worth making a fuss about.

She set the percolator going, tidied the kitchen and opened the door to the garden to let the sun and breeze in. She lingered for a moment in the open doorway, lifting her face to the warmth and the scents on the air, and a feeling of desolation swept over her as she realised how soon she would have to exchange the vibrant, verdant beauty of this place for the concrete pavements and fumes of London. It was amazing how easily she had transplanted to this new environment, how easily she had made it her own. She felt as much a part of this fell as the ravens who chose its shelter in which to live their lives and breed their young. She remembered the glossy feathers of the bird she had seen the day before, and the joyous freedom of its flight, and sighed.

A slight movement behind her invaded her consciousness with the awareness that she was no longer alone. She turned hurriedly and came face to face with Carne.

He was dressed, but his chin was unshaven, and his eyes were bloodshot and deeply shadowed as he stared across the kitchen at her. The silence stretched tautly between them, until at last Rowan said quickly and inanely, 'Good morning. It—it's a lovely day. Would you like some coffee?'

'When I look back on this bloody summer,' he said sardonically, 'my overriding memory will be of you, Rowan, eternally offering me coffee.'

She flushed. 'I'm sorry, but Antonia said . . .'

'I'm quite sure she did,' he returned. 'And don't apologise. Yes, I'll have some of your coffee, and also some aspirin, if you can suggest where I might find some.'

Rowan gave a swift frown. 'I'm not sure there are any. Wait a minute, though. I think there are some in Sybilla's bathroom. I saw them when I tidied the cabinet the other day.'

She walked to the door, but he barred the way. He said, 'The aspirin will wait, Rowan. You and I must talk.'

'There's nothing to talk about.' She stared past him. She could not meet his gaze again. Her mind was tortured by images of Antonia and himself together.

'I think there is.' He took a step nearer to her. 'After last night . . .'

'And last night I want to talk about least of all,' she said raggedly. 'For God's sake let me go, and leave me in peace from here on in.'

There was silence, and then he said, 'If that's what you want, so be it.'

She thought, 'What I want? I want you, Carne. I want you now and for ever, in sickness and in health, as the marriage service says. I want to be close to you, in your thoughts as well as in your arms. I want my child to be yours. I want my life to be built around you, and only you.'

Aloud, she said flatly, 'That's what I want.' Then she walked out of the kitchen and closed the door behind her.

CHAPTER TEN

ALONE in her room, Rowan stayed by the window for a while, looking out at the view with blank unseeing eyes. Wherever her life might lead her, she thought, a vista of pale skies, grey and amethyst fells and a distant glimmer of water would always rouse her to remembered sadness.

She glanced down at the sheet of paper in the typewriter, trying to make sense of the words, but they danced in front of her in a meaningless blur, and after a moment she tore the sheet out and crumpled it into a ball. She had no business to be writing love stories—especially love stories with happy endings. She didn't want to write about people at all, if it came to that. She wanted something as removed from her own sphere of experience as possible. Something Carne has said came back to her. 'Tales of derring-do for tiny tots.' Well, why not? At least it would be an occupation.

Listlessly, she sat down at the typewriter, fitting another piece of paper into the machine, touching the keys here and there, trying to recapture the germ of an idea which had occurred to her the day before when she was out on the fells with Carne. It was the sight of the raven, wheeling and turning with the sun glinting on its feathers, which had done it—which had made her wonder how one of the ravens from the Tower would manage if it changed places with one of those from the fell. In her mind's eye she could see the raven, its coat drab and a little dusty like a City commuter, its movements precise and ordered with none of the grace and freedom she had sensed out on the fell.

She would have to do some research, she thought, find out as much as possible about ravens, what they fed on, how they made their nests, their breeding habits. She would read up the ancient myths and legends concerning them too. As her story was intended for young children, she wouldn't labour this part of her research, but if she could make it interesting enough, perhaps some of the children would be prompted to find out more for themselves.

Her mouth twisted a little. She was getting much too far ahead of herself. The story wasn't written yet, let alone published and being seized on by eager young hands.

But even if her story never saw the light of day, she thought, at least it would give her something to think about except her own unhappiness. She needed something, some interest to fill her days. The emptiness of the nights was something she did not want to contemplate.

She had been working for about two hours, drafting a possible outline for her story, when there was a knock at the door and Carne walked in without further preamble.

'What is it?' Her voice was slightly defensive, and she stationed herself between him and the work in her machine. She didn't want him to come over and read what she had written. This was her defence against him, against the world, and it was too new and vulnerable to be shared.

'It's a number of things,' he said briefly. He had shaved, she noticed inconsequentially, but he still looked weary, and the lines on his face had deepened, the scar beside his mouth showing up white against his tan. 'Firstly, I've been on to an employment agency, and they're sending over a possible housekeeper, so that should take the pressure off a little.'

'Well—yes.' She was a little at a loss, wondering why he should bother to tell her. 'The house is rather big for Antonia to look after. She—she isn't altogether used to housework, as you must have realised.'

'Yes, I realised,' he said rather grimly. 'I was a fool to expect . . . but that doesn't matter now. The woman will be arriving tomorrow, and perhaps you could spare an hour or two to show her about, and provide an explanation if it's necessary.'

'Very well.' Rowan wasn't sure why he was asking her to do this. Antonia was the mistress of the house now, all but legally, and it was surely her place to talk to the new housekeeper and give her her instructions. But all too probably, Antonia had no relish for the task. She would consider it a bore.

'You might stress how important it is for her to keep out

of the studio,' said Carne, after a brief pause. 'I tolerate no one in there when I'm working.'

'You're going to start painting again? I—I'm very pleased.'

'Are you?' His voice was cool, his eyes and face remote. 'I'm taking your advice and starting a portrait of Antonia.'

'That's—good,' she managed. It wasn't good, but it was appropriate, setting the seal on their relationship, she supposed. Antonia would like to be painted. She would see it as a tribute to her beauty from the man who enjoyed it, just as she had regarded the furs and jewels Victor Winslow had lavished on her in the same way. She would like to see that beauty encapsulated, preserved for all time on canvas.

'The other thing I have to tell you is that Grace is downstairs. She wants to talk to you—to apologise. David has revived sufficiently to give a full account of last night's happenings, and she's realised how hasty she's been.'

'I see.' Rowan's fingers drummed restlessly on the typewriter keys for a moment. 'Well, there's no need to apologise. I can understand why she reacted as she did. Perhaps you'd thank her for me.'

'And perhaps I won't,' he said impatiently. 'Come downstairs and speak to her, at least, Rowan. She wants you to go back to work at the pottery, and you can't pretend you don't need the job—or the money anyway.'

She said, 'I'll make out.'

'Don't be a stubborn fool,' he said icily. 'And don't punish Grace for something she said when she was half out of her mind with anxiety. She doesn't deserve it and she's come to make amends. You can at least give her the courtesy of a hearing.'

He turned and went out of the room, and she glared after him, but after a moment she got up and followed.

Grace was waiting in the sitting room, looking rather nervous.

She said immediately Rowan appeared, 'I'm sorry, love. I leapt to conclusions. Will you forgive me and come back and work for us again? I don't think we can do without you.'

They were alone, and Rowan had closed the door behind her. She said slowly, 'I'll come back willingly,

Grace, but I can't promise to stay the summer. As soon as I've saved enough money, I'm leaving, but if you're prepared to have me under those conditions . . .'

'You've quarrelled with Carne? Oh, I was afraid that might happen. Clive said this morning that he'd been furious with you, and it's our fault.'

'It isn't.' Rowan gave a little sigh. 'Well, only indirectly. You see, because of what happened last night, he realised that I'd been making a fool of him—that I was in fact several years older than I'd let him think.'

'Well, of course you are,' Grace said surprisingly. 'Clive and I had figured that out when we first met you, but then we've had more experience of adolescents than Carne has. What we couldn't understand was why. You're still far too young to need to lie about your age.'

Rowan made a weary gesture. 'Let's just say it seemed like a good idea at the time, and leave it at that. But Carne was very angry when he found out—justifiably so, I suppose.'

'I suppose too,' Grace agreed. 'And he can be a swine when he loses his temper, although I must say I've never known him bear a grudge.'

'I could be the first.' Rowan's voice shook a little, but she made herself smile. 'But it doesn't really matter. It just gives me a greater incentive to get away from here. Anyway, that's enough of me. How's David?'

'Praying for death, I imagine. He's got the most terrifying hangover, but the doctor thinks there'll be no ill-effects.' Grace's brightness was shadowed for a moment. 'But it was a terrible thing to do. He could have had alcoholic poisoning and died.'

'What about Jeff Wainwright?'

'Taken himself off to Manchester very conveniently. Clive went round this morning, only to find the bird had flown. The mother and sister were there, both obviously upset, so Clive guessed they knew what had happened last night, or at least part of it. There's a rumour in the village that they're putting the shop and their cottage up for sale and moving away, and I must say I shan't be sorry if they do. And nor, I suspect, will anyone else.' She sighed, then pulled herself briskly together. 'So it's settled, then, is it?

You'll come in to work as usual on Monday?'

'I'll be there,' Rowan promised, and after a few moments Grace went off.

Rowan wandered over to the window and stood looking out for a moment. She supposed she could go back upstairs and get on with her story, but she felt she had done as much as she could for now. She glanced rather ruefully round the room. She could usefully employ herself restoring a little order in here and other parts of the house before the new housekeeper arrived. She didn't want the woman to turn tail and flee, appalled at the magnitude of the task confronting her. She couldn't hope in a few brief hours to restore the gloss and sheen Raven's Crag had worn when they arrived, but maybe she could do something to make the place look a little less neglected and uncared-for.

She was plugging in the Hoover when Antonia walked in.

'No need to play the little menial any more, sweetie. Carne's getting some real help in at long last,' she tossed at her carelessly, as she kicked off her shoes and sank down on the sofa. 'Was that Grace Lister's car I saw leaving here?'

'Yes, she came to offer me my job back at the pottery.'

'Big deal.' Antonia paused in the middle of rummaging in her bag for the inevitable cigarette, and stared at her stepdaughter. 'And you're going to take it?'

'Yes, of course.'

'There's no "of course" about it.' Antonia's voice was suddenly a little shrill. 'You know exactly how I feel about you hanging round here endlessly, making sheep's eyes at Carne. I thought you were going to look for something in Keswick. You might have found another girl to share a bedsit with.'

'Thank you for your generous concern!' Rowan could not disguise her bitterness. 'What a pity I ever came here at all.'

'Yes, it is,' Antonia snapped. 'The whole thing was a ghastly mistake. I must have been mad—and all for the sake of that piffling little allowance from the Winslow estate. Well, thank God I needn't look forward to that sort of penury any longer.'

'You were more than glad of it at one time,' Rowan snapped back.

'Well, that time is long past.' Antonia would have said more, but at that moment the sitting room door opened and Carne came in frowning.

'What's the trouble now?' he demanded grimly. 'I hope you two aren't going to make a habit of shouting at each other when there's resident staff in the house.'

'Oh, darling, I'm so sorry.' Antonia rose from the sofa and went over to him, smiling up at him beguilingly. In her stockinged feet, and against his height, she looked very small and fragile. 'I'm afraid all our tempers are a little frayed today.'

He looked down at her, his face enigmatic. 'Is that a fact?' He looked at Rowan over her head, and his eyes were expressionless. She felt herself tremble. She wanted to put out her hand, to go to him, but pride kept her rooted to the spot. And anyway, Antonia stood between them, as she always would, so close to him that she might as well have been in his arms. He said quietly and coldly, 'There's really no need for you to do the housework, but if you insist, perhaps you'd check Sybilla's flat. I've been on to the nursing home, and she's coming home in a few days. I naturally want everything ready to welcome her.'

'Naturally,' Rowan said ironically. She could sense the shock in Antonia, the disbelief and the rejection. She must have been so sure, so very sure that Sybilla would never return to Raven's Crag. 'I'll make sure that the flat is ready for her.'

'You'd better make up the bed in her spare room too. I've arranged for a nurse to accompany her. She'll need to take care, at least for the first few weeks.'

Rowan nodded and left the room. As she went into the hall, she heard Antonia's voice husky with resentment. 'But Carne—oh, darling, do you think you're doing the right thing . . .'

Rowan didn't wait to hear any more, but she smiled rather grimly as she went up to her room to fetch Sybilla's keys. It took longer than she expected. They weren't in the place she'd thought she'd left them, and she was involved in a tiresome search for quite a time.

When she went down to the flat, she looked around her with a certain amount of pride. It was clean and tidy, just as Sybilla had wanted, but there was no denying, it wore rather a forlorn air. It wasn't just that it was uninhabited— in some odd way, it looked bare. She shrugged, telling herself that she was just being fanciful, but as she cleaned the windows, and dusted and polished, the thought nagged at her.

It was an odd few days which followed. The new house-keeper arrived, a large slow-moving woman called Mrs Ramsden. Bovine she might appear, but Rowan soon discovered there was no need for any explanation of her duties. Silently and efficiently, Mrs Ramsden took over the housework and the cooking, indicating firmly that she needed neither help nor interference from anyone, and Rowan found herself left more to her own devices than she had ever dreamed possible.

The good weather held, and on Sunday afternoon she slipped out of the house and away up the fell, following the route she had taken with Carne. When she reached the plateau where they had seen the raven, she sat down in the sunlight with her back to a rock and waited, but this time there was no flurry, no ripple of blue-black feathers to beguile her, just her own wearying thoughts beating inside her skull, and at last she got up abruptly, and went back to the house. The magic of the fell had withered for her.

She was glad to find herself back at the pottery again, learning to pack up the postal orders for pots as well as serve the customers who were coming in ever-increasing numbers. She saw little of David, who had been inclined to be sheepish at their first encounter, until she had laughed him out of it. The immediate prospect of exams was engaging his attention, but she guessed the fact that he knew now she was older than he was was also tending to keep him at a distance, and she couldn't feel altogether regretful. Even if there had been no age difference, all he could ever have been, as far as she was concerned, was a nice boy. And she had already given her heart and mind to someone who had left boyhood behind him a long time ago.

Nor did she see a great deal of Antonia, who was clearly sulking at the prospect of Sybilla's return, but who was also very much occupied with the sittings for her portrait up in Carne's studio. Not that painting was all that occurred, according to Antonia. Rowan was so sickened by the pin-pricks of sexual innuendo that Antonia introduced every time the portrait was mentioned that she had stopped asking after its progress. If all Antonia said was true, it would probably never be finished anyway, she thought cynically. Yet Carne didn't have to make excuses about portrait painting to have Antonia all to himself. It was his house, and if he and Antonia wanted to stay in bed together all day long making love, then they could do so.

But however besotted he might be, it seemed that Antonia had been unable to change his mind about Sybilla, however hard she had tried, and Rowan remembered only too well all the little tricks Antonia had used to wind Victor Winslow around her little finger. It was a bitter triumph to know that Carne was not so easily beguiled.

But at least her stepmother's preoccupation with Carne meant that she had no time for the high-flying bridge players any more. Rowan had tried once, rather awkwardly, to find out what had happened about the money and whether Antonia had managed to pay her debts, but was told in no uncertain terms to mind her own business.

In the circumstances that hadn't been difficult, Rowan thought wryly, as she walked back to Raven's Crag at the end of her first week back at the pottery. After Mrs Ramsden's plain but excellent dinner, she usually went up to her room and worked on her story. It was drafted to her satisfaction now, and she was busily re-writing it, trying to find the correct level of vocabulary to suit the age of the audience for which it was intended, but without appearing to 'talk down' to her young readers.

She had told Grace rather shyly what she was doing, and Grace had obligingly supplied her with some large sheets of cartridge paper so that she could set out her text and leave space for the illustrations that would be needed. Rowan was no draughtswoman, but she sketched in faintly her ideas for the drawings, although she guessed that if by some remote chance a publisher became interested in her story she would probably have very little say in that side of it.

She was eager to get back to her story. It couldn't stop the hurt inside her when she thought of Carne and Antonia together, but while she was working on it, it demanded all her absorption and concentration, and she could keep her pain at a distance, at least for a while.

As she approached the gates of the house an ambulance came out slowly and turned up the road. Rowan's steps quickened; Sybilla must be home, she thought delightedly.

She sped up the drive and went up the steps to the front door two at a time. At first the house appeared to be deserted, then she heard the murmur of voices in the distance and realised that everyone must be in Sybilla's flat.

She pushed the door open and went into the little sitting room. Her first dismayed thought was how white and ill Sybilla looked—far worse than the last time she had seen her at the clinic. Perhaps the excitement of the journey home had tired her. Her second thought was how grim everyone looked, especially Carne.

She said, 'Sybilla—oh, it's lovely to see you! The flat has seemed so empty without you.'

Antonia gave a little strained crack of laughter, quelled to silence by the blazing look Carne turned on her.

Sybilla looked across the room at Rowan, and she was appalled to see there were tears on the older woman's cheeks.

'You can say that?' Sybilla's voice shook. 'You can honestly stand there and say that to me, after I trusted you . . .'

Rowan stared back at her in mingled bewilderment and compassion. 'I don't understand,' she began. 'Is something wrong?'

Carne said tightly, 'A great deal is wrong. I don't have to ask if you recognise these?' He moved slightly and Rowan saw that his body had been shielding a small table. To her surprise she saw that two of the velvet-framed Victorian miniatures which normally hung beside the fireplace were lying there.

'Of course I do.' Involuntarily her eyes went to the place on the wall where they usually hung, then returned to meet Carne's gaze. The silver eyes were bitter with anger and contempt and her heart began to thud with huge sickening strokes. She said, 'What is it? Why are you all looking at me as if I'm a criminal?'

'Not really a criminal, darling,' Antonia's voice was honey, poisonously sweet. 'Just rather a nasty little petty thief who forgot to dispose of the evidence.'

Carne said slowly, quoting, 'I'll do anything I have to—anything to get out of this place.' His eyes still held hers. They might have been alone together in a suddenly reeling universe. 'But I didn't realise you intended to go to these lengths, Rowan. What did you do with the rest of the things you took?'

'Took?' Her voice was shrill with shock. 'What are you talking about? What am I supposed to have taken?'

'Some candlesticks, a snuffbox, some ivory figures—you know the list as well as I do. Sybilla noticed the things were missing as soon as she came in. Did you think she wouldn't? Or were you counting on the fact that she wasn't going to return here and your depredations would never be noticed?'

It was a nightmare, but soon she would waken from it. She had to.

She took a step forward, towards the small shrunken figure in the chair. She said, 'Sybilla, I never took a thing from you. I wouldn't—I couldn't! You must believe me.'

'She might have done,' Carne said coldly, 'if I hadn't found these——' he gestured towards the miniatures—'stuffed into a drawer in your bedroom.'

'You searched my room? But why?'

'Because you had free access here. You were the only one who had Sybilla's keys. That's what I was looking for when I found the miniatures. I told myself there had to be some rational explanation, but as soon as Sybilla got here she knew something was wrong.'

And so did I, Rowan thought numbly. The other day, I knew the room was too bare, but I didn't know the contents well enough to check—and anyway why should I have done?

Carne said quietly, 'Your bank statement arrived this morning, Rowan. I think, in the circumstances, we have the right to ask to see it.'

A feeling of nausea threatened to overwhelm her, but

she hung on to her self-control.

'See it if you like. It—it won't tell you anything, because there's nothing to tell. I came in here to do the cleaning, not steal. I had no reason to steal.'

His voice was bitter. 'None—except your overwhelming, obsessive desire to have enough money to return to London. All you had to do was ask me, Rowan. Didn't you realise I'd have paid anything to protect Sybilla from this kind of hurt?'

She stood silently, her arms wrapped across herself in automatic defence, until Antonia returned with the bank's long brown envelope.

'Open it yourself,' Carne handed it to her. 'We don't want to pry more than we have to, so all we want to know is the balance.'

'I've nothing to hide.' There was anger stirring in her now, and hurt pride that just because of some monstrous mistake she should be suspected and accused. She tore open the envelope and thrust the sheet it contained back at him.

He looked at the row of figures and his mouth hardened. 'Saved from your wages at the pottery?' he asked defeatedly. 'I don't think so, Rowan.'

Surprised, she took the statement back and glanced at it, her eyes widening as she assimilated the amount of the balance in her account. Then she realised what must have happened. Her quarterly allowance had been transferred directly into the account in accordance with the instructions she had given the estate's solicitors in London. The quarterly allowance that Carne knew nothing about, but which had been one of the levers Antonia had used to persuade her to come to Raven's Crag.

She lifted her eyes and looked across at her stepmother, mutely prompting her to intervene, to tell Carne about the allowance, to remove the last piece of deception from their tortuous relationship.

But as their glances met and locked, Rowan knew with a sinking heart that Antonia was going to say nothing. She was going to let Carne go on thinking that the money in her account had been obtained by criminal means. Her lips were already parting in protest when the whole truth struck her like a blow on the back of the head, stunning her to horrified silence.

She had seen it in Antonia's face for one unguarded moment—guilt, shame and defiance. There was no need to wonder any more where Sybilla's treasures had gone, or even deceive herself that her stepmother had obtained the money to pay her gambling debts from her lover.

Relying on her conviction that Sybilla would never return to Raven's Crag—even, horrifyingly, relying on her death, for that matter—Antonia had taken the missing articles and sold them. Rowan knew it now, and was sickened by it.

She thought agonisingly, 'How could she? Oh God, how could she?'

But in her heart, she knew precisely how. She had always suspected the degree of ruthlessness that Antonia could possess if pushed, and realised that her determination to establish her own security once and for all by marrying Carne had provided the necessary push. Nothing was to be allowed to stand in the way of the plans she had made for her future. Nothing—and no one—especially the step-daughter in whom the habits of loyalty and protectiveness were already too deeply ingrained.

Rowan thought, 'She's betrayed me. She's stabbed me in the back in the worst possible way, but she knows I won't give her away.'

All the mysteries were solved. Antonia's keenness to get her out of the house and back to London became under-standable. Any more thefts, and she, Rowan, would have been bound to have noticed something and mentioned the matter. As it was, she had already had that indefinable sense that all was not well.

But Antonia hadn't had time to dispose of the minia-tures, so in a panic she must have put them in Rowan's room, deliberately foisting suspicion on to her. And then Carne was sent up to look for the keys so that he would be the one to find them—the one to think . . .

She sank her teeth into her lower lip. She wouldn't think about that now. All she had to think about was getting away from here, escaping from this trap which had been set for her. Nothing else mattered.

Her father expected her to look after Antonia, even to the extent of protecting her from the consequences of her own actions. And what did it matter, anyway? Carne did not love her. It was Antonia he wanted, and so the truth could only hurt him.

And she didn't want him to be hurt. Let him preserve what few illusions he had about his future wife, she thought painfully.

She made herself look at Sybilla. 'I'm sorry,' she said, steadying her voice. 'More sorry than I can say. You were honestly never intended to know.'

Sybilla was very straight in her chair, her eyes fixed unswervingly on Rowan's face.

'May I ask how you disposed of my things? I ask only because it may be possible to recover some of them. Old women are sentimental about such things.'

And about trust, and about affection, her eyes were telling Rowan.

Rowan bent her head. 'I can't say where any of them are now.'

It was the truth, she supposed wryly, or at least as much of the truth as it was possible to tell.

Carne said, 'Don't worry, Sybilla. We'll pick up the pieces somehow.' He hesitated, and when he spoke again his voice had roughened. 'I assume you don't want to report this to the police.'

'I think not,' Sybilla said precisely. 'I think under the circumstances, it would be best to keep the matter in the family. However, I feel it might be preferable if Rowan was to leave.'

Rowan lifted her chin. She said coolly, 'As that was the whole purpose of the exercise, I think it would be infinitely preferable.'

She was afraid to look at Antonia in case the triumph in her eyes destroyed her tenuous self-control, but she made herself face Carne.

'I'm sorry,' she said.

'And so am I,' he said, quietly and courteously, as if she was a stranger. 'You'll never know how sorry. Now, you'd better go. Just take what you need. I'll arrange to have your things sent on when you're settled.'

She said with equal politeness, 'Thank you.' And then she walked out, closing the door carefully behind her.

It was a pleasant room. Each evening when she returned to it, Rowan thought how lucky she had been, since that disastrous evening three weeks before when she had run like a hunted animal straight to Grace.

There, her self-command had collapsed under the pressure of Grace's concern, and she had sobbed the whole sordid story into her amazed ears. When she had finished, Grace's lips were set firmly, and Rowan had to swear her to secrecy to prevent her going straight to Raven's Crag and exposing Antonia for the thief and the liar that she was.

Grace had conceded finally, but she did not understand why, and said so bluntly. 'You're a fool, Rowan. She deserves nothing from you. She's played you one dirty trick after another. You don't imagine that Carne won't find out eventually what she's like?'

'He may. He may not.' Rowan's hands twisted together. 'But the important thing is that he won't find out through me. And she may change—once she's got what she wants.'

'People don't change,' Grace said dourly. 'They just become more the same. Haven't you noticed?'

Then she became practical. Rowan would stay the night with them, that went without saying. When she was calmer, they would see she got to London, if that was what she wanted, and they could help in the matter of accommodation too. A cousin of Clive's, whose family had all grown up and married, had converted her big terraced house into a number of bedsitting rooms, mostly for students.

'Livvy isn't in it for the money,' Grace explained. 'She likes the house, and she likes young company around her, so this way she gets the best of both worlds. And with the long vacation coming up she may well have a vacancy.'

And so it proved, although Rowan suspected that Grace could well have pulled a few strings on her behalf. Before they said goodbye, she begged Grace to take temporary charge of the things she had left there but not to tell anyone at Raven's Crag where she had gone.

'No problem.' Grace studied her drawn white face with a frown. 'But are you sure that's what you want? I'm not blind, you know, even though I may have promised to be dumb.'

Rowan forced a smile. 'That's what I want,' she said.

Livvy had proved to be a large, practical humorous lady whom Rowan liked on sight. The rooms in her tall house had been furnished from junk shops but with flair and imagination, and she liked to keep a motherly eye on her young tenants, while pursuing a policy of non-interference.

Rowan managed to find a job in a small newsagents and tobacconists a few streets away, and while the pay she received would not have set the Thames on fire, coupled with her allowance, it meant she could get by until she could think coherently about the future.

She received a couple of letters from Grace, full of general news, including that David had finished his exams and was in the depths of despondency, convinced he had failed. About Raven's Crag she said not a word, and Rowan wondered in spite of herself whether Carne and Antonia were married yet.

She wrote back to Grace reassuring her that she was nicely settled, and asking her to arrange to have the rest of her things sent on. She had only brought one small suitcase away with her, and this imposed strict limitations on her wardrobe. Besides, she wanted her typewriter and her manuscript back, even if she did not relish the memories it would inevitably revive.

But at least it would give her something with which to fill her evenings, apart from going down to Livvy's large, untidy, colourful sitting room and sitting watching television programmes she couldn't remember a single detail about afterwards.

There were other alternatives, of course. Two of her fellow-lodgers, both in their early twenties had eyed her appreciatively and made noises about taking her out, but she deliberately remained aloof. She wanted no more emotional involvement, even of the lightest variety, for quite some time to come.

Besides, she was amazed that anyone would seriously consider dating her. She still looked pale. She wasn't sleeping properly, and it was beginning to show in her hair and complexion, and her nails were bitten down to the quicks again. Not an appetising sight, she thought, viewing herself in the long mirror attached to one wall, with a swift grimace.

There was a knock on the door, and Livvy's head appeared round it.

'You have a visitor, petal. Shall I send him up, or will you see him down in the sitting room?'

'I'll come down. It will be someone from my father's solicitors. I wrote to them to let them know where I was, and also that my stepmother was remarrying shortly, and they said they'd be in touch.'

Rowan was a little on edge as she went into the sitting room. She supposed that technically both she and Antonia had disqualified themselves from their respective allowances, under the terms of the will, and hoped very much that this was not what her unknown caller had come to tell her.

Then she stopped, whatever remark she had been about to make shrivelling on her parted lips as Carne rose unhurriedly from the sofa and stood looking at her.

When she spoke, it was in a whisper. 'What are you doing here?'

He raised an eyebrow. 'Looking for you. And before you start calling Grace names, she kept her word stalwartly to the end. I found your address through the Winslow estate lawyers.'

'But I've only just got in touch with them.'

'So I discovered,' he said. 'I'd asked them to let me know as soon as they heard from you, if they ever did.'

'I see.' She didn't really. She didn't know anything any more, least of all whether seeing him again was more pleasure than pain. 'I—I suppose you had to contact them to let them know you were marrying Antonia.'

'I didn't,' he said. 'And I haven't—married Antonia, that is. I never had any intention of marrying her, although I gather her plans were rather different. She always did take altogether too much for granted. She should have left it at that.' There was a sudden grimness in his voice that made her look at him with dazed comprehension.

'Then—you know?'

He nodded. 'Everything. Or I think I do, and you can fill me in on any points that have been missed.' He looked at her, at the white, strained features, the tears welling up in her eyes, and his voice altered, roughened. 'You stupid, proud little fool! Why did you let me think you'd been helping yourself to Sybilla's things? Why didn't you damn Antonia to hell and tell the truth about her?'

'Because I didn't think that was what you wanted to hear,' she confessed, the tears pouring down her face. 'I thought . . .'

'You thought altogether too bloody much,' he said harshly, and then she was in his arms and his mouth was seeking hers with a demand that combined passion and tenderness. She clung to him, her head swimming, her whole existence crystallised into the reality of his mouth exploring hers, and the gentleness of his hands on her body. He was gentle too as he cradled her face in his hands and looked down at her when the long kiss was over.

'My poor little love! Will you ever forgive me for doubting you? If I'd been thinking straight I'd never have given it credence, but I was haunted by you telling me you'd do anything to get away from me. And I had to admit I hardly knew you. Every time I tried to get near to you, mentally as well as physically, you pushed me away.'

'I didn't want to.' She had to try and explain. 'But Antonia made me believe that you were hers—that I embarrassed you even.'

'She hasn't changed.' There was real anger in his voice as he drew her down to sit beside him on the sofa. 'Even as a girl she had a way of twisting everything to suit her own ends. Oh, I admit for a while it seemed as if she was trying to make something of her life. That's why I lent her the money for the boutique, but when I found she was blithely prepared to write it off, and expected me to do the same, I got angry and decided she needed a lesson. That I'd make her work, if it was the last thing I did. Only I soon realised that the plan had misfired when Sybilla told me that you were waiting on her hand and foot.' He was silent for a moment. 'Sybilla's very fond of you. Even when things looked blackest, she told me privately that she couldn't believe you'd stolen her treasures, and pointed out what

I'd missed—that you'd never actually admitted having done so, but that you were obviously deeply shocked and upset. So I wrote a list of what was missing and combed every antique shop for miles until I found a man who remembered the candlesticks and the snuffbox and gave me a vivid description of the woman who'd sold him the stuff.' He shook his head wryly. 'It didn't resemble you in the slightest. When I faced Antonia with him, she broke down and admitted everything, including how she'd forced you to come north with her originally.'

'Is she still at the house?'

'She is not,' he said grimly. 'When last heard of, she was staying with "friends" in Keswick. From what I can gather, one of her bridge-playing cronies is a retired industrialist, and she has her sights set on him now.'

'But I thought you loved her. She's so beautiful—and you did paint her portrait.'

'I didn't. I made some preliminary sketches, but Antonia's a lousy model. She wants to be admired, and she won't keep still. Besides, her portrait was very much second best, you know.' He kissed her again. 'Come back to me, dryad. Let me paint what's been filling my head to the exclusion of everything else for weeks.'

She said shyly, 'I thought perhaps you'd brought my things.'

'Your luggage is still at Raven's Crag, waiting for you. Sybilla's waiting too, not to mention Mrs Ramsden, who informs me you were "a nice young lady" and was quite put out because you fled without saying goodbye to her.'

Rowan said, 'Did I? Oh dear, but I wasn't thinking very clearly . . .'

'None of us were—but her.'

'But Carne——' she hesitated, 'you were her lover. I saw her coming from your room the morning after our—quarrel.'

He shrugged. 'Perhaps she was. I don't remember. But I hadn't slept with her, whatever impression she may have given you. Years ago I fancied her—sure, why not? But I soon found that any affair with Antonia would be strictly one-sided. All that sexy, come-hither stuff is a façade. There's nothing there. No passion, no warmth, no generosity, and every favour granted on a strictly quid pro quo basis. That's not love, Rowan. I want more from a wife than the occasional, barely tolerated use of her body in return for a roof over her head, and my money to spend.'

Rowan did not speak, and after a pause he said huskily, 'Aren't you going to ask what I do want?' She shook her head, and he gave a slight, shaken laugh. 'Then I'll tell you anyway. I want everything you have to give, and more, Rowan. I want you—all of you, dryad, now and for ever. I'm too old for you. I've made every mistake I could make, I know that. But for God's sake, give me another chance. Things can only get better.'

She said slowly, not looking at him, 'Carne, how can it work? I'm naïve and stupid, and I bite my nails. I'm not fit to be married to anyone, especially someone who moves in your sort of sophisticated world. I'd be out of my depth.'

'I'll teach you to swim.'

'You'd regret it within a year,' she gasped. He was touching her again, and her body was melting.

'Darling, without you there'd be nothing but regrets. And my jet-setting days are over. I told you that some time ago, and I meant it. My life is at Raven's Crag, with you if you'll have me.' He kissed her again, and she yielded against him in passionate abandon, her arms lifting to encircle his neck and draw him even closer. When they drew apart they were both breathless.

'In any case,' said Carne, 'you can't turn me down. Clive and Grace are making us a dinner service as a wedding present.'

'Oh!' Rowan pummelled his chest in mock rage. 'So you were that sure of me!'

'I was never sure of you at all,' he said seriously. 'I'll only be sure when my ring's on your finger. But I do have a small bribe for you.' He reached down beside the sofa and brought up a portfolio. 'Don't be angry, darling, but the manuscript was there in your room. I had to read it. It was like discovering part of you.'

Wonderingly, she opened the portfolio, and cried out in joy. A cascade of ravens emptied on to her lap—prime City ravens in morning coats with bowler hats and umbrellas, and plump country ravens with knowing twinkles in their

eyes and straws in their beaks, each and every one of them
with a character of his own.

'Carne, they're wonderful! They're exactly right. Oh,
how did you know?'

'I didn't. But it bodes well for the future, don't you think?'
He put his arm round her, drawing her to him. His voice
was gentle. 'Marry me, love. Marry me soon. I'm empty
without you.'

'And I've been so unhappy.' She gave a little wondering
laugh. 'I can hardly believe this is happening.'

'You'd better believe it,' he said softly, and close in the
shelter of his arms, his mouth warm on hers, Rowan sur-
rendered herself to the joy of a dream come true.

Take romance with you on your holiday.

Holiday time is almost here again. So look out for the special Mills & Boon Holiday Reading Pack.* Four new romances by four favourite authors. Attractive, smart, easy to pack and only £3.00.

*Available from 12th June.

Dakota Dreamin'
Janet Dailey

Devil Lover
Carole Mortimer

Forbidden Flame
Anne Mather

Gold to Remember
Mary Wibberley